MAYBE
THIS CHRISTMAS...?

BY
ALISON ROBERTS

MILLS &
BOON

First published in Great Britain 2012
by Mills & Boon, an imprint of Harlequin (UK) Limited.
Harlequin (UK) Limited, Eton House, 18-24 Paradise Road,
Richmond, Surrey TW9 1SR

© Alison Roberts 2012

ISBN: 978 0 263 89206 2

Harlequin (UK) policy is to use papers that are natural, renewable and recyclable products and made from wood grown in sustainable forests. The logging and manufacturing process conform to the legal environmental regulations of the country of origin.

Printed and bound in Spain
by Blackprint CPI, Barcelona

CHAPTER ONE

'HER name's Sophie Gillespie. She's six months old.'

A surprisingly heavy burden, but perhaps that was because Gemma hadn't thought to bring a pushchair and she'd been holding the baby on her hip for far too long already. The A and E department of the Queen Mary Infirmary in Manchester, England, was heaving and, because it was Christmas Eve, it all seemed rather surreal.

Reams of tired-looking tinsel had been strung in loops along the walls. A bunch of red and green balloons had been tied to the display screen, currently advertising the waiting time as being an hour and a half. And if they were this busy when it wasn't quite seven p.m., Gemma knew that the waiting time would only increase as new cases came in by ambulance and demanded the attention of the doctors and nurses on duty in the department.

'Look…this is an emergency.'

'Uh-huh?'

The middle-aged receptionist looked as if she'd seen it all. And she probably had. There was a group of very drunk teenage girls in naughty elf costumes singing and shouting loudly in a corner of the reception area. One of them was holding a bloodstained cloth to her face. Another was holding a vomit bag. A trio of equally drunk young men was watching the elves with apprecia- tion and trying to outdo each other with wolf whistles. The expressions on the faces of the people between the groups were long-suffering. A woman sitting beside a small, crying boy looked to be at the end of her tether and she was glaring at Gemma, who appeared to be at- tempting to queue jump.

The receptionist peered over her glasses at Sophie, who wasn't helping. Thanks to the dose of paracetamol she'd given her as she'd left the house, the baby was looking a lot better than she had been. Her face was still flushed and her eyes over-bright but she wasn't crying with that frightening, high-pitched note any more. She was, in fact, smiling at the receptionist.

'She's running a temperature,' Gemma said. 'She's got a rash.'

'It's probably just a virus. Take a seat, please, ma'am. We'll get her seen as soon as possible.'

'What—in a couple of *hours*?'

Gemma could feel the heat radiating off the baby in her arms. She could feel the way Sophie was slumped listlessly against her body. The smile was fading and any moment now Sophie would start crying again. She took a deep breath.

'As soon as possible might be too late,' she snapped. 'She needs to be seen *now*. Please...' she added, trying to keep her voice from wavering. 'I just need to rule out the possibility that it's meningitis.'

'Rule out?' The receptionist peered over her glasses again, this time at Gemma. 'What are you, a doctor?'

'Yes, I am.' Gemma knew her tone lacked conviction. Could she still claim to be a doctor when it had been so long since she'd been anywhere near a patient?

'Not at this hospital you're not.'

Gemma closed her eyes for a heartbeat. 'I used to be.'

'And you're an expert in meningitis, then? What… you're going to tell me you're a paediatrician?'

Like the other woman waiting with a child, the receptionist clearly thought Gemma was trying to queue jump. And now there were people behind her, waiting to check in. One was a man in a dinner suit with a firm hold around the waist of a woman in an elegant black dress who had a halo of silver tinsel on her head.

'Can you hurry up?' the man said loudly. 'My wife needs help here.'

Sophie whimpered and Gemma knew she had to do something fast. Something she had sworn not to do. She took another deep breath and leaned closer to the hole in the bulletproof glass protecting the reception area.

'No, I'm not a paediatrician and I don't work at this hospital.' Her tone of voice was enough to encourage the receptionist to make eye contact. 'But my husband does.' At least, he did, as far as she knew. He could have moved on, though, couldn't he? In more ways than just where he worked. 'And he *is* a paediatrician,' she added, mentally crossing her fingers that this information would be enough to get her seen faster.

'Oh? What's his name, then?'

'Andrew Baxter.'

The woman behind her groaned and clutched her stomach. The man pushed past Gemma.

'For God's sake, I think my wife might be having a miscarriage.'

The receptionist's eyes had widened at Gemma's words. Now they widened even further as her gaze flicked to the next person in the queue and a look of alarm crossed her face. She leapt to her feet, signalling for assistance from other staff members. Moments later, the man and his wife were being ushered through the internal doors. The receptionist gave Gemma an apologetic glance.

'I won't be long. I'll get you seen next and...and I'll find out if your husband's on call.'

No. That was the last thing Gemma wanted.

Oh...Lord. What would Andy think if someone told him that his wife was in Reception? That she was holding a child that she thought might have meningitis?

He'd think it was his worst nightmare. The ghost of a Christmas past that he'd probably spent the last six years trying to forget.

Just like she had.

Dr Andrew Baxter was in his favourite place in the world. The large dayroom at the end of Queen Mary's paediatric ward.

He was admiring the enormous Christmas tree the staff had just finished decorating and he found himself smiling as he thought about the huge sack of gifts hiding in the sluice room that he would be in charge of distributing tomorrow when he was suitably dressed in his Santa costume.

It was hard to believe there had been a time when he hadn't been able to bring himself to come into this area of the ward. Especially at this particular time of year. When he'd been focused purely on the children who were too sick to enjoy this room with its bright decorations and abundance of toys.

Time really did heal, didn't it?

It couldn't wipe out the scars, of course. Andy knew there was a poignant ache behind his smile and he knew that he'd have to field a few significantly sympathetic glances from his colleagues tomorrow, but he could handle it now.

Enjoy it, even. And that was more than he'd ever hoped would be the case.

With it being after seven p.m., the dayroom would normally be empty as children were settled into bed for the night but here, just like in the outside world, Christmas Eve sparkled with a particular kind of magic that meant normal rules became rather flexible.

Four-year-old Ruth, who was recovering from a bone-marrow transplant to treat her leukaemia, was still at risk for infection but her dad, David, had carried her as far as the door so that she could see the tree. They were both wearing gowns and hats and had masks covering their faces but Andy saw the way David whispered in his daughter's ear and then pointed. He could see the way the child's eyes grew wide with wonder and then sense the urgency of the whisper back to her father.

Andy stepped closer.

'Hello, gorgeous.' He smiled at Ruth. 'Do you like our Christmas tree?'

A shy nod but then Ruth buried her face against her father's neck.

'Ruthie's worried that Father Christmas won't come to the hospital.'

'He *always* comes,' Andy said.

His confidence was absolute and why wouldn't it be? He'd been filling the role for years now and knew he could carry it off to perfection. Being tall and broad, it was easy to pad himself out with a couple of pillows so that his body shape was unrecognisable. The latest beard and moustache was a glue-on variety that couldn't be tugged off by a curious child and it was luxuriant enough to disguise him completely once the hat was in place.

Ruth's eyes appeared again and, after a brief glance at Andy, she whispered in her father's ear again. David grinned at Andy.

'She wants to know if he's going to bring her a present.'

'Sure is.' Andy nodded. There would be more than one that had Ruth's name on it. Every child on the ward had a parcel set aside for them from the pile of the donated gifts and parents were invited to put something special into Santa's sack as well. Not that Ruth would be able to join the throng that gathered around the tree for the ceremony but, if her latest test results were good, she should be able to watch from behind the windows and receive her gifts at a safer distance.

'Of course, he can't come to deliver the presents until all the girls and boys are asleep,' Andy added, with a wink at David. 'Might be time for bed?'

Ruth looked at him properly this time. 'But…how does he know I'm in hos—in…hostible?'

Andy knew his face was solemn. 'He just does,' he said calmly. 'Santa's magic. *Christmas* is magic.'

He watched David carry Ruth back to her room, making a mental note to chase up the latest lab results on this patient later tonight. He might put in a quick call to her specialist consultant as well, to discuss what participation might be allowable tomorrow.

Andrew Baxter was a general paediatrician. He was the primary consultant for medical cases that were admitted to the ward and stayed involved if they were referred on to surgeons, but he was also involved in every other case that came through these doors in some way. The 'outside' world was pretty irrelevant these days. This was *his* world. His home.

It didn't matter if the young patients were admitted under an oncologist for cancer treatment or a specialist paediatric cardiologist for heart problems or an orthopaedic surgeon who was dealing with a traumatic injury. Andy was an automatic part of the team. He knew every child who was in here and some of them he knew extremely well because they got admitted more than once or stayed for a long time.

Like John Boy, who was still in the dayroom, circling the tree as he watched the fairy-lights sparkling. Eleven years old, John Boy had a progressive and debilitating syndrome that led to myriad physical challenges and his life expectancy was no more than fifteen to twenty years at best. If the cardiologists couldn't deal with the abnormalities that were causing a degree of heart failure this time, that life expectancy could be drastically reduced.

Of mixed race, with ultra-curly black hair and a wide, white smile, the lad had been fostered out since birth but had spent more of his life in hospital than out of it and he was a firm favourite on this ward. With his frail, twisted body now confined to a wheelchair, John Boy had lost none of his sense of humour and determination to cause mischief.

Right now, he was making some loud and rather disgusting noises, his head hanging almost between his knees. Andy moved swiftly.

'Hey, John Boy! What's going on?'

John Boy groaned impressively and waved his hand feebly. Andy looked down and stepped back hurriedly from the pile of vomit on the floor.

'Oh…*no*…'

A nurse, Carla, was climbing down the ladder she had used to fasten the huge star on the top of the tree.

'Oh *no*,' she echoed, but she was laughing. 'Not

again, John Boy. That plastic vomit joke is getting old, you know?'

Andy nudged the offensive-looking puddle with his foot. Sure enough, the edge lifted cleanly. John Boy was laughing so hard he had to hold onto the side of his wheelchair to stop him falling out and the sound was so contagious everybody in the room was either laughing or smiling. The noise level was almost enough to drown out the sound of Andy's pager.

Still grinning, he walked to the wall phone and took the call. Within seconds his grin was only a memory and the frown on his face was enough to raise Carla's eyebrows. She straightened swiftly from picking up the plastic vomit. She dropped it in John Boy's lap, which caused a new paroxysm of mirth.

'What's up, Andy?'

But he couldn't tell her. He didn't want to tell anyone. It couldn't be true, surely? He kept his eyes focused on John Boy instead. On a patient. An anchor in his real world.

'His lips are getting blue,' he growled. 'Get him back to his room and get some oxygen on, would you, please, Carla?'

He knew they were both staring at him as he left the room. He knew that the tone of his voice had been enough to stop John Boy laughing as if a switch had been flicked off and he hated it that he'd been responsible for that.

But he hadn't been able to prevent that tone. Not

when he was struggling to hold back so many memories. Bad memories.

Oh…God… If this was really happening, why on earth did it have to happen *tonight* of all nights?

The emergency department was packed to the gills.

Andy entered through the internal double doors. Serious cases were filling the resuscitation bays. He could see an elderly man hooked up to monitors, sitting up and struggling to breathe even with the assistance of CPAP. Heart failure secondary to an infarction, probably. Ambulance officers were still hovering in the next bay where a trauma victim was being assessed. One of them was holding a cyclist's helmet, which was in two pieces. The next bay had staff intubating an unconscious man. A woman was standing in the corner of the bay, sobbing.

'I told him not to go up on the roof,' Andy heard her gasp. 'I didn't even *want* a stupid flashing reindeer.'

The cubicles were next and they were also full. One had a very well-dressed woman lying on the bed, a crooked tinsel halo still on her head.

'Can't you do something?' The man with her was glaring at the poor junior registrar. 'She's pregnant, for God's sake…'

So many people who were having their Christmas Eves ruined by illness or accident. This would have been a very depressing place to be except for the numerous staff members. Some of the nurses were wearing Santa hats or had flashing earrings. All of them, even the ones having to deal with life-threatening situations, were doing it with skill and patience and as much good cheer as was possible. Andy caught more than one smile of greeting. These people were his colleagues. The closest thing he had to family, in fact.

He smiled back and reached the central station to find a nurse he'd actually taken out once, a long time ago. Julia had made it very clear that she was disappointed it had never gone any further and she greeted him now with a very warm smile.

'Andy… Merry Christmas, almost.'

'You, too.' Julia's long blonde hair was tied back in a ponytail that had tinsel wound around the top. 'You guys look busy.'

'One of our biggest nights. Have you just come to visit?'

'No, I got paged. A baby…' Andy had to swallow rather hard. 'Query meningitis?'

Julia looked up at the glass board with the spaces for each cubicle had names and details that it was her job tonight to keep updated. 'Doesn't ring a bell…'

'Brought in by a woman called Gemma…Baxter.' The hesitation was momentary but significant. Would Gemma have gone back to her maiden name by now? She couldn't have got married again. Not when they'd never formalised a divorce. Julia didn't seem to notice the surname and Andy hurried on. 'Someone called Janice called it through.'

'Janice?' Julia looked puzzled. 'She's on Reception. In the waiting room.' Julia frowned. 'If she's got a query meningitis it should have come through as a priority. I hope she's not waiting for a bed or something. Let me go and check.'

'That's OK, I'll do that.' He could almost hear the wheels turning for Julia now. She was staring at him with an odd expression.

'Did you say her name was *Baxter*? Is she a relative?'

Was she? Did it still count if you were still legally married to someone even if they'd simply walked out of your life?

Andy had reached the external set of double doors that led into the waiting room. He spotted Gemma the instant he pushed through the doors. It didn't matter that the place was crowded and it should have been hard to find anybody—his gaze went unswervingly straight towards her as if it was some kind of magnetic force.

The impact was enough to stop him in his tracks for a moment.

His head was telling him that it didn't count. Their marriage had been over a very long time ago and there was nothing there for him now.

His heart was telling him something very different.

This was the woman he had vowed to love, honour and cherish until they were parted by death. He'd meant every single word of those marriage vows.

For a moment, Andy could ignore everything that had happened since the day those vows had been spoken. He could forget about the way they'd been driven apart by forces too overwhelming for either of them to even begin to fight. He could forget that it had been years since he'd seen Gemma or heard the sound of her voice.

What he couldn't forget was what had drawn them together in the first place. That absolute surety that they were perfect for each other.

True soul mates.

For just that blink of time that pure feeling, one far too big to be enclosed by a tiny word like love, shone out of the dark corner of his heart that had been locked and abandoned for so long.

And…and that glow *hurt*, dammit.

Sophie was starting to grizzle again.

Gemma bounced her gently and started walking in a small circle, away from the queue waiting to see the receptionist. What was going on? She'd been told to wait but she'd expected to at least be shown through to a cubicle in the department. With the drama of the staff rushing to attend to the woman having a threatened miscarriage she seemed to have been forgotten.

Had they rung Andy? Was he on call or…even worse, had they rung him at home and made him feel obliged to come in on Christmas Eve and sort out a ghost from his past?

Oh…Lord. He probably had a new partner by now. He might even have his own kids. Except, if that was the case, why hadn't he contacted her to ask for a divorce? She'd had no contact at all. For four years. Ever since she'd packed that bag and—

'Gemma?'

The voice was angry. And it was male, but even before Gemma whirled to face the speaker she knew it wasn't Andy.

'Simon! What are you doing here?'

Not only was it Simon, he had the children in tow. All of them. Seven-year-old Hazel, five-year-old Jamie and the twins, Chloe and Ben, who were three and a half.

'Go on,' she heard him snap. 'There she is.'

Hazel, bless her, was hanging onto a twin with each hand and hauling them forward. No easy task because they were clearly exhausted. What were they doing out of bed? They'd been asleep when Gemma had left the house and they were in their pyjamas and rubbing bleary eyes now, as though they hadn't woken up properly. Ben was clutching his favourite soft toy as if afraid someone was about to rip it out of his arms.

A sudden fear gripped Gemma. They were sick. With whatever Sophie had wrong with her.

But why was Simon here? OK, he'd arrived at the house a few minutes before the babysitter had been due and she'd had to rush off with Sophie but…but Hazel's bottom lip was wobbling and she was like another little mother to these children and *never* cried.

'Oh…hon come here.' Gemma balanced Sophie with one arm and held the other one out to gather Hazel and the twins close. 'It's all right…'

'No, it's not.' Simon had a hand on Jamie's shoulder,

pushing the small boy towards her. 'Your babysitter decided not to show.'

'What? Oh, no...'

'She rang. Had a car accident or some such excuse.'

'Oh, my God! Is she all right?'

'She sounded fine.' Simon shook his head. 'Look, I'm sorry, Gemma but, you know...I had no idea what I was signing up for here.'

'No.' Of course he hadn't. This had been a blind date that an old friend had insisted on setting her up with. Just a glass of wine, she'd said. At your local. Just see if you like him. He's gorgeous. And rich. And *single*.

There was no denying that Simon was good looking. Blond, blue-eyed and extremely well dressed, too. And...smooth was the first thought that had come to mind when she'd let him into the house. But definitely not her type. He'd been horrified when she'd said she had to get Sophie to the hospital and could he please wait until the babysitter arrived.

And...

'How did you get them here?'

'I drove, of course. You practically live in the next county.'

Hardly. The house was rural, certainly, but on the very edge of the city, which made Queen Mary's the closest hospital, otherwise Gemma would have gone somewhere else.

'What about the car seats?'

'Ooh, look...' Jamie was pointing to the area of the

waiting room set up to cater for children. 'There's toys.' He trotted off.

'He didn't use them,' Hazel said. 'I told him and he...' Her breath hitched. 'He told me to shut up.'

Gemma's jaw dropped. She stared at Simon, who simply shrugged.

'Look, I could've left them in the house. If Jane had told me anything more than that you were a cute, single chick who was desperate for a date, I wouldn't have come near you with a bargepole. I don't *do* kids.'

Chloe chose that moment to hold her arms up, asking to be cuddled. When it didn't happen instantly, she burst into tears. Sophie's grizzles turned into a full-blown wail. Ben sat down on the floor and buried his face against the well-worn fluff of his toy. Simon looked at them all for a second, shook his head in disbelief, turned on his heel and walked out.

Gemma had no idea what to do first. Hazel was pressed against her, her skinny little body shaking with repressed sobs. Gemma didn't need to look down. She knew that there would be tears streaming down Hazel's cheeks. Both Chloe and Sophie were howling and... Where on earth had Jamie got to?

Wildly, Gemma scanned the waiting room as she tried to tamp down the escalating tension from the sounds of miserable children all around her. The action came to a juddering halt, however, when her gaze collided with a person who'd been standing there watching the whole, horrible scene with Simon.

A man who had shaggy brown hair instead of

groomed blond waves. Brown eyes, not blue. Who couldn't be considered well dressed with his crooked tie and shirtsleeves that were trying to come down from where they'd been rolled up. But her type?

Oh…yes. The archetype, in fact. Because this was Andy. The man she'd fallen in love with. The man she'd known would be the only one for her for the rest of her life. For just an instant, Gemma could forget that this was the man whose life she'd done her best to ruin because the first wave of emotion to hit her was one of…

Relief.

Thank *God*. No matter what happened in this next micro-chapter of her life, she could deal with it if she had Andy nearby.

Her touchstone.

The rock that had been missing from her life for so long. Yes, she'd learned to stand on her own two feet but the ground had never felt solid enough to trust. To put roots into.

The blessed relief that felt like a homecoming twisted almost instantly into something else, however. Fear?

He hadn't said her name but he looked as angry as Simon had been when he'd stormed into the waiting room of Queen Mary's.

Or…maybe it wasn't anger. She'd seen that kind of look before, during a fight. Partly anger but also pain. And bewilderment. The result of being attacked when you didn't know quite what it was about and why you deserved it in the first place.

Gemma didn't know what to say. Maybe Andy didn't either. He was looking at the baby in her arms.

'I'll take her,' he said. 'You bring the others and follow me.'

CHAPTER TWO

THANK heavens there was a sick baby to assess.

It was another blessing that Andy had had plenty of practice in using a professional mode to override personal pain. This might be the best test yet, mind you.

Gemma's baby?

She had found someone to take his place in her life and she'd had his *baby*? A baby he now had cradled in his own arms as he led the way from the waiting room into the business area of the emergency department. Gemma was a good few steps behind him. He hadn't waited quite long enough for her to scoop up the youngest girl and send the oldest one to fetch the boy called Jamie from the playpen.

Jamie?

Something was struggling to escape from the part of his brain he was overriding but Andy didn't dare release the circuit breaker he'd had to slam on within seconds of walking into that waiting room.

That first glimpse of Gemma had hit him like an emotional sledgehammer. The power of that initial, soul-deep response had had the potential to destroy him utterly if he hadn't been able to shut it down fast. Fortunately, some automatic survival instinct had kicked in and extinguished that blinding glow. Shutting off his emotional response had left him with a lens focused on physical attributes and...astonishingly, it could have been yesterday that he'd last seen her.

OK, her hair was longer. Those luxuriant brown waves had barely touched her shoulders back then and they were in a loose plait that hung down to the middle of her back now. Same colour, though, and even in the artificial glare of the neon strip lighting in here it was alive with sparks of russet and deep gold. She'd filled out a little, too, but that only made her look more like the woman he'd fallen in love with instead of the pale shadow that had slipped out of his life four years ago.

How much worse was it going to be when he was close enough to see her eyes? Nobody else in the world had Gemma's eyes. They might share that glowing hazel shade but he'd never seen anyone with the unusual gold rims around the irises and the matching chips in their depths.

So far, by concentrating on the small people around her, Andy had managed to avoid more than a grazing glance. He was still avoiding direct eye contact as he walked briskly ahead of her.

He was getting close to the triage desk now and Julia was watching his approach. Or rather she was staring at the small train of followers he knew he had. Gemma must look like the old woman from the shoe, he thought grimly. So many children she didn't know what to do.

The irony would be unbearable if he let himself go there.

'Space?' he queried crisply. 'Query meningitis here.'

'Um...' Julia gave her head a tiny shake and turned it to glance over her shoulder at the board. 'Resus One's just been cleared...but—'

'Thanks.' Andy didn't give her time to say that it probably needed to be kept clear for a more urgent case. The privacy and space of one of the larger areas would be ideal to contain this unacceptably large group. It wasn't until he led them all into the space he realised that isolating himself from the hubbub of the cubicles would only intensify the undercurrents happening here but, by then, it was too late.

A nurse had just finished smoothing a clean sheet onto the bed. Andy laid the baby down gently. Her wails had diminished as he'd carried her here but the volume got turned up as he put her down and she was rubbing her eyes with small, tight fists. Was the light hurting her? Andy angled the lamp away.

'What's going on?' he asked. It was quite easy to ask the question without looking directly at Gemma. Right now she was just another parent of a sick child.

'Fever, irritability, refusing food.' Gemma's voice was strained. 'She vomited once and her cry sounded...' her voice wavered '...kind of high-pitched.'

Andy focused on the baby. He slid one hand behind her head. Lifting it gently, he was relieved to see her neck flex. If this was a case of meningitis, it was at an early stage but he could feel the heat from the skin beneath wisps of golden hair darkened by perspiration.

'Let's get her undressed,' he told the nurse. 'I'd like some baseline vital signs, too, thanks.'

Hard to assess a rate of breathing when a baby was this distressed, of course. And the bulging fontanelle could be the result of the effort of crying rather than anything more sinister. Andy straightened for a moment, frowning, as he tried to take in an overall impression.

It didn't help that there were so many other children in here. The small girl in Gemma's arms was still whimpering and the older boy was whining.

'But *why* can't I go and play with the toys?'

'Shh, Jamie.' The older girl gave him a shove. 'Sophie's *sick*. She might be going to *die*.'

Andy's eyebrows reversed direction and shot up. The matter-of-fact tone of the child was shocking. He heard Gemma gasp and it was impossible to prevent his gaze going straight to her face.

She was looking straight back at him.

He could see a mirror of his own shock at Sophie's statement. And see a flash of despair in Gemma's eyes.

And he could see something else. A plea? No, it was more like an entire library of unspoken words. Instant understanding and...trust that what was known wouldn't be used for harm.

And there was that glow again, dammit. Rays of intense light and warmth seeping out from the mental lid he'd slammed over the hole in his heart. Andy struggled to push the lid more firmly into place. To find something to screw it down with.

She's moved on, a small voice reminded Andy. *She's got children. Another man's children.*

It was Gemma who dragged her gaze clear.

'She's *not* going to die, Hazel.' But was there an edge of desperation in Gemma's voice?

'She's here so that we can look after her,' Andy added in his most reassuring adult-to-child tone. 'And make sure that she doesn't…' The stare he was receiving from Jamie was disconcerting. 'That nothing bad happens.'

The nurse was pulling Sophie's arms from the sleeves of a soft, hand-knitted cardigan. Sophie was not co-operating. She was flexing her arms tightly and kicking out with her feet. Nothing floppy about her, Andy thought. It was a good sign that she was so upset. It wouldn't be much fun for anybody if a lumbar puncture was needed to confirm the possibility of meningitis, though. He certainly wouldn't be doing a procedure like that with an audience of young children, especially when one of them was calmly expecting a catastrophe.

Hazel was giving him a stare as direct as Jamie's had been. She looked far older than her years and there was something familiar about that serious scrutiny. The penny finally dropped.

Hazel? Jamie? There was no way he could ignore the pull into the forbidden area now. Not that he was going to raise that lid, even a millimetre, but he could tread—carefully—around its perimeter. Andy directed a cautious glance at Gemma.

'These are your sister's children? Laura and Evan's kids?'

He didn't need to see her nodding. Of course they were. Four years was a long time in a child's life. The last time he'd seen Hazel she'd been a three-year-old. James had been a baby not much older than Sophie and...and Laura had been pregnant with twins, hadn't she?

The nurse had succeeded in undressing Sophie now, removing sheepskin bootees and peeling away the soft stretchy suit to leave her in just a singlet and nappy. Sophie was still protesting the procedure and she was starting to sound exhausted on top of being so unhappy. Gemma stepped closer. She tried to reach out a hand to touch the baby but the child she was holding wrapped her arms more tightly around her neck.

'No-o-o... Don't put me down, Aunty Gemma.'

Hazel was peering under the bed. 'You come out of there, Ben. Right *now*.'

'And Sophie?' Andy couldn't stem a wash of relief so strong it made his chest feel too tight to take a new breath. 'She's Laura's baby?'

'She was.' Gemma managed to secure her burden with one arm and touch Sophie's head with her other hand. She looked up at Andy. 'She's mine now. They all are.'

Andy said nothing. He knew his question was written all over his face.

'They were bringing Sophie home from the hospital,' Gemma said quietly. 'There was a head-on collision with a truck at the intersection where their lane joins the main road. A car came out of the lane without giving way and Evan swerved and that put them over the centre line. They...they both died at the scene.' She pressed her lips together hard and squeezed her eyes shut for a heartbeat.

'Oh, my God,' Andy breathed. Laura had been his sister-in-law. Bright and bubbly and so full of life. Gemma had been more than a big sister to her. She had been her mother as well. The news must have been unbelievably devastating. 'Gemma...I'm so sorry.'

Gemma opened her eyes again, avoiding his gaze. Because accepting sympathy might undo her in front of the children? Her voice was stronger. Artificially bright. 'Luckily the car seat saved Sophie from any injury.'

'And you were here in Manchester?' Andy still couldn't get his head around it. How long had she been here and why hadn't he known anything about it? It felt...wrong.

'No. I was in Sydney. Australia.'

Of course she had been. In the place she'd taken off to four years ago. The point on the globe where she could be as far as possible away from him. Andy could feel his own lips tightening. Could feel himself stepping back from that dangerous, personal ground.

'But you came back. To look after the kids.'

'Of course.'

Two tiny words that said *so* much. Andy knew exactly why Gemma had come back. But the simple statement prised open a completely separate can of worms at the same time. She could abandon her career and traverse the globe to care for children for her sister's sake?

She hadn't been able to do even half of that for him, had she?

There was anger trapped amongst the pain and grief in that no-go area. Plenty of it. Especially now that he had successfully extinguished that glow. He turned back to his patient.

'Let's get her singlet off as well. I want to check for any sign of a rash.'

Gemma wasn't sure who she felt the most sorry for.

Sophie? A tiny baby who was not only feeling sick but had to be frightened by the bright lights and strange environment and unfamiliar people pulling her clothes off and poking at her.

Hazel? A child who was disturbingly solemn these days. It was scary the way she seemed to be braced for fate to wipe another member of her family from the face of the earth.

The twins, who were so tired they didn't know what to do with themselves?

Herself?

Oh, yes...it would be all too easy to make it about herself at this particular moment.

Not because she was half out of her mind with worry. Or that her arms were beginning to ache unbearably from holding the heavy weight of three-year-old Chloe who was slumped and almost asleep, with her head buried against Gemma's shoulder, but still making sad, whimpering sounds.

No. The real pain was coming from watching Andy. Seeing the changes that four years had etched into his face. The fine lines that had deepened around his eyes. The flecks of silver amongst the warm brown hair at his temples. The five-o'clock shadow that looked…coarser than she remembered.

Or maybe it wasn't the changes that were making her feel like this. Maybe it was the things that *hadn't* changed that were squeezing her heart until it ached harder than her arms.

That crease of genuine concern between his eyebrows. The confident but gentle movements of his hands as they touched the baby, seeking answers to so many questions. The way she could almost see his mind working with that absolute thoroughness and speed and intelligence she knew he possessed.

'She's got a bit of a rash on her trunk but that could be a heat rash from running a fever. This could be petechiae around her eyes, though.' Andy was bent over the baby, cupping her head reassuringly with one hand, using a single finger of his other hand to press an area close to her eyes, checking to see if the tiny spots would vanish with pressure. He glanced up at Gemma. 'Has she been vomiting at all?'

'Just the once. After a feed. She refused her bottle after that.'

Andy's nod was thoughtful. 'Could have been enough

to push her venous pressure up and cause these.' But he was frowning. 'We'll have to keep an eye on them.'

He took his stethoscope out to listen to the tiny chest but paused for a moment when Sophie stretched out her hand. He gave her a finger to clutch. Gemma watched those tiny starfish fingers curl around Andy's finger and she could actually feel how warm and strong it must seem. Something curled inside her at the same time. The memory of what it was like to touch Andy? To feel his strength and his warmth and the steady, comforting beat of his heart?

It was so, so easy to remember how much she had loved this man.

How much she *still* loved him.

That's why you set him free, her mind whispered. *You have no claim on him any more. He wouldn't want you to have one.*

His voice was soft enough to bring a lump to her throat.

'It's all right, chicken,' he told Sophie. 'You'll get a proper cuddle soon, I promise.'

He might well give her that cuddle himself, Gemma thought, and the fresh shaft of misery told her exactly who it was that she felt most sorry for here.

Andy.

No wonder she had felt that edge of anger when she'd told him she'd come rushing back from Australia to step into the terrible gap left by her sister's death.

Andy had been the one who'd wanted a big family. For Gemma it had come well down the list of any priorities. A list that had always been headed by her determination to achieve a stellar career.

The irony of what she was throwing in his face to-night was undeserved. Cruel, even.

Andy was the one with the stellar career now. The grapevine that existed in the medical world easily extended as far as Australia and she'd heard about his growing reputation as a leader in his field.

And her career?

Snuffed out. For the last six months and for as far as she could see into the future, she would be a stay-at-home mum.

To a ridiculous number of children. The big family Andy had always wanted and she had refused to consider. In those days, she hadn't even wanted one child, had she?

Sophie's exhausted cries had settled into the occasional miserable hiccup as Andy completed his initial examination, which included peering into her ears with an otoscope.

'I don't think it's meningitis,' he told Gemma finally.

'Oh…thank God for that.' The tight knot in Gemma's stomach eased just a little, knowing that Sophie might not have to go through an invasive procedure like a lumbar puncture.

Andy could see the relief in Gemma's eyes but he couldn't smile at her. He knew she wasn't going to be happy with what he was about to say.

'I'm going to take some bloods.'

Sure enough, the fear was there again. Enough to

show Andy that Gemma was totally committed to this
family of orphans. Their welfare was *her* welfare.

'Her right eardrum is pretty inflamed,' he continued, 'and otitis media could well be enough to explain
her symptoms but I'm concerned about that rash. We've
had a local outbreak of measles recently and one or
two of those children have had some unpleasant com-
plications.'

Gemma was listening carefully. So was Hazel.

'Kirsty's got measles,' she said.

'Who's Kirsty?' Andy's voice was deceptively calm.
'A friend of yours?'

Hazel nodded. 'She comes to play at my house sometimes.'

Andy's glance held Gemma. 'Have the other children been vaccinated?'

'I…don't know, sorry.'

'We can find out. But not tonight, obviously.' Andy
straightened. He could see the nurse preparing a tray for
taking blood samples from Sophie but it wasn't something he wanted the other children to watch. He'd ask
Gemma to take them all into the relatives' room for a
few minutes.

She could take them all home. Even Sophie. He could
issue instructions to keep them quarantined at home
until the results came in and that way he'd be doing his
duty in not risking the spread of a potentially dangerous
illness. Gemma was more than capable of watching for
any signs of deterioration in the baby's condition but…
if he sent them home, would he see any of them again?

Did he want to?

Andy didn't know the answer to that so he wasn't willing to take the risk of losing what little control he had over the situation. And even the possibility of a potentially serious illness like measles made it perfectly justifiable to keep Sophie here until they were confident of the diagnosis.

To keep them all here, for that matter.

Quarantined, in fact.

'I'll be back in a minute,' he excused himself. 'I've got a phone call I need to make.'

Thirty minutes later, Gemma found herself in a single room at the end of the paediatric ward. Already containing two single beds and armchairs suitable for parents to crash in, the staff had squeezed in two extra cots and a bassinette.

'Just for a while,' Andy told her. 'Until we get the results back on those blood tests and we can rule out measles.'

Sophie was sound asleep in the bassinette with a dose of paracetamol and antibiotics on board. The twins were eyeing the cots dubiously. Jamie and Hazel were eyeing the hospital-issue pyjamas a nurse had provided.

'I want to go home,' Hazel whispered sadly.

'I know, hon, but we can't. Not yet.'

'But it's Christmas Eve.'

Gemma couldn't say anything. The true irony of this situation was pressing down on her. An unbearable weight that made it impossible to look directly at Andy.

She heard him clear his throat. An uncomfortable sound.

'Will you be all right getting the kids settled? I… have a patient in the PICU I really need to follow up on.'

'Of course. Thanks for all your help.'

'I'll come back later.'

Gemma said nothing. She couldn't because the lump in her throat was too huge.

It was Christmas Eve and Andy was going to the paediatric intensive care unit.

The place it had all begun, ten years ago.

CHAPTER THREE

Christmas: ten years ago

'It's a big ask, Gemma. I know that.'

The PICU consultant was dressed in a dinner suit, complete with a black velvet bow-tie. He was running late for a Christmas Eve function. Gemma already felt guilty for calling him in but she'd had no choice, had she? Her senior registrar and the consultant on duty were caught up dealing with a six-month-old baby in heart failure and a new admission with a severe asthma attack.

The deterioration in five-year-old Jessica's condition had been inevitable but the decision to withdraw treatment and end the child's suffering had certainly not been one a junior doctor could make.

'You don't have to do it immediately,' her consultant continued. 'Any time tonight is all right. Wait until you've got the support you need. I'm sorry…but I really can't stay. This function is a huge deal for my daughter. She's leading in the carol choir doing a solo of "Once

in Royal David's City" and if I don't make it my name
will be mud and tomorrow's…'

'Christmas.' Gemma nodded. She managed a smile.
'Family time that shouldn't be spoiled if it can be
helped.'

'You've got it.' The older man sighed. 'If there was
any chance of improving the outcome by heroic mea-
sures right now I'd stay, of course. But we'd only be
prolonging the inevitable.'

'I know.'

They'd all known that almost as soon as Jessica had
been admitted. The battle against cancer had been going
on for half the little girl's life and she'd seemed to be
in remission but any infection in someone with a com-
promised immune system was potentially catastrophic.

Over the last few days they had been fighting multi-
organ failure and the decision that had been made over
the last hour had been much bigger than whether or
not to begin dialysis to cope with her kidneys shutting down.

Gemma had to swallow the lump in her throat. 'I just
don't understand why her mother won't come back in.'

'She's a foster-mother, Gemma,' he reminded her.
'She loves Jessica dearly but she's got six other children
at home and…it's Christmas Eve. She was in here for
most of the day and she's said her goodbyes. It's not as
if Jessica's going to wake up. You'll take her off the life
support and she'll just stop breathing. It probably won't
take very long.' The consultant glanced at his watch as
he reached for a pen. 'I'll write it up. As I said, I know

it's a big ask. No one will blame you if you're not up for it but I know how much time you've spent with her since her admission and I thought…'

Gemma took a shaky inward breath. Yes, she'd spent a lot of time with Jessica. Too much, probably, especially before she'd been sedated and put on life support. Certainly enough time to have fallen in love with the child and, if the closest thing to a mother she had couldn't be here at the end then someone who loved her was surely next best.

'I can do it,' she whispered. 'But…not just yet.'

'Take all the time you need.' The consultant signed his name on the order and turned to leave. He paused to offer Gemma a sympathetic smile. 'You're one of the best junior doctors I've ever had the pleasure of working with,' he said, 'but this isn't a time for being brave and trying to cope on your own. Every person who works in here will understand how tough this is. Take your pick but find someone to lean on, OK?'

Gemma couldn't speak. She could only nod.

It was the way she was standing that caught his attention.

She looked as though she was gathering resolution to dive into a pool of icy water. Or knock on a door when she knew that somebody she really didn't want to see was going to answer the summons. What was going on in that closed room of the PICU? Andrew Baxter had to focus to tune back into what his registrar was saying.

'So we'll keep up the inotropic support overnight.

Keep an eye on all the parameters, especially urine output. If it hasn't picked up by morning we'll be looking at some more invasive treatment for the heart failure.' The registrar yawned. 'Call me if anything changes but, in the meantime, I'm going to get my head down for a bit.' His smile was cheerful. 'You get to stay up and mind the shop. One of the perks of being the new kid on the block.'

'I don't mind.' Andy returned the smile, aware of the woman still standing as still as a statue outside that room. He hesitated only briefly after his companion left.

'Hey.' His greeting was quiet. 'Do you…um…need any help?'

She looked up at him and Andy was struck by two things. The first, and most obvious, was the level of distress in her eyes. The second was the eyes themselves. He'd never seen anything like them. Flecks of gold in the rich hazel depths and an extraordinary rim of the same gold around the edges of the irises. He couldn't help holding the eye contact for longer than he should with someone he'd never met but she didn't seem to mind. One side of her mouth curved upwards in a wry smile.

'Got a bit of courage to spare?'

Andy could feel himself standing a little bit taller. Feeling more confident than he knew he had a right to. 'You bet,' he said. 'How much would you like?'

'Buckets,' she said, a tiny wobble in her voice. 'Have you ever had to turn off someone's life support?'

Andy blew out a slow breath. 'Hardly. I'm a baby

doctor. I started in the August intake and I've only just begun my second rotation.'

'Me, too.'

'And your team has left you to deal with this on your own?' Andy was horrified.

She shook her head. 'I get to choose a support person. My registrar is busy with the other consultant on the asthma case that came in a little while ago and the other registrar on duty is in with a baby. I think it's a cardiac case.'

Andy nodded. 'It is. I'm on a cardiology run. Six-month-old that's come in with heart failure. I'll probably be here all night, monitoring him. At the moment they're trying to decide whether to take him up to the cath lab for a procedure. I got sent out to check availability.'

'Sounds full on.'

'It won't be. If we're not going to the cath lab immediately I'll be floating around here pretty much for hours.' Andy tried to sound casual but her words were echoing in his head. She was allowed to choose a support person. The desire to *be* that person came from nowhere but it was disturbingly strong. It was emotional support she needed, not medical expertise, and surely he would understand how she would be feeling better than anyone else around here. They were both baby doctors and he knew how nervous he'd be in her position. How hard something like this would be.

Andy gave her an encouraging smile. 'I could be your support person.'

* * *

Gemma could feel her eyes widening.

She didn't even know this guy's name and he was being so...*nice*.

Genuine, too. He had dark brown eyes that radiated warmth. And understanding. Well, that made sense. He was at the same stage of his career as she was with hers and he'd never been in this position. Maybe, like her, he still hadn't even seen someone actually die. Gemma could be quite sure that anyone else here in the PICU had seen it before. It didn't mean that they wouldn't be able to support her but they might have forgotten just how scary it was that first time. Not knowing how it might hit you. How unprofessional you might end up looking...

Gemma didn't want to look unprofessional. Not in front of people who were more senior to herself and might judge her for it.

Kind eyes was smiling at her. 'Sorry—I haven't even introduced myself. Andrew Baxter. Andy...' He held out his hand.

Gemma automatically took the hand. It was warm and big and gave hers a friendly squeeze rather than a formal shake. He let go almost immediately but she could still feel the warmth. And the strength.

'I'm Gemma,' she told him.

'Hello, Gemma.' Andy's smile faded and he looked suddenly sombre. 'Would you like me to check with my consultant about whether it's OK for me to hang out with you for a while?'

Gemma found herself nodding. 'I'll ask whether

someone more senior has to be there. But there's no rush,' she added hurriedly. 'I wanted to just sit with Jessie for a bit first.'

He held her gaze for a moment, a question in his eyes. And then he nodded as though he approved of the plan.

'I'll come and find you,' he promised.

It was remarkably private in one of these areas of the PICU when the curtains were drawn over the big windows and the door was closed.

Remarkably quiet, too, with just the gentle hiss of the ventilator and muted beeping from the bank of monitoring equipment.

The nurse had given Gemma a concerned look before she'd left her alone in there with Jessica.

'Are you sure you don't want me to stay?'

Gemma shook her head and offered a faint smile. 'Thanks, but I need to do this in my own time,' she said. 'And...I think one of the other house officers is going to come and keep me company for a bit.'

The door opened quietly a few minutes later and then closed again. Andy moved with unusual grace for a big man as he positioned a chair and then sat down so that he was looking across the bed at Gemma.

Except he wasn't looking at Gemma. His gaze was fixed on Jessica's pale little face. He reached out and made her hand disappear beneath his.

'Hello, there, Jessie,' he whispered. 'I'm Andy. I'm Gemma's friend.'

Gemma liked that. She certainly needed a friend right now.

For several minutes they simply sat there in silence.

'Do you think she's aware of anything?' Gemma asked softly.

'I had a look at her chart on the way in,' Andy responded. 'She's well sedated so I'm sure she's not in any pain.'

'But nobody really knows, do they? Whether there's an awareness of...something.'

'Something like whether there's somebody there that cares about you?'

'Mmm.' Gemma took hold of Jessie's other hand as she looked up. Away from the harsh strip lighting of the main area of the PICU, Andy's face looked softer. His dark hair was just as tousled, the strong planes of his cheeks and jaw a little less craggy and his eyes were even warmer.

But what was really appealing was that he seemed to get what she was doing in here. Why it was important. His posture was also relaxed enough to suggest he wasn't going to put any pressure on her to hurry what had to be done.

'I saw she had a guardian listed as next of kin rather than family but...' Andy shook his head. 'I still don't understand why it's just us in here.'

'She's fostered,' Gemma told him. 'She was in foster-care even before she was diagnosed with a brain tumour over two years ago and she's had major medical issues ever since. There are very few foster-parents out there who would be prepared to cope with that.' She knew she was sounding a bit defensive but she knew how hard it could be.

'And the woman who's been doing it has a bunch of other kids who need her tonight. She's been in here half the day and…she couldn't face this.'

'But you can.' The statement was quiet and had a strong undercurrent of admiration.

Gemma's breath came out in a short huff. 'I don't know about that. It's…' For some strange reason she found herself on the verge of dumping her whole life history onto someone who was a stranger to her, which was pretty weird when she was such a fiercely private person. 'It's complicated.'

Andy said nothing for another minute or so. Then he cleared his throat. 'So…where did you do your training?'

'Birmingham.' Gemma felt herself frowning. What on earth did this have to do with anything? Then she got it. Andy wanted to give her some time to get used to him. To trust him? Given that she'd learned not to trust people very early in life it was a strategy she could appreciate. Oddly, it felt redundant. How could she not instinctively trust someone who had such kind eyes?

Her abrupt response was still hanging in the air. Gemma cleared her throat. 'How 'bout you? Where did you train?'

'Cambridge.'

'Nice.'

Andy nodded. 'What made you choose Birmingham?'

'I lived there. With my younger sister.' Gemma

paused for a heartbeat. Reminded herself that Andy was trying to build trust here and it couldn't hurt to help. 'She was still at school,' she added, 'and I didn't want to move her.'

Andy's eyebrows rose. 'There was just the two of you?'

It was Gemma's turn to nod. And then she took a deep breath. Maybe she needed to accelerate this 'getting to know you' phase because she really did need a friend here. Someone she could trust. Someone who knew they could trust her. Or maybe it had already been accelerated because of an instant connection that somehow disengaged all her normal protective mechanisms.

'We were foster-kids,' she told him quietly. 'I got guardianship of Laura as soon as I turned eighteen. She was thirteen then.'

She could feel the way his gaze was fixed on her even though she was keeping her head bowed, watching as she rubbed the back of Jessie's hand with her thumb.

'Wow... That's not something siblings often do for each other. Laura's very lucky to have you for a sister.'

'No. I'm the lucky one. Laura's an amazing person. One of those naturally happy people, you know? She can make everyone around her feel better just by being there.'

'You're both lucky, then,' Andy said. 'Me, I'm an only child. I dreamt of having a sibling. Lots of them, in fact. I couldn't think of anything better than having a really big family but it never happened.' He shrugged, as though excusing Gemma from feeling sorry for him.

'Guess it'll be up to me to change the next Baxter generation.'

'You want lots of kids?'

'At least half a dozen.' Andy grinned. 'What about you?'

Gemma shook her head sharply.

'You don't want kids?'

'Sure. One or two. But that's so far into the future it doesn't register yet.' She could feel her spine straighten a little. 'I haven't worked as hard as I have not to make sure I get my career exactly where I want it before I take time off to have a baby.'

'Going to be rich and famous, huh?'

'That's the plan.' Oh, help…that had sounded shallow hadn't it? 'Secure, anyway,' Gemma added. 'And… respected, I guess.'

Andy nodded as though he understood where she was coming from. 'How old were you when you went into foster-care?'

'I was eight. Laura was only three. Luckily we got sent places together. Probably because I kicked up such a fuss if they made noises about separating us and also because I was prepared to take care of Laura myself.' She looked up then and offered a smile. 'I was quite likely to bite anybody that tried to take over.'

Andy grinned. 'I can believe that.' Then his face sobered again. He looked at Jessie and then back at Gemma. He didn't say anything but she knew he was joining the dots. She didn't need to spell out the complexities of why she felt a bond with this child and why it was important for her to be here with her at the end of her short life.

'You're quite something, aren't you?' he said finally.

A warm glow unfurled somewhere deep inside Gemma but outwardly all she did was shrug. 'I wouldn't say that.'

'I would. You completed your medical degree. It was hard enough for me and I had family support and no responsibilities. I've still got a pretty impressive student debt.'

'Tell me about it.' But Gemma didn't want to go there. She'd shared more than enough of her difficult background. Any more and they'd need to bring in the violins and that was definitely not an atmosphere that was going to help get her into the right space for what had to come. The task she still wasn't quite ready for. Time to change the subject and get to know her new friend a little better. 'What made you choose to go into medicine?'

'I think I always wanted to be a doctor. My dad's a GP in Norwich.'

'Family tradition?'

Andy grinned. 'Familiar, anyway. I just grew up knowing that the only thing I wanted to be was a doctor. Maybe I was too lazy to think of anything else I wanted to be.' His gaze was interested. 'How 'bout you?'

'Laura had to have her appendix out when she was seven and the surgeon was the loveliest woman, who arranged permission for me to stay in the hospital with her for a couple of days. I fell in love with both the surgeon and the hospital. Plus, I had to choose a career that would enable me to always be able to take care of my sister.'

'So you're going into surgery for a speciality?'

Gemma smiled. 'Haven't thought about that too much yet. I'm concentrating on surviving the next couple of years.'

'Me, too. I figure that it could be a process of elimination. It's a good thing we get all these rotations. I'll cross off the ones that don't feel right along the way.' He looked at Jessie and sighed. 'Might have to cross off PICU. It's pretty intense, isn't it?'

'But awesome when the outcome is good. What's happening with that baby that came in under your team?'

'He's been off colour for a few days but his mother brought him in because he was so breathless he couldn't finish his bottle. We started diuretics in ED but his blood gases showed metabolic acidosis.'

'Has he got a congenital abnormality?'

Andy shook his head. 'Echocardiography was normal. The likely scenario is an infection of some kind. Viral or bacterial.'

'Will he make it?'

Andy looked grim. 'About thirty per cent of kids that are like this die or require transplantation in the first year after the infection. His parents are distraught. It's their first baby.'

His empathy for those parents was transparent and Gemma felt a flash of sympathy. Maybe it was a hazard of the job for junior doctors that they became too emotionally involved with their cases. Andy wasn't only prepared to care about his own case, he was now in, boots and all, to Gemma's.

He not only had kind eyes, this man. He had a huge heart.

'They're not bad odds,' she offered. 'Worth fighting for, that's for sure.'

'Mmm. Speaking of which, I'd better go and check on things. Like his urine output.' Andy got to his feet. 'Will you be OK for a bit?'

Gemma nodded. 'I...might take her lines out.'

'But you won't do anything else? Until I get back?'

He looked so anxious. So concerned. For *her*.

Gemma felt something very big squeeze in her chest as she smiled at him. 'No. I won't do anything until you get back.'

By the time Andy got back to Jessica's room, he could see that things had changed. Gemma had taken off all the cardiac monitoring patches and the ECG machine was silent. The IV lines were out as well, including the central line that had been in place beneath a tiny collar bone. No blood pressure or heart rate or other vital signs were being recorded now. The screens on the monitors were blank, which accentuated the soft lighting. The only thing left to remove was the breathing tube. The only sound in the room was the gentle hiss of mechanically moving air.

Gemma had not only removed the invasive lines, she

had covered the wounds with sticky dots and cleaned away any trace of blood.

'She hardly bled at all,' she told Andy. 'Her blood pressure must be really low.'

'Would you like me to remove the ET tube?'

He was watching Gemma's face carefully. He saw the fear in her eyes that was quickly shuttered by their lids. She had amazing eyelashes, a part of his brain registered. Thick and dark, like her hair, and he was sure she wasn't wearing any make-up. Right now, her lips were unnaturally pale. It was the tiny tremble in her lips that really undid Andy, though. He stepped closer and put his arm around her shoulders.

'Let's do it together.'

So they did. Gemma peeled away the tape securing the tube in place with as much care as if Jessica had been awake and feeling the unpleasant sensation. It was Andy who slipped the tube out and turned off the hiss of the ventilator.

For a long, long moment, they simply stood there. One of Gemma's hands was holding Jessie's. The other had somehow found its way into Andy's and he gripped it firmly.

They watched as the little girl struggled to take a breath on her own. Her face was still. Peaceful, even, but the small chest rose and fell slowly.

Andy could actually hear Gemma swallow. Her voice sounded thick. So quiet he had to lean closer to hear the words.

'How long do you think...?'

'I don't know.'

They watched for another breath. And another.

'Do you think…?' Gemma had to swallow again. Andy could see a tear trickling down the side of her nose. 'Do you think it would be OK to hold her?'

Andy felt dangerously close to tears himself. 'Of course it would.'

He guided Gemma to one of the comfortable chairs that were always in these rooms for exhausted parents. He gathered Jessica's limp body into his arms and gently transferred her into Gemma's. She eased the little girl's head into the crook of her elbow and stroked away a few strands of hair.

'It's OK, hon,' she whispered. 'We're here. You're not alone.'

God…this was hard. Much harder than Andy had expected it to be. He had to look away and try to breathe past the painful lump in his throat.

He heard Gemma start to hum. Shakily at first, with no discernible tune, but then the sound grew stronger and he recognised it.

'The "Skye Boat Song",' he whispered.

Gemma looked up and her smile was poignant. 'It was Laura's favourite,' she said very softly. 'It always helped her get to sleep, no matter what was happening around us.'

The tight feeling in Andy's chest got bigger. What kind of childhood had Gemma had? She had an inner strength that shone through, despite the vulnerability he was witnessing in having to deal with this heart-breaking event.

She was, quite simply…astonishing.

Jessica's breathing pattern had changed. She would take a deep breath and then several shallow ones and then there would be a pause before the next deep breath. Cheyne Stokes breathing, it was called. A sign that death was close.

Andy kept an eye on the clock in case Gemma didn't remember to record the time of death. He moved closer too, perching a hip on the arm of the chair so that he could put a hand on Gemma's shoulder and let her know that he was connected here.

He could look down. At a brave young woman holding a child as if she was hers. As if she was loved and would be mourned when she was gone.

Jessica was gone a short time later but neither of them moved for several minutes and they both had tears running freely.

It was hours later that Andy saw Gemma again. Waiting for a lift. The doors opened just as he got close so he got into the lift with her. He hadn't intended to but she'd looked wrecked the last time he'd seen her in the PICU and he had to make sure she was OK.

It was Gemma who spoke first as the doors of the lift closed.

'Thank you,' she said quietly. 'For…before. I couldn't have done that without you.'

'Yes, you could.' Andy was embarrassed by her gratitude. He looked down and nudged something with his foot. What was it? He stooped and picked it up.

'What's that?'

'A bit of rubbish.'

Gemma looked at the sprig of green plastic with tiny white balls. 'It's mistletoe,' she said. Her breath was a huff. 'I'd almost forgotten but it's Christmas Day now, isn't it?'

'It is indeed.' Andy turned his head to smile at her. 'Merry Christmas, Gemma.'

She held his gaze and Andy knew in that moment that he was going to see her again. That something had started tonight that he wouldn't be able to stop. Wouldn't want to stop. He raised the twig of mistletoe above their heads as the lift slowed.

He only meant to give her a peck on the cheek but she moved her head as the doors opened and her lips brushed his.

For a heartbeat, she stood very still.

As stunned as he was?

'Um…Merry Christmas, Andy,' she whispered. 'See you around.' And then she was gone.

'Yes,' Andy told the silent corridor before he pushed the button to go back to the floor he needed. 'You certainly will.'

CHAPTER FOUR

THE children weren't at all happy about having to go to sleep in a strange room on Christmas Eve.

'No!' Ben shouted when Gemma tried to lift him into the cot. 'No, no, *n-o-o…*'

'Shh,' Gemma commanded. 'Don't wake Sophie up.' Or disturb any of the other sick children in this ward, she thought. It was a privilege to be keeping all these children together right now, she knew that. Of course she would have been allowed to stay with Sophie but if the others had been banned, she had nobody to step in and help out at such short notice and she would have had to leave the baby alone.

With her spirits sinking a little further, Gemma remembered she hadn't even texted the babysitter she had arranged for tonight to see if she was all right after her car accident.

Ben curled into a mutinous ball on the floor, having squirmed out of her arms. He also began crying. So did Chloe.

'I want Mummy,' she sobbed.

Even though the door to the room was firmly closed,

Gemma could hear the faint wail of another miserable child somewhere. Set off by Ben and Chloe?

'Come on, guys,' she pleaded. 'It's not for long. Here…' She crouched on the floor and held out her arms. 'Cuddles?'

Chloe stuck out a quivering bottom lip. 'You're… not…Mummy.'

Oh…*God*…

Gemma felt like crying herself. She wasn't Mummy. She wasn't even a beloved aunty, was she? She'd fled from being involved in the lives of these children four years ago before the twins had even been born so she'd been no better than a complete stranger to them when she'd rushed back into their world six months ago.

It had seemed like she'd been making progress. The children had gradually got used to her and she'd done her best to make them feel loved and as secure as possible. But Chloe's whimpered words had taken her straight back to square one.

Or maybe not quite.

Hazel heaved a world-weary sigh that should only have been able to come from someone with several decades more life experience than a seven-year-old.

'Aunty Gemma is our mummy now, Chloe.'

Chloe eyed her older sister. Big, blue eyes swam with tears. She turned back to Gemma, sticking her thumb into her mouth. Thinking mode.

The nurses had provided a box of toys in the room and Jamie was sitting in the corner, doing a big-piece jigsaw puzzle of a squirrel. He looked up at Chloe.

'I love Aunty Gemma,' he said. 'She's a good mummy.'

The matter-of-fact words were sweet praise indeed. Gemma had to blink hard. The smile she gave Chloe was distinctly wobbly.

Chloe gave an enormous sniffle, pulled her thumb from her mouth with a popping sound and then held her arms wide to launch herself at Gemma.

Ben wanted in on the cuddle, of course, and Gemma suddenly had her arms overloaded with a warm tangle of chunky, three-year-old limbs and sweet-smelling, still baby-soft hair. She even got a sticky kiss from Chloe.

'Bed now?' Gemma suggested hopefully a minute or two later.

'Will you tell us a story?'

'Of course I will.'

But with Ben in one cot, Chloe shook her head firmly when Gemma went to lift her into the other cot.

'Want Ben,' she said. 'Same bed.'

'Hmm.' Gemma was dubious. 'It would be a bit of a squash, wouldn't it?'

But Ben, bless him, wriggled to one side. 'Lotsa room,' he declared. 'Digger's not big.'

'Digger' was Ben's favourite toy—a soft, brightly coloured bulldozer. Thank goodness it hadn't been left behind when Simon had brought the children in because Ben would never get to sleep without it. Chloe was the same about Raggy Doll.

Gemma's heart sank. Where *was* Raggy Doll?

Chloe didn't seem to have noticed yet that her cuddly was missing.

'I think sleeping with Ben is a great idea.' Gemma lifted Chloe into the cot. 'You can snuggle up like kittens in a basket.'

'I want a kitten,' Chloe said wistfully. 'Is Santa going to bring me one?'

'Maybe.' Gemma knew about the Christmas wish. She had a very cute, soft toy kitten wrapped and ready to go under the tree. Hopefully that would defer the longing for the real thing. 'Jamie? Can you find a story in the box, please? Then you could come and sit on my knee and listen too.'

Had the nurse deliberately put a story about Christmas in the box for the children? Gemma wasn't sure if it was going to be helpful to remind them about how much their own Christmas was being disrupted this year but the two older children listened with rapt attention to a tale of siblings who thought Christmas was boring until they both became involved in the magic of a pantomime performance. The twins were asleep by the time Gemma was halfway through the story and Jamie was struggling to keep his eyes open by the end.

'I want to go to a pantomime,' Hazel said as Gemma lifted Jamie into a bed. 'Mummy always said she'd take us. "Next year."'

'I'll take you,' Gemma promised, tucking Jamie in. 'Your mummy and I saw *Cinderella* when she was about your age. It was her favourite game for ages afterwards, playing pantomimes.'

'I want to see *Jack and the Beanstalk*,' Jamie mumbled drowsily. 'Like in the story.'

And with that, he was asleep. Hazel, however, looked far from tired.

'When will you take us?' she demanded.

It was on the tip of Gemma's tongue to say 'Next year', which was only logical. It was far too late to arrange anything for this Christmas season. But then she looked into her niece's wide, blue eyes and she could see something that just shouldn't be there. An understanding that life did not necessarily deliver what you most wanted. That dreams weren't worth having because they were most likely not going to come true.

If she said 'Next year', Hazel would hear an echo of her mother's voice and maybe she would try and protect her heart from yet more pain by assuming it wasn't going to happen. Terrible accidents happened all the time, didn't they? 'Next year' her aunt might not be here any more.

'I think…' Gemma was speaking cautiously because she wasn't a hundred per cent sure '…that some pantomines go at least until the end of December. If we can find one that does and I can find someone to look after Sophie, I'll take you all.' She offered Hazel a hopeful smile. 'I'll go on the internet on my phone and see what I can find out.'

To Gemma's surprise, she discovered there was a lot of entertainment for children available in and around the city. Why had it not occurred to her to look into this before?

'*The Wind in the Willows* is on for another couple of weeks,' she told Hazel. 'That would be fun.'

'Mmm.' Hazel had a fingertip against her teeth.

'Don't bite your nails, hon.'

She checked her phone again. 'Oh…*Jack and the Beanstalk* is on until the end of December. Shall I see if I can book some tickets?'

''Kay.'

'You're still biting.'

'Can't help it.'

Gemma sighed. The bad habit had only started in the last six months and it was always worse if Hazel was upset or worried about something. She closed her phone for the moment and went to give the little girl a hug.

'Sophie's going to be fine,' she told her. 'Try not to worry so much.'

'But it's not Sophie that I'm worried about.'

'What is it?'

Hazel kept her chin lowered. 'We're supposed to leave Santa a snack. We always put a glass of milk and a chocolate biscuit beside the fireplace. Sometimes he's not so hungry because all the boys and girls give him snacks but he always drinks some of the milk and takes a big bite out of the biccie.'

Hazel gave a huge sniff as she turned to stare at her little brother. Jamie was as soundly asleep as the twins but Hazel lowered her voice anyway.

'I know it's your mummy and daddy that give you most of the presents,' she whispered, 'but there's always a special one that they don't know about. It's wrapped in special paper and it doesn't have a label. *That's* the one that Santa brings.'

Another little piece broke off Gemma's heart as she thought of the family traditions Laura and Evan had been creating for their children. The kind that would get carried on for generations.

She hadn't known and it was too late to find different, special paper and leave those gifts without a label. Worse, she'd labelled more than one already as having been given by Father Christmas.

Oh…help…

'If he sees that we don't care enough to leave him something to eat and drink, he might think we don't even believe in him and he won't leave the special present,' Hazel continued sadly. 'And then it won't be really Christmas, will it?'

'Oh…hon…'

How could she fix this? Take a label off some of the gifts? Suggest that Santa had liked their Christmas paper enough to use it again on *his* special gifts?

But it was only a small part of the real problem here, wasn't it?

The bigger issue was that it wasn't going to be really Christmas because Christmas was all about family.

These children had been precious to their parents, who had created the best possible environment in which to raise them. It wasn't just the gorgeous, semi-rural property with the good school available nearby. It was more the loving environment. Parents that could weave positive family values and unique traditions into the upbringing of their children and celebrate them with joy on occasions like birthdays and Christmas.

That was what was missing from their lives now. The absolute security of that love and the demonstration of it through little things like the details of what happened on Christmas Eve.

Gemma was at a loss but she had to try and make this better somehow.

'I love you,' she said, pulling Hazel into her arms for a cuddle. 'I'm not going anywhere. I will always be here for all of you and I will always love you.' She took a deep breath. 'Christmas *is* different this year and I'm really, really sorry about that, but it's still Christmas and we'll make it special because we love each other and we'll be together.' She tightened her hold into an extra squeeze and kissed the top of Hazel's head. 'We'll do it together, OK? Make it really special for everybody.'

Hazel wrapped her arms around Gemma's neck. 'You're nice, Aunty Gemma,' she whispered. 'I love you, too.'

For the second time that evening Gemma felt herself far too close to tears. Partly, it was from relief that she had managed to slot into the lives of her nieces and nephews and earn their trust.

Their love was a huge bonus.

Sophie was stirring as Gemma blinked back her tears. A whimper became a cry that threatened to wake the other children. Gemma hurried to lift her from the bassinette.

'I can hold her,' Hazel offered.

Gemma shook her head, bouncing the baby gently in her arms. 'It's late, sweetheart, and you need to try and get some rest, too.' Tension was rising at the same pace as Sophie's volume. Chloe stirred and whimpered in the cot.

Gemma thought quickly. 'I'll take Sophie for a bit of a walk and see if I can get a bottle heated for her. She's probably hungry by now.' She eyed Hazel anxiously. 'I won't be far away. Just out in the corridor.'

'I'll be OK.' Hazel nodded.

'Look…there's a button beside the bed, on the end of that cord thing. If you push that, a nurse will come. Why don't you curl up on the bed and try and go to sleep?'

''Kay.' Hazel came close enough to drop a kiss onto the back of her smallest sister's head. 'Shh…' she told the baby. 'It's OK. Aunty Gemma's looking after you. She's looking after all of us.'

Hazel's words echoed in Gemma's mind as she slipped out of the room and closed the door behind her. The ward corridor was dim but she could see the lighted area of the nurses' station and wondered if it would be acceptable to walk that far. Or were they being strictly quarantined until blood tests revealed whether Sophie might have a contagious disease like measles?

A smaller, bobbing light came towards her. The nurse was pointing the torch at the floor but raised it to illuminate Sophie's face.

'Problems?'

'The other children are asleep so I didn't want her to wake them. Sometimes walking up and down and singing is enough to get her to settle again but I think she might be hungry.'

'Might be a good time to change her nappy. We can take her temperature and check on what's happening with that rash, too. Then I can see about a bottle for you.'

'Thank you.' Gemma eyed the door of the private room they had been assigned. 'Are we still being quarantined? Do we need to do the nappy in there?'

The nurse also eyed the door. There were several children asleep in there and Sophie's cries stepped up a level in volume again. She shook her head.

'We can use the treatment room,' she said. 'It's not as though you're going to come anywhere near any other children at this time of night.'

She led the way. 'I'm Lisa Jones, by the way. Night shift nurse manager.'

'I'm Gemma Ba—' Gemma caught herself but Lisa smiled.

'Baxter, yes?' Even in the dim periphery of the torchlight Gemma could see the curiosity in Lisa's glance. 'None of us knew that Andy was still married.' Her smile widened. 'It explains why so many women got so disappointed by never getting past first base.'

For Gemma, it raised more questions rather than provided any kind of explanation. Had Andy avoided having any kind of meaningful relationship with another woman?

Why?

And why on earth did it give her a frisson of...what... *relief*?

'We've been separated for some time,' she informed

Lisa, her voice tight enough to let the nurse know that the topic of conversation was not welcome. 'I've been working in Australia.'

The lights in the treatment room were overly bright. Sophie's increasing distress made further personal conversation impossible, which was fine by Gemma. She'd had no intention of gossiping about her personal life but Lisa had nodded at her statement as though she knew already.

And why wouldn't she? The kind of tragedy and its aftermath that she and Andy had been through would have been hot news on any hospital grapevine. She had to assume everybody knew virtually everything around here.

Was that the explanation for Andy's apparently monastic existence in the last few years? Had he simply been successful in keeping his private life private? Or did he have the same problem she knew she would always face—of knowing that any relationship she might find could never adequately take the place of what was missing from her life? And, therefore, what was the point of even going there?

No. Sadly, Gemma was quite sure that wouldn't be what, if anything, was holding Andy back. She had been the one who had failed to live up to being a good partner in their marriage. It would be easy for Andy to find more than a replacement to fill that gap in his life. He would have no trouble finding a vastly improved model.

The casually uttered words of the nurse went round

and round in the back of Gemma's mind as she watched Lisa remove Sophie's nappy and expertly assess her skin for any sign of a rash.

So *many* women?

So disappointed?

'Her skin's looking good,' Lisa declared. 'Let's get some fresh pants on her and take her temp.'

Sophie's temperature had come down a little.

'That's excellent,' Lisa told the baby. 'We'll get you dressed again, give you a bit more paracetamol and then you can have some supper. Maybe that will stop you howling, yes?'

But Sophie stopped crying even before the formula was prepared and heated for her. She stopped when she'd been buttoned back into her stretchy suit and Gemma had picked her up for a cuddle. Rubbing her face in the dip beneath Gemma's collarbone, the ear-splitting shrieks subsided with remarkable speed, although she could still feel the tiny body in her arms jerking with deep, gulping breaths.

'Ohh...' Lisa smiled at them. 'Look at that. She just wanted her mummy.'

Gemma opened her mouth to deny the title and say she was only her aunt but then she closed it again.

She *was* Sophie's mummy now, wasn't she? She always would be. Maybe her bond with her, her sister's last child, would be the strongest because Sophie would have no memories of anyone else being there for her.

And at this moment the sweetness of being able to

comfort this tiny person was overwhelming. The best feeling in the world?

Holding the bottle as Sophie sucked on it was just as good. Something in the way she held eye contact with Gemma as she drank tugged on a very deep place in her heart. The tiny hand curled over her big finger on top of the bottle added another poignant beat every time it squeezed rhythmically. Like a kitten kneading its mother's stomach.

Another nurse came into the central station as Gemma sat there, feeding Sophie. Her face was creased with concern.

'Lisa? Ruth's awake and complaining of a tummy-ache. Should I give her something?'

'What's her temperature?'

'Normal. Everything seems fine…but…'

'I'll come and see her. Did you check on John Boy?'

'His sats are down. Jules is watching him and she put his oxygen flow up to six litres. He's awake, too, I'm afraid. He's not complaining of anything, as usual, but I think he might need some additional pain relief. Should we page Andy?'

'Give me a minute or two to double-check. We don't want to pull him away from the PICU unless we have to.'

'John Boy?' Gemma queried as Lisa draped a stetho-scope around her neck and picked up a chart. 'Is that really his name?'

Lisa grinned. 'Maybe somebody was a fan of *The Waltons*, way back.' Her smile faded. 'Or maybe it was

just because he was one of far too many children before he went into foster-care. He's a neat kid. Has some
pretty serious heart failure to contend with at the moment.' She picked up another chart.

'And Ruthie's battling leukaemia. We need to keep
a close eye on any symptoms in case it's infection or
rejection after her bone-marrow transplant. I'll need to
check them both and maybe drag Andy back from the
PICU. Not that he'll mind,' she added. 'They're both
favourites with him.' She paused by the door to glance
back at Gemma. 'Will you be OK?'

Gemma nodded. The bottle was almost empty. 'I'll
take Sophie back to the room. She'll probably be asleep
again by the time I get there.'

She could hear the muted sounds of increased activity in the ward as she walked slowly back to the
room. Maybe Lisa shouldn't have been giving her any
details of her patients' histories but that kind of confi-
dentiality was more relaxed on a paediatric ward and
she was a doctor herself. She certainly couldn't accuse
any of the people she'd met so far of being unprofessional. Young lives were at stake here and the staff were
clearly dedicated.

Including Andy, obviously. Both these sick children
were favourites? And he wouldn't mind a late-night call
to pull him back to the ward?

Gemma's steps slowed to the point where she actually stopped and turned for a long look down the ward

corridor. She could see doors that were open and hear the squeak of a trolley being moved.

Right at the end of the corridor she could see small flashes of red and green and blue. There must be a Christmas tree in the dayroom, she decided. Of course there would be. She might have been away from dealing with patients for a long time but she remembered the extra lengths medical staff went to in order to make a day like Christmas special for anyone unfortunate enough to be confined in a hospital. That kind of effort always reached its peak when children were involved.

Rapid footsteps sounded and Gemma saw a nurse hurrying into the nurses' station. She could hear the low buzz of an urgent conversation, which was probably summoning Andy back to the ward.

To his world, in fact.

And suddenly Gemma understood.

She looked down at the baby in her arms and remembered that feeling she'd had when she'd picked her up and Sophie had stopped crying.

She'd never understood how Andy could have chosen to go into paediatrics after what had happened. It had felt like he was rubbing salt into her wounds. Like he was telling the world it didn't matter and that he could move on.

But did he get that same kind of feeling from comforting these sick children? And their families? How much would it be magnified by being able to save their lives or at least improve them, instead of only offering the comfort of cleanliness and warmth and food?

She got it.

Finally. Too late, of course, but Gemma felt humbled by the knowledge.

She tiptoed back into the room to find that Hazel had fallen asleep as well. She and Sophie were the only ones awake now and Sophie's eyelids were showing no sign of drooping. She grinned up at Gemma, who found herself smiling back.

She began to walk between the door and window. Back and forth. Humming softly to the tune of a song she knew would only soothe the other children and was therefore very unlikely to wake them. A tune that was automatic enough to allow her thoughts to continue tumbling unchecked.

Dear Lord...was that the *'Skye Boat Song'* he could hear?

It stopped Andy in his tracks outside the room that Gemma and the children were in. The door was slightly ajar, which was how he could hear the sound. The curtains on the corridor side of the room had not been completely closed either, so Andy could see inside.

He couldn't stop for more than a few seconds because he was needed elsewhere. The nursing staff was worried about Ruth. And John Boy. Neither problem sounded serious but he needed to check to reassure himself as much as his colleagues.

A few seconds was enough to take in the picture,

though. Hazel was asleep on one of the beds, curled up with a blanket carefully draped over her. Jamie was asleep on the other bed, flat on his back and looking angelic with his blond curls and an amused tilt to the corners of his mouth. An opened story book lay on the floor near his bed.

The twins were in the same cot, a tangle of limbs in fluffy pyjamas that made them look like puppies in a box. A brightly coloured toy had been pushed to one end and was threatening to fall through the bars.

And there was Gemma. Walking slowly back and forth with her head bent low enough for her cheek to be resting gently on the baby's head.

It was the picture of a mother caring for her children. Andy could imagine the lilt of her voice as she'd read them a story. See her drawing up the blanket to tuck it around Hazel. Soon she would probably rescue the falling toy and put it back beside Ben and maybe she would smooth strands of hair off his forehead and give him a kiss.

The tenderness of the picture made Andy's heart ache. The yearning sensation stayed with him as he moved on to deal with his young patients.

It was still with him a little while later when he'd checked both Ruth and John Boy and charted extra medications to help them both get a good night's sleep.

He could feel the pull back to that room at the end of the corridor and it was so strong it hurt.

Or maybe it was something else that was causing the pain.

Trying to get his head straight, Andy walked in the opposite direction from the room that held Gemma and all the Gillespie children in it. He found himself in the ward's dayroom, staring at the coloured flashes coming from the lights on the Christmas tree.

Christmas was such a part of his and Gemma's story, wasn't it?

That first Christmas, ten years ago, had been when he'd met the woman he'd known was going to be the love of his life.

What if someone had asked him, a few weeks later, what he saw for his future? OK, maybe it had been later than that that the dream had taken firm shape but the longing had always been there, hadn't it?

A variation on the picture he'd been caught by when he'd come back into the ward a short time ago.

A loving family with Gemma at its heart.

Oh...how he wanted to go back to that room. But he couldn't make his feet move. What if she was still singing to get Sophie back to sleep?

The song she had sung to her little sister so many years ago to help her sleep no matter what had been happening around them.

The song she had sung to a dying child who'd had nobody around to love them at the end.

The song she had sung to Max.

The lights on the Christmas tree seemed to intensify and grow spikes of colour that blurred until Andy could blink the extra moisture away.

Christmas...

Family…
Gemma…
…Heartache.

CHAPTER FIVE

Christmas: eight years ago

THE cafeteria on the first floor of Queen Mary's hospital was even more crowded and noisy than usual.

The vast room was still decorated with huge, rainbow-hued paper bells and chains thanks to the staff party that had been hosted in here last night. The festive spirit seemed to have lingered as well judging by the peals of laughter amongst the hubbub of conversation, clash of cutlery on china and pagers and mobile phones going off. The faint strains of a Christmas carol could be heard coming from a CD player near the cash register.

Gemma eyed the food selection dubiously. 'Have you got any sushi left?'

'Long gone. Sorry, love. You're a bit late for lunch.'

'Tell me about it.' Gemma heaved a sigh. 'I'll have some macaroni cheese, thanks.'

'Good choice.' The kitchen hand nodded. 'You need a bit of meat on your bones, you do.'

As she pushed her tray further along the counter,

Gemma's smile had nothing to do with the gelatinous heap of hot food on her plate. She was happy because she knew that somewhere in this crowded space Andy was waiting for her. And, if the Christmas fairies were kind, they might get a whole thirty minutes of each other's company.

It should have been almost impossible to spot a single person quickly amongst the hordes but Gemma simply stood still near the till, holding her tray. She closed her eyes for a moment, listening to the sound of a choir singing 'Oh, Come, All Ye Faithful' from the CD player and then opened her eyes and let something she couldn't name direct her gaze.

'Joyful and triumphant...' the choir sang, and they were right because it had worked.

It always worked.

Andy broke off the conversation he was having with someone at an adjoining table and his gaze zeroed in to meet Gemma's. He waved and smiled and Gemma let out the breath she hadn't noticed she was holding.

How long would it last? she wondered as she got closer. It had been two years since she'd met Andy in the PICU that night. Over a year since they'd moved in together and yet her stomach still did that odd little flip when she saw him smile at her. A flip that sent waves of something rippling through her body. Something strong and safe that had become her touchstone in a world that was often exhausting and challenging and difficult. Something that was also thrilling because it reminded her of what the world was like when it was just the two of them and they had a whole night to be together. Something that was joyous, too, because it held a promise of how good the future might be.

'Good grief, what *is* that?'

'Macaroni cheese. Want some?' Gemma held up a loaded fork and laughed as Andy's eyes widened in mock horror.

'I'm OK, thanks. Up to coffee already, see? I had a turkey roll. With stuffing and cranberry sauce. Probably leftovers from the supper last night but it was still great.'

'Didn't see any of them. Anyway…' Gemma wolfed the forkful. 'I'm starving and carb loading is a good idea because I'll need the energy to cope with the marathon that will probably be the rest of my shift.'

'How's it going in babyland?'

'Flat out. You'd think people would time getting pregnant a bit better, wouldn't you?' Gemma spoke around another forkful of cheesy pasta. 'Two Caesars, a forceps and a breech. And that was all by elevenses.'

'Well, I've had two heart attacks, an amputated finger, critical asthma and unexplained abdominal pain.'

Gemma grinned. 'You're looking surprisingly well, in that case. Good job on the finger, too. Can't see a scar, even.'

It was an old joke but Andy had no trouble smiling back. For a heartbeat the cacophony of sounds, the harsh lighting and even the competing smells of various foodstuffs faded away. He could even forget about that awful stuff

Gemma was eating. His outward breath was a sigh of pure contentment.

He could lose himself in her eyes like this every time. Especially when she smiled. It made him feel…good.

Really good. As if he was in exactly the right place in his life. With exactly the right person.

'Still OK for tonight?' It wasn't beyond the realms of possibility that Gemma would have put her hand up for an extra shift if things were desperate.

'Can't wait.' Gemma ate another mouthful and chased a drop of cheese sauce from her lips with her tongue.

Andy's gut tightened pleasurably. He couldn't wait either.

'How good is it that we've both got Christmas Eve off duty?'

'I know. Sometimes I wonder why we bothered moving in together when we only see each other in here or when we bump into each other in some corridor.'

'Because we've both got horrendous student debts and two can live as cheaply as one.'

They both smiled. They both knew the real reason why they had moved in together and it wasn't simply to save money. It had been the logical next step in a relationship that had the potential to last for ever.

'Speaking of debt,' Andy said, 'I've checked online and the bank holidays mean we've got a few days' grace to pay the power bill. That means you've got a bit extra for the groceries.'

'Hooray.' Gemma's eyes lit up. 'Chocolate.'

'I was thinking maybe a bottle of wine? For tonight?'

'Mmm. Chocolate *and* wine. Heaven.'

'Maybe some food, too?'

'Hmm.' Still eating, Gemma pulled a notebook and pen from her pocket. 'I'd better write a list. You're on a late day, aren't you?'

'Yeah...sorry. Won't finish till eight p.m. at the earliest. Supermarkets will be shut by then, otherwise I'd come and help you shop.'

Gemma shook her head. 'How often do we get an evening with neither of us rostered on? I don't want to waste it in the aisles of a supermarket.' She glanced at Andy as he drained his coffee cup. 'We're out of coffee at home, aren't we?'

'Yep. And milk and bread. And I used the last of the shampoo this morning.'

Gemma scribbled the items on the list. 'I'll get some bacon and eggs for Christmas breakfast. It's good that we're working tomorrow, isn't it? We should get a nice Christmas lunch and that'll save us buying our own turkey.'

'The perks of being a junior doctor,' Andy agreed wryly. 'Overworked and underpaid but...hey...we get a free Christmas lunch.'

'At least you don't have to dress up in a Santa suit. You should see the party they're organising in the paediatric ward.'

'I did. I went up to check on that kid that came into A and E last night. The one that got hit by the car that lost control on the ice?'

'Oh…how's she doing?'

'Fractured pelvis and ribs but it was the head injury I was really worried about. CT was clear. Just bad concussion.' Andy knew he was sounding pleased. It had been a full-on resuscitation that he'd run by himself. He *was* pleased with the outcome.

Gemma looked up from her expanding list. She smiled. 'You're loving Emergency, aren't you?'

'Who wouldn't? You get a bit of everything. Neonates to geriatrics. Superficial to critical. Medical, surgical and trauma. It's a roller-coaster.'

'You want to choose it for a specialty?'

'You know? I think I might.' The thought of taking another step into shaping the future into exactly what he wanted it to look like was a great feeling. It would be perfect if Gemma could find that kind of satisfaction as well. They were due to nominate the specialty they would become a registrar in for the coming year but Gemma was using her head rather than her heart to try and make the decisions that would shape the rest of her career.

She wanted something that would have a research component that could take that career to medical-rockstar level. So far, the real contenders were either oncology or anaesthetics with a sub-specialty of pain control.

'You're going to cross O&G off your list, aren't you?'

Gemma nodded emphatically. 'It's not for me. All those *babies*…'

She was pulling an overly dramatic face but her final word seemed to hang in the air and suddenly a charged silence fell between them. A kitchen hand pushed a trolley past their table. She gathered up Andy's plate and cup and stacked them. She eyed Gemma's unfinished plate.

'You all done with that?'

'What? Oh...yes. I've had enough.'

Clearly, Gemma had lost the voracious appetite she'd arrived with. They both watched her plate being scraped and stacked and the cutlery being dropped into a bucket of sudsy water. Then they looked at each other and Andy raised his eyebrows in a silent question.

Gemma shook her head and looked away again.

Oh...*hell*...

He reached out to give Gemma's hand a reassuring squeeze. 'It's only been a couple of days, babe. You're on the Pill and the percentage failure rate is ridiculously small. Stop stressing.'

'One per cent isn't ridiculously small, you know. Not if it happens to be you.'

'Try to think of it as a ninety-nine per cent chance of there being nothing to worry about.'

The sound of pagers going off was just part of the background noise in the busy cafeteria full of medics but this time it was close enough to make them both reach for the devices clipped to their belts.

'It's me.' Gemma sighed. 'Probably another Caesar, the rate we're going today. Nobody wants to wait and have their baby on Christmas Day.'

'I'll come with you. I was due back downstairs about five minutes ago, I think.'

Saying nothing as they edged their way between tables was fine but the silence was noticeable as soon as they left the cafeteria. A short walk took them to the bank of lifts where they had to part company. Gemma had to wait for a lift while Andy took the stairs down to the ground level. It wasn't much of a wait. The light glowed and a pinging sound announced the arrival of the lift.

'See you tonight.' Gemma's smile was a bit tight and Andy could see the shadow of anxiety in her eyes.

To hell with hospital etiquette, he decided, bending his head to brush her lips with his own.

'Stop worrying,' he said softly. 'Doctor's orders.'

Stop worrying?

Fat chance. But it was possible to shove the worry into a parking lot at the back of her brain. It was something that junior doctors got very practised at. All that worry over the last couple of years...

Could they handle the responsibility of being *real* doctors with lives affected by their decisions?

Could they cope with the exhaustion of long hours and having every job that more senior staff couldn't be bothered doing thrown their way?

Could they even begin to make a dent in the massive amount of debt they'd accumulated in their training?

You had to be dedicated to a career in medicine, that was for sure. But that was part of what had drawn Gemma and Andy together in the first place. They might have come into medicine from different directions but the determination to excel in a career they were both in love with was something they shared. Maybe that was why the relationship worked so well even when it was hard to find any quality time together to nurture it. They both understood the pressures and made allowances for it. Most of the time, anyway.

Gemma filled her trolley at the supermarket rapidly but she was being careful of what she pulled from the shelves and freezers. Only the essentials and the least expensive options. Except she had leeway to be just a little bit extravagant today, didn't she? It was Christmas and although they'd made a pact not to spend anything on buying presents for each other, it would be a gift in itself to have a special evening together. A nice dinner by candlelight. Wine. An early night...

A smile tugged at Gemma's lips as she chose Andy's favourite red wine and then went to find some steak to go with it. Maybe it was partly due to the pressure and small amount of time they had together at home that meant their love-making had never lost the magic of that first time, only a few days after their first meeting. If anything, it had got better and better as they learned more about each other and had fallen in love and chosen to make a commitment.

That love was growing stronger as time went by as well. Just thinking about Andy as she manoeuvred the trolley through crowded aisles gave Gemma the kind of warm internal glow that only her little sister had ever evoked in her before. The kind that made you want to cherish and nurture someone. The kind of giving that actually meant you could receive more than you gave.

Passing a Christmas confectionery stand, Gemma added a couple of candy canes, a big bag of cheesy ring snacks and the ultimate treat of her favourite brand of Swiss chocolate that came in the shape of gold-wrapped reindeer with red ribbons and bells around their necks. Andy wouldn't be as excited about the chocolate as she was and, still feeling the glow, Gemma wanted to find something special just for him. She headed for the toiletries section with the intention of at least checking out the price of aftershave or something. They needed shampoo, anyway, didn't they?

She walked past the over-the-counter medications first and the slim, blue and white boxes on the bottom shelf seemed to be glowing. The price on the home pregnancy test kits was high but Gemma stopped in her tracks. She even picked a box up.

It would be the best Christmas gift for both of them, wouldn't it? To find that they weren't in that unlucky one per cent? To know that the future was still wide open and full of promise?

After a long moment she reluctantly returned the box to the shelf. She could do a test for free at work and what possible difference could waiting a day or two make? What if the news was what she so desperately didn't want it to be and Christmas was ruined for both of them? Gemma turned and fled the aisle, any thoughts of aftershave or even shampoo forgotten.

Her mobile was ringing as she headed out into the freezing, dark evening, laden with shopping bags. She had to put down two of the bags to reach her phone but she couldn't ignore the call. What if it was Andy, saying he was going to have to work later than expected? It would be an awful waste if she'd spent so much on a special dinner and then it was ruined by having to be kept warm for too long.

But it wasn't Andy.

'Laura!' Gemma forgot about how cold it was, standing out here. 'Hey, hon...how *are* you? Merry almost Christmas. Did you get my card?'

Her little sister was laughing. 'Good and yes and same to you...'

'Did you get some time off work? Are you going to be able to come up?'

'Yes, but—'

'Oh...' Gemma couldn't help interrupting. 'It'll be so good to see you. It's been way too long.'

'I know. Gem?'

Gemma caught her breath. 'What?'

'I've got something to tell you.'

Gemma was still holding that breath. 'Oh, my God, you're not pregnant, are you?'

'*No*...' Laura was laughing again. 'At least, not yet.'

'What does that mean? You're *planning* to be pregnant?' Gemma had to shake her head. This was more than ironic.

'Ev's asked me to marry him, Gem. We're *engaged*. I've got a ring and everything.'

'Oh...' Gemma was lost for words. Laura sounded *so* happy. She was only twenty-two but her boyfriend Evan had been in her life for longer than Andy had been in hers. A builder with a solid future ahead of him, Evan had met Laura when he'd gone into the kitchen shop she worked in. 'That's fantastic, hon. I'm so happy for you.'

'That's not even the best bit. You know how Evan's always had a dream of finding some ramshackle old barn and converting it into a dream house? Well, he's found one on the internet and...you'll never guess.'

Gemma's heart skipped a beat. 'Don't tell me it's in Australia or somewhere.'

'No, silly. It's in spitting distance of you. Outskirts of Manchester. We've put an offer in. We should know whether we've got it or not by the time we come up to see you for New Year...' Laura's excitement was almost palpable. 'I can't wait... Will you help me plan my wedding?'

'Of course I will.'

'It'll be your turn next. We can make an extra scrapbook of ideas for you.'

It was Gemma's turn to laugh. 'As if... It'll be ten years before I've got time to even think about a wedding.' After all, why would you go to the expense of having a wedding unless you were ready to settle down and start a family?

'And keep your fingers crossed for us about the barn. How good would it be if we got it? There's even room for a pony for the kids. Hey...is it snowing up your way?'

Gemma looked around. The freezing sleet had, indeed, turned to fluffy white flakes while she'd been standing here, talking. 'Sure is, and I'm freezing. I need to get my groceries home and get some dinner on. Love you. I'll call you tomorrow.'

'Love you, too. Say hi to Andy for me.'

The snow was beginning to settle as Gemma reached the iron railing that marked her destination. She glanced below street level at the two-metre square of concrete that was the garden their basement bedsit looked out on.

A converted semi-rural barn? Settling down to make babies and even planning ahead for the pets those children would have?

Did she feel envious of her little sister?

Maybe a little but only because Laura was achieving her dream. They wanted very different things from life and Gemma still had a mountain to climb before she reached hers. There was a touch of sadness there too, letting go of the responsibility she'd had since childhood of protecting the person she loved most in the world. She could turn over that responsibility to Evan now, with the absolute confidence that he would step up to the mark.

Mixed in with both those realisations was also a definite fizzle of excitement. Background parental-type anxiety about Laura had always been there and had sometimes distracted her from her own goals.

That distraction was gone. She could focus on climbing her personal mountain now and eventually, like Laura, she would achieve everything she'd always dreamed of.

Andy spotted the tree branch beside a rubbish skip near the bus stop.

It must have broken off a good-sized Christmas tree a few days ago, he decided, because it was a bit wilted and had a ragged strip of bark at its base. Still…it was a good three feet high and not that lopsided. If he held it at an angle it looked like a small Christmas tree.

Just the right size for a very small apartment.

His feet crunched in a thin layer of snow when he got off the bus. A white Christmas this year, then. The best kind. Even a thin layer smoothed out the rough edges and made everything look a bit softer and prettier. The bare concrete yard beside the steps down to his front door looked positively festive with the glow of light coming through the gap where the curtain was frayed.

The smell of hot food as he went inside was mouthwatering. Gemma's face when she saw what he was carrying was priceless.

'For me? You shouldn't have…' She was laughing as Andy propped the branch against the end of the couch and swept her into a hug.

'Nothing's too much trouble for the woman I love,' he said. 'I had to put up with several people who didn't want to be close to a prickly pine tree on the bus but I just said, "Merry Christmas to you, too". And I smiled a lot.'

Gemma was smiling now. Right into his eyes. And then she gave him a kiss that was a promise of things to come. 'It's gorgeous,' she told him. 'And I know just what we can use to decorate it.'

They propped the branch up with medical textbooks from their bookshelf. Gemma ripped open the bag of cheesy rings and held one up. 'Perfect, yes?'

'Mmm.' Andy snatched the ring and ate it.

'No-o-o…' Gemma held the bag out of reach. 'Look.' She took a ring out and poked the end of a branch through its centre. The lurid yellow coating of the snack food stood out against the dark green of the pine needles.

By the time the bag was empty their fingers had a thick yellow coating as well but the small tree looked as though it was covered with oddly shaped golden lights. Gemma put her head on one side as she considered the final result. Grinning, she went to fetch something from a grocery bag beside the kitchen bench.

Using a knife, she poked a hole into the bottom of the gold-wrapped chocolate reindeer and then poked the uppermost point of the tree inside. The heavy ornament tipped sideways at a drunken angle but it didn't fall off. Gemma nodded with satisfaction.

'Perfect,' she declared. 'All it needs now is a pile of gifts underneath.' She caught her bottom lip between her teeth, turning to Andy. 'I haven't got a gift for you, babe, I'm sorry.'

'We made a pact, remember? But…I do have a gift for you…kind of.'

Gemma thumped his shoulder. 'How could you? What about the pact? Now I feel *really* awful.'

'I didn't spend any money on it,' Andy said. 'I nicked it from work. And…you might not like it, anyway.'

'Show me.'

Andy felt in the pocket of the coat he'd dropped over the end of the couch when the tree decoration had got properly under way. He held up the slim, rectangular box with some trepidation. It wasn't much of a gift.

'Peace of mind?' he offered softly.

The laughter and lightness was sucked out of the room so fast Andy cursed himself for even having the idea in the first place, but Gemma, her face completely neutral, took the box and disappeared into the tiny bathroom of the apartment.

She didn't come out.

Andy waited for two minutes and then paced back and forth for another three. These tests only took a minute to cook, didn't they? He knocked on the door.

'You OK?'

He got no answer. Unsure whether to burst in on her, Andy leaned his forehead on the door and that was when he heard it.

A stifled sob.

He threw the door open. Gemma was sitting on the toilet lid, staring at the stick she held in one hand. Her other hand was cradling her forehead. She had tears coursing down her face.

Andy dropped to his knees in front of her and reached

to spread his hands and hold as much of Gemma as he could grasp.

'It's OK,' he told her. 'We'll cope.'

But Gemma shook her head, shaking with sobs. Andy waited and finally, she started to force some words out.

'I thought...you know...I thought if the worst happened, it wasn't that big a deal... Lots of people have terminations because...they can't afford a baby...or it's just totally the wrong time in their lives...'

The chill that ran down Andy's spine made it hard to stay silent and keep listening but Gemma wasn't finished yet.

'But then it hit me...you know? This is a *baby*, Andy. *Our* baby...and I just can't...'

'No...of course you can't.' His relief was astonishingly strong. Andy stood up, gathering Gemma in his arms. Holding her tight.

'It's over,' Gemma sobbed against his chest. 'My career. All those dreams...'

'No,' he said fiercely. 'They're not over. I won't let that happen, Gem. We're in this together. We'll make it work.'

'But...*how*?'

'I don't know yet.' Andy took a deep breath, thinking fast. 'We're going to be specialist registrars. We'll have more defined hours. We can juggle shifts and use the hospital day-care facilities. I'll make sure I do half the chores. My parents would help us with a deposit for a bigger apartment. A house, even.'

'But you swore you would never accept financial help from your family. You wanted to make it on your own.'

'This is more important. We all have to compromise sometimes in life. It'll be temporary. Just like how hard it might be for the first year or so of having a baby. It's temporary. You have to look at the bigger picture.'

Gemma seemed calmer now. 'What's that?'

'Us.' Andy pulled back far enough to meet Gemma's gaze. 'I love you,' he said softly. 'I want to be with you for the rest of my life. I want us to have a family together. Maybe we're getting pushed into it a bit faster than would have been ideal but…God, Gemma. I love you *so* much…'

'I love you, too.'

'Marry me.' The words came from nowhere but the moment they left his lips Andy knew they were exactly what he wanted to say. What he wanted to happen, with all his heart. Gemma was staring at him, open-mouthed. 'Please?' he added.

She was still staring. He could almost see the whirl of her thoughts. The fear of how hard it would be now to achieve the career she wanted so much. Trying to process the concept of marriage and family when it had been the last thing she'd wanted. What had she always said? That she'd spent virtually her whole life being a parent to her younger sister and it would be a very long time before she wanted to go there again. But mixed in with the negative, difficult thoughts Andy could also see something glowing. Her trust in him.

Her love.

'I could go down on one knee,' he offered with a crooked smile.

Gemma's lips twitched. 'I think you already did that when I was sitting on the loo.' She bit her lip. 'Oh, my God, Andy. You just proposed to me in the *bathroom*.'

'Easily fixed.' Andy led her back into their small living area. The chocolate reindeer on the top of their joke of a Christmas tree was hanging upside down now.

But it gave Andy inspiration.

'Don't move,' he told Gemma.

It was there somewhere, he knew it was. In a box at the back of the crowded wardrobe in the bedroom. Amongst a collection of old snapshots and Scout badges and odd treasures that marked important milestones in his life. When he found it, he went back to Gemma and held it aloft triumphantly.

'Remember this?'

Gemma smiled but her eyes filled with tears again as she nodded.

Andy kept hold of the piece of plastic mistletoe. He moved his hand so that it was above Gemma's head. And then he kissed her. Maybe he couldn't put how much he loved her into the right words but he could *show* her.

Her eyes were still closed when he finally broke the tender kiss. When she opened them, they were as misty as her smile.

'Yes,' she whispered. 'I'd love to marry you.' Her smile wobbled. 'Laura's coming next week to talk about *her* wedding. She's the one who actually wants to have a baby soon. She's not going to believe this. I don't think I believe it.'

Andy kissed her again. He believed it. He knew it wasn't going to be easy but the confidence that they would make it through and that it was the right thing to do was growing. He just needed to convince Gemma.

'Let's have dinner,' he suggested. 'Don't know about you, but I'm absolutely *starving*.' He rescued the upside-down reindeer and gave it to Gemma. 'Dessert.' He grinned.

She smiled back and that was the moment Andy knew that everything would be all right. They could do this.

Together.

CHAPTER SIX

THE yearning wouldn't go away.

If anything, standing in front of the ward Christmas tree and letting memories from the past out of their locked cage had made it worse.

Andy could feel that moment when he'd proposed to Gemma as if it had just happened. The confidence of his love for her that he'd been so sure would carry them through anything life could throw at them. The excitement at the thought of being a father, which had been so unexpected because he'd known that Gemma would have resisted starting a family for as long as possible. The sheer joy of her acceptance of his proposal… Knowing that he'd won. He'd found the holy grail of winning a partner for life.

Something that huge and that real couldn't have simply faded into nothingness, could it?

Bled to death in the wake of the trauma of Gemma leaving him?

No.

Those few minutes in front of the Christmas tree

had let Andy know without a shadow of a doubt that it was all still there.

On his side, at least.

But what about Gemma? There'd been that moment earlier this evening when he'd thought he could see something that suggested it hadn't changed for her either. Not below the surface.

That look in her eyes when Hazel had dropped the verbal bombshell that Sophie might be going to die.

He hadn't imagined that link. The kind of connection that only came from knowing somebody else almost as well as you knew yourself.

If it had just been the knowledge it would have little more than a shared memory but there had been something much bigger in that shared glance. An expectation of trust, because that was what was being offered.

And somehow, putting those components together had added up to much, much more than he would have expected the total to be. The combination of a shared past and continued trust could only be fused by love.

Yes. If he chose to interpret that moment with an open mind—or rather heart—he might believe that beneath the landslide of rubble they'd piled onto their relationship and tried to bury it with there was still a rock-solid foundation. It was possible that Gemma still loved him.

As much as he still loved her?

Could he go there with some emotional rescue dogs and sniff out some signs of life beneath that rubble?

Did he want to?

Maybe he didn't but maybe he had no choice.

He'd never moved on, had he? He'd tried. God knew, he'd tried so many times but the initial flash of attraction he might have discovered with other women soon flickered out. As much as he desperately wanted to find them, the channels that created the kind of connection he'd had with Gemma didn't seem to exist with anybody else.

Without any conscious decision, Andy found his feet moving him back towards Gemma's room. The route took him past the nurses' station.

'Andy?' Lisa was sitting at the desk beside the phone. She looked up, about to say something, but then frowned. 'You OK?'

Oh...help. Did his disturbed emotional state show on his face that clearly? 'I'm fine,' he said. 'What's up?'

'Two things. You remember Chantelle Simms?'

'Of course. Three-year-old with severe abdominal pain and diarrhoea. No fever, nothing showing on a scan and normal bloods. We discharged her this morning.'

'Yes, well, she's just been brought back into Emergency. Screaming with pain and the mother is beside herself. They're having trouble calming either of them down but when they have, they're going to send her back up.'

Andy was frowning now. 'What on earth did we miss? She seemed absolutely fine when we sent her home this morning. And her mum was so relieved that they didn't have to stay in for Christmas. What was the mum's name again?'

'Deirdre.'

'Hmm.' Something was nagging at the back of Andy's mind. She'd been a young, single mother. So worried about her daughter.

'She's all I have in the world, Dr Baxter. I couldn't bear it if something happened to her.'

There'd been tears. Uncontrolled sobbing, in fact, that had needed a fair bit of reassurance and shoulder patting.

A perfectly normal parental reaction to having a child who was clearly unwell. But...

'The other thing...' Lisa was reaching for a piece of paper. 'Results on the Gillespie baby have come through. Looks like it's not measles or meningitis or anything nasty.'

Andy scanned the results himself. 'Thank goodness for that. I guess the ear infection is definitely the culprit.'

'Her temperature was well down when I checked her vital signs a wee while ago. Will you discharge her?'

Andy glanced at his watch. 'It's after midnight,' he observed. 'It would be a bit rough to send Gemma home with five kids to try and settle again.'

'Mmm.' Lisa's tone was neutral but her gaze was steady. Curious.

'She might want to go, of course.' Andy did his best to keep his own tone just as neutral. 'I'll give her the option.' He turned away, before Lisa could try and read anything more into the situation. 'Give me a call as soon as Chantelle and her mum arrive on the ward.'

* * *

There was a brief period of absolute peace when Gemma had finally settled Sophie back into the bassinette. For a long minute or two she simply stood there in the midst of this little tribe of sleeping children and listened to the sound of their breathing.

Feeling the tension of this extraordinarily difficult night ebbing to a point where it could become quite manageable.

And then there was a soft tap at the door and it opened and there was Andy.

'Hi...' His smile seemed tentative in the half-light and his voice was too quiet to read anything into his tone. 'How's it going?'

Gemma knew her own smile was also tentative but she was struggling here. With an echo of that relief that Andy's presence had brought with it from the moment she'd first seen him again in Queen Mary's waiting room. With the yearning for it to be more than what it could possibly be now. With...*missing* him so much.

It shouldn't be this hard, she told herself in those split seconds of trying to pull herself together enough to give him a coherent response and not just burst into tears and throw herself into his arms or something.

Missing Andy was just a part of life for her now, wasn't it?

In the beginning, she had missed him in the way you might miss a limb that had been torn off in a dreadful accident. An unbearably painful injury and, even though you knew the limb was no longer there, you could *feel* it. And you'd go to do things that required its presence, forgetting for a split second that it was no longer available. And with the realisation of the way things really were now would come a fresh wave of that excruciating pain.

But nobody could live like that for ever and, as trite as it sounded, time was a great healer. Well, a pretty good one, anyway. Protective mechanisms like blocking emails, not picking up those early phone calls and deleting the voice mail before listening had also helped.

And, at some point, it had become the safe and sensible thing to continue to do. Contacting Andy would be to invite news that he'd moved on. That he had found someone who could give him all the things that she hadn't been able to. That might have been the object of the exercise, of course, but Gemma wasn't ready to hear about it.

Maybe she never would be.

Because, while she thought she'd become used to missing Andy, she'd been wrong.

And being this close, where she could see him and hear him and even touch him, but what they'd once had was gone.

And…oh, God…she missed that *so* much and there was no way she could tell him that because he'd moved on with his life. He had a career he clearly loved and he was admired and respected by his colleagues. He might have someone else in his private life. He seemed to have found peace, at least, and he didn't deserve her coming back and damaging the good space he was in.

'It's all good,' she heard herself whispering finally, in response to Andy's query. 'They're all asleep.'

Andy was looking around the room. Slowly. His gaze rested on each child and lingered longest on Sophie. He looked about to speak but then beckoned Gemma. She followed him out of the room.

'Don't want to wake anybody,' Andy said. 'Unless you do?'

Gemma blinked. 'Why would I want to do that?'

'We've got the lab results back. There's no reason to keep Sophie or any of the other children in any kind of quarantine. It's not measles.'

'Thank goodness.'

'And it's certainly not...anything else that's serious.' Andy's hesitation might not have been noticeable to anybody else but it shouted a single word to Gemma.

Her indrawn breath was a gulp. She had to look away. To break that connection that had the potential to open such deep, deep wounds.

'So...' Andy cleared his throat. 'If you wanted, you could take all the children home, but...'

Gemma's gaze flew back to meet his. There was a 'but'? A potential complication for Sophie?

'I thought you might like to let them sleep until morning. It would be a shame to start Christmas Day with overtired and unhappy children, wouldn't it?'

'Would that be OK?'

Andy nodded. 'I have a feeling that both I and my registrar will be far too busy to sign the discharge papers before morning.'

'Oh…' The decision was a no-brainer. 'Thanks, Andy.'

'No problem.' He cleared his throat again and glanced at his watch. 'I'm going to hang around for a bit because there's a re-admission coming up from Emergency soon.' His tone was both confident and casual but the glance he sent Gemma held a question that he seemed unsure of even asking. 'Would you…like a coffee?'

What Gemma really needed was a few hours' sleep so that she would be able to take care of the children in the morning so a stimulant like coffee would not be a good idea.

But that wasn't what Andy was offering, was it?

He was asking if she'd like the chance to talk. To him. Alone? Her heart gave a thump and picked up speed. This was unexpected. She'd had no way of preparing for such a conversation. Did Andy want to know something in particular or did he feel the need to go over old, painful ground? And, if he did, could she bring herself to refuse?

There were things she would like to know herself. Like whether there *was* someone special in his life that his colleagues didn't know about.

Like how he was feeling seeing her again like this. Had he missed her the way she'd missed him? Was he aware of the sheet of seemingly unbreakable glass between them that could move and reshape itself to provide a barrier for even physical touch?

'I'd l—' The word died on Gemma's lips. *Like* wasn't

really an appropriate expectation in accepting this invitation. *Love* even less so. 'Um…yes,' she said quietly instead.

'Come with me.' Andy turned. 'I'll ask Lisa to get one of the nurses to keep an eye on the children. We can make a drink in the kitchen and then take it into my office.'

He'd done it now.

Engineered a situation that could well make everything far harder than it needed to be.

He'd taken Gemma away from the children. Removed himself from any distraction or the chaperonage of colleagues.

He'd brought her into a private space. Not even a neutral space. This was his office. More than a home away from home because the apartment he lived in was merely a space to exist when he was away from work.

This office was his real home because home was where the heart was. It was here that he kept his favourite books and CDs and…oh, yeah…

How could he have forgotten that photo on his desk? The one of he and Gemma in the park that day. Standing in several inches of snow, kissing beneath the frosted branches of an old, weeping elm tree. A photo that had been taken on a day's leave that they had laughingly deemed their honeymoon. When they'd gone to Cambridge to tell his parents that a new generation of the Baxter family was on its way.

Maybe Gemma couldn't see the photograph from

where she was sitting in the leather armchair reserved
for visitors. Andy pulled the chair from behind his desk,
both to sit without the barrier of furniture between them
but also to distract Gemma from spotting the photograph.

He really didn't want her to see it. She'd moved on
with her life, having chosen to leave him behind. He
didn't want her to know that he hadn't managed to do
the same. He didn't want to make himself so vulnerable all over again.

'So...' Andy took a sip of his coffee, watching
Gemma over the rim of the mug. 'Here we are, then.'

'Mmm.' Gemma was staring at the liquid in her mug
as though trying to decide whether she wanted to drink
it or not. Her body language suggested she felt as awkward as Andy suddenly did.

The silence that fell seemed impossible to break but
then Gemma raised her chin for just an instant to meet
his eyes before she looked down again.

'Sorry,' she said.

Why was she sorry? Because seeing him again was
the last thing she had wanted?

Andy felt his breath leave his chest in a sigh. If someone had asked him that morning, he might have said
that seeing Gemma was the last thing *he* would want,
but, now that it had happened, he knew it would have
been a lie. A huge lie.

'I'm not,' he said quietly. 'It's good to see you, Gem.'

Her face lifted sharply, revealing a startled gaze instead of an apologetic one. She hadn't expected him to

say that but something was shining through the surprise. Hope?

'You're looking good,' Andy added with a smile.

Gemma gave an incredulous huff. 'Are you kidding? I'm like the walking dead. I've never been as tired as I've been in the last six months. Not even when we were doing a hundred-plus hours a week as junior doctors.'

'Running on adrenaline,' Andy sympathised. 'It catches up with you eventually.'

His gaze held hers for a heartbeat longer. Did she remember the rare occasions that their days off had coincided back then? They'd have such big plans to make the most of the day but, so often, they would end up on the couch, wrapped in each other's arms. Sound asleep. A tangle of limbs like the twins in their shared cot down the corridor.

Andy could actually remember the feel of being that close to Gemma. Hearing the sound of her soft breathing. Feeling the steady thump of her heart. Being aware of the solid security of knowing that he was not, and never would be, alone in the world.

He had to look away but his traitorous glance slid towards that photograph on his desk.

'Yeah...I'm a wreck,' Gemma was saying. 'Haven't been near a hairdresser since I got back. Can't even remember where I left my mascara.'

'You don't need it.' Andy could hear the raw edge in his voice but couldn't stop the words from emerging. 'You never did.'

Another silence fell, just as awkward as the last one.

Andy had to break it this time because he could feel Gemma waiting. Poised, as if she didn't know what direction to jump. He was being given the choice here, but he was nowhere near ready to take the unexpected route that was becoming so visible.

So tempting.

And then Andy saw Gemma's gaze rake his desk and get caught by the photograph. Something like panic pushed him forward. He found a bright, casual tone to use.

'What's it like, living in Sydney?' he asked.

The disappointment was absolutely crushing.

It was the kind of question you might ask a complete stranger. Virtually the complete opposite of the last words he'd spoken—telling her that she didn't need to wear mascara.

Reminding her that he'd always thought she was beautiful, even first thing in the morning or after a solid night on call when she'd had no sleep and had felt like a zombie. And…he had *that* photograph on his desk. A reminder of just how close they had once been there in front of him. Every day. Why?

And why had he said something that had brought them so close again and then pushed her away so abruptly by saying something so impersonal?

He needs time, she reminded herself. We both do. Time to get used to breathing the same air again.

'Sydney's great,' she said. 'Gorgeous city.'

'What part do you live in?'

'I had an apartment close to where I worked at Sydney Harbour Hospital.' Gemma emphasised the past tense. 'Top floor of a block and I had a balcony that looked over the Harbour Bridge and the Opera House. Pretty much like a postcard.'

She couldn't read any expression on Andy's face and Gemma knew he had to work hard to appear that impassive. Especially when she'd never had any trouble reading the tiny changes that could happen around his eyes and mouth. She realised she could still read the impassiveness just as easily. He didn't like what he was hearing.

Sure enough, his voice was tightly controlled when he spoke again.

'And the job? Was that perfect, too?'

There was anger behind those words. Hurt. Fair enough. Gemma closed her eyes for a moment.

'I became a consultant radiologist a year ago. Specialising in MRI and ultrasound.'

'Any particular interests?' Andy sounded genuinely interested now. This was safe ground. A professional discussion rather than personal.

'Image-guided procedures,' Gemma responded.

'Like biopsies?'

'And surgeries. I especially like being involved in spinal and neurological cases.'

Andy looked impressed. 'Sounds fascinating. Full on, I bet.'

'Yes. It was.'

He raised an eyebrow. 'Past tense?'

Gemma shrugged. 'For the foreseeable future. And at the rate the technologies change, I doubt that I'll ever catch up again.'

And it didn't matter, she wanted to add. There *were* more important things in life than a high-powered career. She'd learned that the hard way, being thrown in at the deep end as the only living relative for five young orphans. Andy had known it all along, hadn't he?

But how could she tell him that?

If it hadn't taken her so long to learn, they would probably still be together. As an intact family, even.

No…she couldn't go there.

And…it was too late now, anyway.

Wasn't it?

Andy couldn't interpret the look he was getting from Gemma.

Did she think he wouldn't understand how important her career was to her? He almost snorted aloud. It had always been more important than anything else in her life. Including him. He might not like that about her but he'd always understood.

'You could probably get a job here,' he told her. 'There's always a shortage of specialist skills like you have. Part time,' he added, seeing her incredulous expression. 'When you've got childcare organised.'

Gemma was still staring at him. She looked totally lost for words.

'Is…um…money a problem?' How sad that he felt

so uncomfortable asking such a personal question but, if that was what was holding her back, he could help.

Gemma shook her head. 'Not at all. Both Laura and Evan had good life insurance cover. The house is safe and the children will always be well provided for. Financially, I probably never need to work again.'

'But you want to.'

Gemma looked away. 'It's not an option right now. I'm not even thinking about it.'

Really? She'd become the thing she'd sworn she never would be. A full-time stay-at-home mother. And she was OK with that?

The idea was confusing enough to make Andy head for safe territory.

'Is the house the same one? The barn conversion?'

'Yes. Evan made such a fabulous job of it. It's an amazing family home.'

'I remember. He sourced those old beams and stained-glass windows. I helped him shift all those stone slabs for doing the kitchen floor.' Andy smiled ruefully. 'Don't think my back has ever been quite the same.'

'They did heaps more while I've been away, too. Added on a new wing after the twins came along. And Laura somehow found time to create a huge garden. You could just about stock a supermarket from the vegetable patch and orchard.'

'There was a lot of land to play with, that's for sure.'

'A lot of it is in paddocks. There's a few pet sheep and Hazel's got a pony. Lots of hens, too. Laura sold eggs to the neighbours.'

'Sounds…idyllic.'

Andy could have kicked himself as the word came out. The situation was so far from idyllic…for everybody involved. The children had lost their parents. Gemma had lost her sister and brother-in-law and she'd had to leave the career she loved so much. And maybe she'd had to leave more than her career behind in Sydney. The man he'd heard berating her in the reception area had clearly been expecting to go on a date with Gemma but did that necessarily mean she hadn't left someone special behind in Australia?

'Sorry,' he muttered. 'I didn't mean that to sound…I don't know…flippant.'

'It's OK. It *is* idyllic. It was Laura's dream home and lifestyle and I intend to keep it alive for her children, no matter what.'

'Family,' Andy murmured. 'That's what it's all about, isn't it?'

'Yes.'

He could see Gemma swallow hard and take a deep breath. Open her mouth to say something that was obviously difficult.

'What about you, Andy? Are you…? I mean, is there someone…um… Have you got…?'

What? A substitute for the family he could have had with her? Andy waited for her to finish the question, his heart sinking. He didn't want to talk about himself. There was nothing to tell Gemma but too much he wanted to say.

And maybe he could talk to her now. Really talk.

They were closed off from the world here and he could feel the strangeness of being alone with Gemma again wearing off. Every time his eyes met hers, he could feel barriers cracking. Chunks of them falling away, even. Could he tell her the truth? And, if he did, where would that lead them?

But neither of them got the chance to say anything else. A knock on the door heralded the appearance of a nurse.

'Lisa said to tell you that Chantelle's arrived on the ward. Her mother's refusing to let your registrar admit her. She wants you.' From somewhere down the corridor came the faint wail of a frightened child.

'I'll be right there.' Andy pushed himself to his feet. The spell was broken and the outside world had intruded, and maybe that was for the best. He left his coffee where it was on the desk. He'd only taken that one sip and it would be stone cold by the time he got back.

Gemma hadn't drunk hers either.

'Stay here and finish your coffee if you like,' he told her. 'I'll come back and…maybe we could talk some more.'

Gemma gave him another one of those surprised looks. 'If you want to,' she said. Her unfinished question was still hanging in the air.

'I do,' Andy said quietly.

But Gemma didn't seem to be listening to him any more. The silent question on her face was directed at the nurse.

'It's not one of yours crying, don't worry,' the nurse reassured her.

But Gemma was on her feet now and Andy could feel the tension in her body. She was clearly still listening to the baby cry and needed to make sure it wasn't one of her own.

She was scared, Andy realised. Terrified that something horrible was going to happen to one of those precious kids.

Of course she was.

He had to reach out and touch her. To offer his own reassurance. To let her know that he understood.

Really understood.

And when Gemma tilted her chin and met his gaze, he could see that his message was being received with all the nuances that came from their past.

Just like him, she was listening to that cry and thinking about Max.

CHAPTER SEVEN

Christmas: six years ago

'CALL for you, Gemma. Outside line.'

'Thank you.' Gemma dumped the armload of patient notes she was carrying on the desk and reached for the phone. 'Hi hon, how's it going?'

There was surprised laughter on the line. 'How did you know it was me?'

Gemma groaned. 'I didn't. And I didn't think it *was* you, Laura. I thought it was Andy. He was going to call and let me know how Max is.'

'Is he sick?'

'Bit sniffly and grumpy this morning. Probably just a cold coming on but he had me up a few times in the night.'

'Oh, no…poor you. That's all you need when you've got to get up and go to work.'

'Worse for Andy if he's been unsettled all day. There's no guarantee he'll get any sleep on night shift.'

'Poor him, too. Can't believe he has to do a night shift on Christmas Eve.'

'We figured it's a small price to pay for having been able to juggle our rosters so well. Things will get easier in the new year once Max starts day care for more than one day a week.'

'And you've definitely got tomorrow off? You're not going to get called in at the last minute or something?'

'No way. Not when we're going to see your new kitchen in action for the first time. That Aga is going to cook the perfect turkey or there'll be some serious questions being asked.'

Laura laughed. 'Fingers crossed. I'm doing my best. Oh…I can't wait, Gem. Max and Hazel are old enough to know what's going on now. They'll be able to *play* together. It's going to be a real, family Christmas. Dream-come-true stuff…'

'You're not going to start crying on me, are you?'

The sniff was noisy enough to make Gemma wince. 'No-o-o… I'm just…so happy.'

'I will be, too, as soon as I get away from here. I've got a full ward round to get done first, though, so I'll have to go.'

'OK…but…'

'But?' There was an urgency in Laura's tone that made Gemma pause. 'What's wrong?'

'I'm not supposed to tell you yet but…I'm going to *burst* if I don't.'

'Don't do that. It would be messy and I have no idea how to cook turkeys.' Gemma heard another sniff. And then a very happy sigh. Where had she heard that before?

'Oh, my God, Laura...are you *pregnant* again?'

'I think I might be. I *hope* so.'

'Fingers crossed, then.' Gemma closed her eyes as she shook her head. 'Rather you than me.'

'Maybe it'll be a boy this time. So Max won't have to play with girls all his life.'

'Good thinking.'

'You could always have another one...' Laura suggested breathlessly. 'Remember how fun it was when we both had babies at the same time?'

'Fun? Are you kidding? It was a logistical nightmare. One that's only just starting to get manageable. No...' Gemma glanced at her watch. 'I've got to go, Laura. I'll see you in the morning.'

'Are you mad at me?'

'No, of course not. I'm delighted for you. I'm delighted that you're going to provide a whole bunch of cousins for Max so I won't have to feel guilty about him being an only child. But I *have* to go. Now. Love you. 'Bye.'

Gemma eyed the phone after she'd hung up on Laura. She got as far as dialling the outside line, intending to call Andy and see how things were going at home. But what if he'd just got Max down for his nap and was finally grabbing the hour or two's sleep he must desperately need? Gemma put the phone down again. With a resigned sigh she picked up the big stack of patient notes and headed out into the ward.

There were fourteen patients to check on. Some would need physical examinations and some would need results chased up and possibly further investigations ordered. She might even have to call the consultant in if there was anything she was really concerned about. All these patients and probably a few family members would need a chance to talk to their doctor. If she was really, really lucky, she would be able to get through it all in four hours or so.

And then she could go home to the two men in her life and start Christmas.

How good was that going to be?

There were no flowers allowed in the respiratory ward Gemma was working in at the moment so the staff had made up for a year's worth of lacking colour by going to town with non-allergenic Christmas decorations. Tinsel and banners and multicoloured baubles were tied to every handle, strung across doorways and decorated bed ends and trolleys. With a smile, Gemma broke off a piece of bright green tinsel and tied it around the short ponytail taming her hair.

Then she went to collect her junior houseman and a nurse from the staff kitchen. If Andy called she would interrupt the round for a couple of minutes. If he didn't, that meant everything was fine and she'd wait until she got home to catch up.

Gemma and Andy were still living in a basement flat but this one had two bedrooms, a bigger living area and even two chairs and a microscopic patch of grass outside. It also cost nearly twice as much as their first flat had but, with them both working full time finally, it was getting much easier to manage the finances. They were

at last saving for a deposit on a house of their own and
the plan was for them to have moved by next Christmas.

It was nearly six p.m. by the time Gemma arrived home.
Andy was due to start his night shift at nine p.m. so
they would have a good couple of hours together before
he had to head off.

'Hi, honey…I'm home,' she called as she closed the
front door behind her. It was a standing joke but, in the
silence that followed her greeting, Gemma bit her lip. It
didn't always produce a smile. Maybe Andy had had a
rough day, in which case the sing-song announcement
of her arrival to take over the parenting duties could be
met with some built-up resentment. It was something
she'd had to work on herself in those early days when
she'd had the lion's share of caring for Max.

The tiny hallway of the flat was no more than a place
to hang coats and keys. It finished with a bathroom at
the end. A door to the left led to the main bedroom. The
second bedroom opened off that and would probably
get turned into a walk-in wardrobe by a future owner.
A door to the right led to the open-plan living room
and kitchen with the door that opened to the tiny, below
street level courtyard.

At this time of the evening Max would be due for
his bath but the door to the bathroom was closed so
that obviously wasn't happening. Gemma could feel a
knot of tension in her stomach now. Playing with Max
in the bath was such a treat it was the reward for anything not so good that had happened during the day.

The time afterwards, with Max in his fluffy pyjamas, smelling sweetly of baby powder and ready for cuddles and bedtime, was the best of family time. It was when they both knew that the struggle was worth it. That the bond they all had was precious.

Maybe Andy was still feeding Max his dinner but it was too quiet for that to be happening. Max loved his food. He was always messy and noisy, especially when he had his favourite wooden spoon to bang on the tray of his high chair.

And why hadn't the lights been turned on? It was pitch black outside now. And freezing. But the shiver that ran through Gemma as she flung her coat onto a hook didn't feel like it was caused by the cold. The door to the living room was slightly ajar so it made no sound as Gemma pushed it open.

There was a source of light after all. The twinkling lights on the Christmas tree shone green and red and blue in turn. A real Christmas tree this year, albeit an artificial one. Yesterday they had taken far too many photographs of Max sitting beneath it wearing a Santa hat and looking impossibly cute amongst the brightly wrapped parcels.

It took less than the time to draw a breath to see what was going on. Andy was sound asleep on the couch, one arm trailing to leave an upturned palm on the rug, the fingers curled gently. Right beside that hand was the baby monitor so that he would hear the moment Max woke up from his nap.

Gemma's heart sank. Andy must have been desperate to let Max have such a late nap and it meant that she would be lucky to get him back to bed this side of midnight after he'd had his dinner and bath. She couldn't berate Andy for it, though. They did what they had to do as far as coping with parenting and they had a pact to support each other a hundred per cent.

Gemma flicked on a lamp and then the kitchen light. She filled the jug and plugged it in. Andy was going to need a bucket of coffee before setting off to work.

Neither the light nor the sound of her moving around woke Andy up so Gemma went and knelt beside the couch, intending to wake him with a kiss on his cheek.

She simply knelt there for a long moment, however. Andy looked *so* tired. He hadn't shaved today and his jaw was dark enough to make the rest of face look pale. Even in sleep, she could see the weary furrows etched into his forehead and around his eyes and Gemma felt guilty. If she hadn't been so hell-bent on keeping her career on track, she could have made life so much easier for both of them for this early stage of family life but no…she'd worked until she'd been eight and a half months pregnant and then she'd gone back to work when Max had been only six weeks old.

And Andy had kept his promise of making parenthood an equally shared venture. Done more than his share quite often, in fact, and had never argued over some of the big issues, like stopping breastfeeding so they could share night feeds and remove a looming hassle from her return to work.

Yep. He was a hero, all right. Gemma lifted her hand

and gently brushed a lock of unruly hair back from Andy's forehead. The sudden rush of tenderness almost brought tears to her eyes. While having a baby and now a boisterous toddler in their lives had covered a lot of the romance with things like dirty nappies and broken sleep, the underlying love they had for each other had become stronger because of it. Right then, Gemma vowed to try and make life just a bit easier for Andy. Or, at least, to show him, more often, how much she cared about him.

The touch of her hand had been enough to jump-start Andy's journey to consciousness. With his eyes still firmly closed, his lips curled in a smile and his hand came up from the floor to catch Gemma's. He pulled her closer, turning his head and she willingly bent down to kiss his lips.

'Mmm…you're home early…' he murmured.

'Hardly. It's half past six.'

Andy's eyes shot open. *'What?'*

Gemma froze at his horrified tone. 'How long have you been asleep?'

'I put Max down for his nap after lunch.' Andy was pulling himself into a sitting position. With a groan he covered his face with his hands and massaged his forehead. 'It would have been about one o'clock.'

He'd been asleep for five and half hours? Gemma still felt frozen. Oh…God…she was too scared to go and check. Memories of Max as a tiny baby, so soundly asleep that you couldn't see whether he was breathing or not, came back to haunt her. But sixteen months was way too late to be worrying about cot death, wasn't it?

As if to reassure her, there was a crackle from the baby monitor. A snuffling sound and then a grunt. Gemma was half way to being on her feet when a new sound was transmitted.

It was a child's cry but it was not a sound she had ever heard Max making before. Or any child, for that matter. It was a weird, high-pitched keening that made her blood run cold.

Andy was on his feet now as well. Gemma saw the Adam's apple in his throat move as he swallowed hard. His face went white.

With a muttered oath he overtook Gemma as they both rushed into their son's bedroom.

This was a nightmare.

He was supposed to be in the emergency department of the Queen Mary Infirmary as a senior registrar on night duty, not as the parent of a seriously sick child.

Somebody's cellphone was ringing with the tune of 'Jingle Bells'. A young female member of the domestic staff went past with a mop and bucket and a headband sporting reindeer antlers with flashing lights on the top. The nurse doing triage was wearing a Santa hat identical to the one they'd been taking photos of Max wearing last night.

How could anyone be thinking of Christmas right now?

It had ceased to be of any relevance whatsoever from

the moment they had turned the light on in Max's bed-room and seen his flushed, feverish-looking face. The fontanelle on the top of his head had been bulging and tense but what had terrified both Andy and Gemma most had been finding the rash on his abdomen and chest. Just a few spots but they had been bright red and refused to blanch with pressure.

There had been no time to wait for an ambulance and neither of them had seemed to notice that they were breaking the law by having Max wrapped in a blanket in Gemma's arms instead of being in his car seat as they'd rushed him to hospital.

Arriving here—to the expertise and technology geared to save lives should have been a comfort but it only marked the real beginning of the nightmare. Gemma had tears streaming down her face as she helped two nurses hold Max as still as possible, curled up on his side so that the senior ED consultant could perform a lumbar puncture. It was an agonisingly slow wait for the drops of clear fluid to be collected into several different tubes.

Finally, it was over, and Gemma was allowed to pick Max up and cuddle him for a minute.

'We'll get IV access and start the antibiotics now,' the consultant said. 'I'll get a bed organised in the PICU.' He picked up a chart. 'Run through it again for me. He was symptom-free yesterday?'

Gemma rocked Max, who was looking drowsy now. 'He had an unsettled night but he wasn't running a temperature. I thought he might be getting a new tooth or something.'

'And this morning?'

'He was just a bit...irritable. A slight sniffle, that's all. Like the very start of a head cold.'

'He was rubbing his ear at lunchtime,' Andy added. 'He's had ear infections before so I assumed that's what it was. I gave him some paracetamol and he settled for a nap without a fuss.'

'And he slept for five and a half hours.' The consultant's tone held a grim edge. 'How long does he normally nap?'

'An hour. An hour and a half if we're lucky.' It was Gemma who answered. Andy could feel her gaze on him. He swallowed hard.

'I fell asleep as well,' he admitted. 'I have to, when I'm working nights and looking after Max during the day. I didn't think to set an alarm because...'

Because he'd never needed to. He'd had the monitor right beside him and he knew he'd wake at the first squeak. Maybe Max had made a sound at some stage but he'd slipped into such a deep sleep by then it had simply become part of a dream. This was his fault. He should have spotted the signs. Had Max in here with some powerful antibiotics running through his veins hours ago.

Because every minute counted in the war against bacterial meningitis.

'When did he last pass any urine?'

'I changed his nappy before lunch.'

'It's still dry now,' Gemma added quietly.

The consultant had finished scribbling his notes. He turned to his registrar, who was still filling in the forms for the CSF and blood samples collected. 'Make sure you've covered microscopy, culture, protein and glucose analysis. And put a rush on getting the results.'

'Will do.'

'Go up to PICU with the Baxters. I'll come up as soon as I've got a minute. Make sure that plasma and urine electrolytes are carefully monitored and fluids restricted until we see some signs of recovery.'

Recovery.

That was the magic word.

The only gift that mattered this Christmas. Gemma had heard the word as well. Huge eyes in a pale face searched out and locked on his. Andy took a step closer and put his arm around both Gemma and Max. He might be powerless in protecting his family from what was happening but at least he could hold them close.

'We'll start a standard combination antibiotic regime immediately,' the consultant was telling them both. 'And then we'll transfer you upstairs.' He paused and Andy knew that this was the moment to offer a family reassurance if there was any to be had.

'We'd better start both of you on prophylactic antibiotics as well.' The consultant's voice was sympathetic. 'I'm really sorry, but this looks like a clear case of meningococcal disease.'

Recovery was looking further away instead of closer

as the hours ticked past and Christmas Eve became Christmas Day.

'He's in septic shock,' the PICU consultant told them. 'We're going to intubate and get him onto a ventilator.'

The rash was rapidly evolving. Instead of the tiny red pinpricks on Max's chest and abdomen, he now had a rash over his entire body. And it wasn't just little spots. They seemed to be joining together in places to make ugly, dark stains on his skin that looked like inkblots.

He wasn't just put on the ventilator. Their precious little boy had to have a nasogastric tube placed. And a urinary catheter. A larger-bore IV line was inserted as well so that therapy to control his blood pressure and electrolyte abnormalities could be administered.

'Order some fresh frozen plasma, too,' the consultant told his registrar. 'It's highly likely we've got coagulation issues happening.'

For any parents this was terrifying. For Gemma and Andy, who could understand all the terminology and the reasons that particular tests were being ordered or procedures were being done, it was even worse. They knew exactly how dangerous an illness this was. They knew what needed to be done and could have done it themselve...on someone else's child.

But this was their son. Their only child. And even if there hadn't been rules about treating close relatives yourselves, the emotional involvement rendered them incapable of being relied on for objective analysis or the ability to perform invasive procedures.

For a short time, after the initial rush to get ventilation started and new drugs including narcotic pain relief on board, there was a lull in the number of people hovering over Max and disturbing his body with different procedures or tests.

Andy and Gemma could sit beside the bed, holding each other's hands tightly. Almost too scared to breathe.

For a long time neither of them spoke. It was Andy who broke the silence.

'I'm sorry, Gem.'

'What for?'

'I fell asleep. I should have spotted this so much earlier.'

The extra squeeze on his hand was comforting. 'You can't blame yourself. You were exhausted. You have to nap when Maxie's asleep. If he didn't wake up, then of course you wouldn't have either.'

'I know, but—'

'If we're going to go down the "Who can we blame?" track, what about me? I knew he was sniffly this morning and I still went off to work. I'm the mother who wouldn't stay at home full time, which was why you were exhausted in the first place. It's my fault as much as yours.'

'It's nobody's fault,' Andy had to admit. 'It's…' His throat was closing. Clogging with tears that were too deep to come out. 'It's bloody awful, that's what.'

'He can fight this. I remember a case when I was doing Paeds. A nine-month-old girl who had it as badly as this. Full septic shock and organ failure and she was on ventilation for ten days. She ended up having to have surgical debridement of the skin on her fingers and toes but she survived. Nothing got...got amputated...'

Gemma's voice disintegrated into a choked sob and she lowered her head and began sobbing silently, her pain and fear almost palpable things. Andy put his arm around her shoulders and drew her close enough for her head to rest on his chest. The position they still slept in by choice. He rubbed her back gently in big circles.

A nurse came close. 'Your sister's here,' she said. 'Laura Gillespie? I've put her in the relatives' room. Do you want to go and see her?'

Andy's hold on Gemma tightened. They couldn't leave Max by himself even if he was unconscious. He didn't want Gemma out of reach either. He had to hold them all close together. As a family.

But Laura was family, too. A combination of both sister and child to Gemma after she'd practically raised her. She was also the mother of Max's best friend and cousin, Hazel. They couldn't shut her out.

'Bring her in,' he suggested. 'And...she and her family had better start the prophylactic antibiotics, too. They've spent time with us over the last few days.'

They were supposed to be spending the day together tomorrow. Celebrating Christmas.

Laura came in, wearing a gown and mask. She stopped abruptly when she got close to the bed and uttered a soft cry of horror.

It had the effect of showing both Andy and Gemma the scene through fresh eyes.

Max's tiny, naked body lay on the top of the bed,

criss-crossed by the wires connecting electrodes to the monitoring equipment. Numerous IV ports were splashes of colour amongst the clear tubing and white tape. He had tubes in his nose and his mouth and a blood-pressure cuff, which looked far too big, covering an upper arm.

The most shocking thing, however, was the discolouration of his skin. The mottling of the dreadful rash as it spread and intensified.

Laura couldn't cope. Her voice was anguished as she excused herself only minutes later.

'I'll be right outside. Come and get me if…'

Andy nodded. He would go and get her if there was something she could do to help. Or if things got any worse.

Things did get worse within the next couple of hours despite treatment that was as aggressive as this awful disease. Constant monitoring and adjustments to the drug regime were made but Max's blood pressure continued to drop. His renal function declined and it became harder to keep oxygen saturation levels up to an acceptable range.

Worst of all, his little feet and hands were showing marked changes in their colour. The inkblots expanded and darkened until the skin looked almost black. The medical team fought a valiant battle but somewhere just before dawn they knew they had lost. The tubes and wires were taken off and the parents were left alone with their child for the final minutes of his life.

The first stages of grief were a curious phenomenon for Gemma. It was Andy who cried first—great racking sobs of unbearable pain—but she felt completely numb. As though she was sleepwalking through a nightmare that would have to end at some point but not yet.

She held her son as he took his last breath and she had Andy holding them both. It was almost a rerun of the night they'd first met and yet it couldn't have been more different. They hadn't even known each other then and now they had a bond that was so strong it seemed as if nothing could ever break it.

Even this?

Andy didn't seem to think so. When they finally had to leave Max behind, he put his arms around Gemma and held her so tightly she couldn't breathe.

'We'll get through this,' he promised, in a broken whisper. 'Somehow, we're going to get through this together.'

Laura had been distraught. They'd had to call Evan and tell him to come and get her in his work van because there was no way she could drive herself home. She had wanted Gemma and Andy to come with her but couldn't persuade them.

'We need time together,' Gemma told her sister. 'In our own home.'

Only maybe that hadn't been the best idea because walking into the house and feeling how empty it was without Max destroyed Andy all over again and he sat on the couch, his head in his hands, sobbing.

Still Gemma couldn't cry. She knew it would come

and when it did she would fall into a pit of grief that would be terrifying in its depth but she was still in that protective, trance-like state.

She walked around the apartment, touching things. The floppy-eared rabbit toy that had been such a favourite. Why hadn't they remembered to take that to the hospital with them? The presents were still under the tree. They were all for Max. What should she do with them now? Brushing loose strands of hair back from her face, she felt the length of that stupid green tinsel still tied to her ponytail. She pulled it free and let it drift to the floor.

The kitchen was a mess. Dishes from lunch sat in the sink and the tray of the highchair was covered with what looked like dried-up custard. There were things all over the table, too. Paper and scissors and glue.

Andy had been making a card. He'd printed out one of the photos of Max they'd taken yesterday and had made a Christmas card. Inside, in wobbly writing that was supposed to look like a toddler had written it were the words:

Merry Christmas. I love you Mummy. From Max.

There was something else on the table beside the card. Without thinking, Gemma picked it up and carried it through to the living room. And it was then that the words on the home-made card sank in.

The moment the wall of grief hit her.

Andy was on his feet in an instant. Holding her in his arms. Sinking with her to the floor as they started to face the unthinkable.

It was a long, long time later that Andy noticed Gemma's clenched fist.

'What have you got?'

Gemma uncurled her fingers. She was holding a shared memento that somehow managed to never get lost and to make an appearance every Christmas.

The sad little piece of plastic mistletoe that she'd found in the lift the first night they'd met. The one Andy had held above her head after he'd proposed to her when she'd found out she was pregnant.

There would be no kiss this year. Instead, they simply clung to each other and cried.

CHAPTER EIGHT

THE reassurance that it hadn't been one of 'her' children crying hadn't been enough.

Gemma abandoned her own cup of coffee and went back to their room to find that they were, indeed, all fast asleep.

What was it about sleeping children that tugged so hard at the heartstrings? Maybe it was that perfect skin and a baby's cupid bow of a mouth that took years to change shape. The spread-eagled position that advertised utter relaxation. Or was it the innocence of such young faces that had yet to face the harsh realities of the world?

Except that these children had already faced too much. Sophie knew nothing about it, of course, and even the twins were young enough to have accepted the massive change in their lives but Jamie, and especially Hazel, would always be aware of that sad gap left by having their own parents torn away. And, while Gemma was doing her best to fill the gap, she could never replace a father completely.

Standing there in the semi-darkness, letting her

gaze travel from one child to the next and back again, Gemma was overwhelmed by how protective she felt. How much she loved these children. And by the joy of remembering the cuddles and kisses she had received as she'd settled them down tonight. The words the children had said.

I love Aunty Gemma. She's a good mummy.

You're nice, Aunty Gemma. I love you, too.

It's OK. Aunty Gemma's looking after you. She's looking after all of us.

She was. She always would. Always. Oh...help. She had tears running down her cheeks again. Just as well she had lost her mascara but she must still look a mess. With a sniff and a quick scrub at her cheeks Gemma started moving again. Not into the children's room but down towards the bathroom so that she could wash her face and try and make herself look a bit more respectable.

Because it wasn't just the nurse's reassurance about the children that hadn't been enough. The conversation with Andy felt like it had only just begun. That it had been interrupted at a crucial moment even. Andy had invited her to stay and finish her coffee. He'd said he'd come back and that he wanted to talk some more.

Gemma wanted that, too. *So* much.

Despite it being in the early hours of the morning, Gemma found she wasn't alone in the bathroom. While she was splashing her face with some cold water at the basin, a toilet flushed and then the door banged as a young woman came out in a hurry.

'Oh, God, I needed that!' she exclaimed, heading for the basin beside Gemma. 'I've been hanging on for *hours*.'

Gemma glanced sideways as she reached for some paper towels. The woman looked barely more than a teenager. She was wearing leggings and layers of clothing on her upper body but she was painfully thin. She had dark hair that reached her waist and an abundance of silver jewellery that rattled as she moved her hands and dug in an oversized shoulder-bag.

'Rough night, huh?' she said sympathetically.

'Oh, man...you've got no idea.' The girl didn't look at Gemma. She had pulled a mascara wand from the bag that was balanced precariously on the edge of the basin. She leaned forward to peer at herself in the mirror. 'How awful is it to have to come into a *hospital* on Christmas Eve? We'll be in here for Christmas *Day*.'

The words struck an odd note because attending to her eyelashes seemed to be the most important thing on this girl's mind. Gemma took another glance at her own blotchy face, dismissed the reflection and screwed up the paper towels to drop them into the bin.

'They make it special,' she told the girl. 'Everybody knows how tough it is on kids to be in here for Christmas. And on their parents,' she added kindly. 'In fact, it's probably tougher on you than it is on your baby.'

It would have to be a baby she was in with, wouldn't it? She was so young.

'Tell me about it.' The girl was fishing in her bag

again. This time it was for lip gloss. 'We've got the loveliest doctor, though. How 'bout you?'

Did she mean Andy? Was this the mother of his latest admission? And she was in here, trying to make herself look as attractive as possible?

Was that why *she* was beginning to feel judgmental? That there was something about this young woman she really didn't like?

'We're doing fine,' she said coolly, already moving away. 'We'll be going home tomorrow.'

'Lucky you. We'll probably be here for ages. Oh... damn...' A careless nudge as she leaned closer to the mirror had dislodged the bag and sent it flying to the floor. A heap of objects escaped to scatter themselves on the floor.

A small bottle rolled rapidly enough to knock Gemma's foot. She bent down and picked it up to hand it back but all those years of medical training made her glance automatically at the label as she did so.

A well-known brand of laxatives. Well...that might go some way to explaining why this girl was so thin. The bottle was snatched out of her hand with a haste that suggested Gemma was correct in thinking the medication might be being abused.

'Gotta run,' the girl said. 'Catch ya later.'

There wasn't much Andy could do for the three-year-old girl who'd been readmitted tonight, of all nights. The morphine she'd been given for the severe abdominal pain had worked its magic and the child was now comfortably asleep. A new raft of investigations would need to be ordered but that was a task for the morning and most of those tests would have to wait in any case. Only absolute emergencies could be dealt with on Christmas Day.

With some relief, Andy headed back to his office. Would Gemma still be there?

He hoped so.

Or did he? He'd been on the point of confessing how empty his life was without her. Feeling closer to her with every passing minute.

Would the barriers be back in place by now?

Gemma wasn't sitting in the armchair. She was standing beside his desk, staring at that photograph. She jumped when she heard him approach and when her gaze met his, she looked…guilty.

What for?

Nosing around in personal things or because the photograph reminded her of what they'd once had? What she'd thrown away?

Andy's breath came out in a sigh. Yes…the barriers were there again.

'How's it going?' he asked. 'That coffee was probably undrinkable.'

'I forgot about it. I went to check on the children.'

'They OK?'

'Sound asleep.'

'That's good. They'll be fine in the morning and ready to enjoy their Christmas Day.'

'I hope so.' Gemma was biting her bottom lip, a sure

sign that she wasn't feeling comfortable. 'How's your patient?'

'Also asleep.' Andy shook his head. 'I have to confess I have no idea what's going on there. We've done a raft of tests, including a CT, and everything's normal. Her mother's convinced she's got appendicitis. Wanted me to call in a surgeon immediately. She said she had her appendix out a couple of years ago and she reckons Chantelle's got exactly the same symptoms. Plus, she looked it up on the internet.'

'Oh...' Gemma's lips had an amused curve to them. 'Can't argue with the internet, can you?'

Andy smiled. 'Not easily, no.'

Gemma was watching him. The guilty expression had long since vanished. Right now she was looking as if she was concentrating hard on something.

'Chantelle's mother,' she said. 'Does she look about nineteen, long dark hair and a ton of jewellery?'

'That's her. Why?'

'I met her in the bathroom.'

Andy nodded. 'Yeah...she dashed off to the loo when I was examining Chantelle.'

'Does she...I mean...does something strike you as being a bit off key with her?'

Andy frowned. 'She's very young. Needs more reassurance than Chantelle, that's for sure.'

'Hmm.'

The sound that Gemma made took Andy back through the years. Right back to when they had both been junior doctors, in fact, and had spent hours discussing their cases and bouncing ideas around. Sparking off each other like that had been something they'd both loved. It had invariably pushed them both to think harder and perform better. And he recognised that sound. Gemma had thought of something he probably hadn't. The old response came automatically to his lips.

'OK, Einstein. Spill.'

Gemma's lips twitched but then her face became serious. 'Has Munchausen's by proxy occurred to you?'

Andy blinked. 'No. Should it?'

'Difficulty coming up with any kind of definitive diagnosis? A caregiver who's had the same symptoms as the child within the previous five years?'

'Mmm. It's not a conclusion I'd be happy jumping to.' He stared at Gemma, narrowing his eyes. 'You sound a bit too sure of yourself. Did Deidre say something in the bathroom?'

'No. It was more what she wasn't saying.'

'What do you mean?'

'She was busy fixing her make-up. Saying how awful it was to be stuck in hospital. Only she didn't sound that cut up about it, you know? And she didn't even mention her baby. And...'

'And?'

'And it might be nothing but she knocked her bag over and I picked up a bottle of pills. Laxatives.'

Andy could almost hear the penny dropping. 'Oh, hell,' he groaned. 'That would do it. Diarrhoea. Violent abdominal cramps. Normal test results.' He ran his hands through his hair, wondering how he was going to deal with this.

'Have you got access to Chantelle's previous health records?'

'Not yet. She only came in the first time a couple of days ago and they've moved recently from up north. We've requested information but...well, it is Christmas. Silly season.'

'Might be worth having a chat to someone. Maybe looking at the mother's records, too. It's another sign, isn't it? Moving around and going to new hospitals or doctors.'

Andy nodded. 'No time like the present. If I get any red flags, I could at least talk to Deirdre about it. Get those laxatives off her before she makes the poor kid suffer any more, if that is what's happening.'

He caught Gemma's gaze. They were both confident they were on the right track. They both knew that if they *were* right, mother and child would need a lot of help and it would be far better to step in now before any real harm was done.

'I'll come and find you,' Andy said. 'And let you know what they say.'

It was over an hour later when Andy eased open the door of the children's room. Gemma had been dozing in the armchair but came awake instantly when she'd sensed the movement.

The only light came from the nightlights plugged in

low to the floor in both the room and the corridor outside, but Gemma could see how tense Andy was.

Or maybe it was more that she could sense it. The same way she'd picked up the silent opening of the door when she'd been more than half-asleep.

Gemma uncurled her legs and got to her feet. As she got closer to Andy she could see how still he was holding himself. How wary the expression in his eyes was. He wasn't at all sure he wanted to be here, was he? The tension felt like nervousness. Borderline fear, even?

It was instantly contagious. They'd always been able to connect effortlessly. To gauge and respond to each other on both intellectual and emotional levels.

Andy was here because something had changed. He wanted—or needed—time with *her*. A heartbeat later, his words confirmed the impression.

'I need some fresh air,' Andy muttered quietly. 'Want to come with me?'

Did she?

Gemma could feel her heart rate accelerating. Her mouth felt dry. A short time ago, in his office, she had sensed them getting closer and had been so disappointed when Andy had pushed her away with the impersonal questions about her life in Sydney.

The opposite was happening here.

And that was making Gemma feel very, very nervous.

It was Christmas Eve, for heaven's sake. A time of year that bound them together with memories that were very painful. It could be the worst time to try and re-connect on a deeper level.

Or...it might be the only time when emotions could be strong enough to break down barriers.

Andy was holding out his hand and suddenly Gemma had her answer.

Of course she wanted to go with him. She *had* to.

No words were needed on her part. Gemma simply put her hand in Andy's.

He led them at a fast pace along the corridor, out of the ward and up a stairwell.

'Don't worry. I've told Lisa to page me if any of the children wake up.'

Up and up the stairs they went until they came to a heavy metal fire door. Gemma knew exactly where they were going. It was the place they'd often headed for as young doctors, when the only time they'd seemed to get alone together had been moments they'd been able to escape from work and come here.

On to the roof of Queen Mary Infirmary.

The air was fresh all right.

Freezing, in fact, but Gemma wasn't about to complain. It wasn't bothering her yet because she was so aware of the warmth of Andy's hand.

He was still holding it. Up all those stairs and even when he'd pushed open the heavy door to the roof space. Now, as the blast of icy air hit, he increased the pressure of his grip.

'Can you stand it?'

Gemma could only nod. Oh...yes...

'It's pretty cold,' Andy added as he led them on a route that had once been so well trodden. Round the back of the structure that held the workings of the nearest set of lifts. Into a sheltered corner well away from the heli-pad. A private place that had a great view over the city of Manchester. The blinking light of a plane coming in to land could be seen beneath the heavy, low-slung clouds.

'Santa's sleigh, you reckon?' Gemma smiled but couldn't repress a small shiver.

Andy didn't smile at her weak joke. 'I just need a minute,' he apologised. 'Head-clearing stuff. The cold is...cleansing or something, I guess.'

'Oh...' Gemma understood instantly. 'We were right, then.'

'*You* were.' But something made Andy pause and take a slow, inward breath.

'We' was more accurate. He'd been reminded at the time of the way they'd once sparked off each other professionally and come up with things that had been more than the sum of different ideas. Something that had pushed them both into being better doctors. Better people even?

It had been the same as parenting together.

The same as making love.

They had always been a perfect team. Two halves of a whole that was impossible to achieve alone. Or with anybody else.

God...how could he have forgotten how powerful that was? How much...*less* his life was without it?

Feeling it again now was terrifying. How the hell was he going to say goodbye to her tomorrow and watch her walk out of his life again?

Andy cleared his throat and deliberately avoided catching Gemma's gaze. Avoided saying anything remotely personal. The only thing he couldn't bring himself to do was break the handclasp. He needed that touch. That warmth. To feel that connection for just a little longer.

'First hospital I rang where she was last living was able to fill me in. Mind you, it wouldn't have mattered what hospital I rang. She's well known in the system up there. Had a perfectly normal appendix removed the year before she had a baby and someone finally flagged the possibility of Munchausen's.

'Maybe that procedure was major enough to keep her happy for a while. Or maybe becoming a mother changed something. This is the first time Chantelle's been the patient instead of Deirdre.'

'Thank goodness it's been caught early. I've heard of cases that went on for years and years before the truth came out.'

'Mmm. This could have gone the same way if I didn't have so much faith in your instincts. She denied it all fiercely at first. Until I called her bluff and said there was an easy blood test I could do to check for something like laxatives in Chantelle's blood and then she knew she was busted and it all came out along with a lot of tears.'

* * *

Gemma squeezed his hand. It would have been an emotional and difficult conversation to have had. And he still had faith in her instincts? For some reason, it felt like a much bigger compliment than telling her she had never needed to wear mascara. It felt like the way they'd once been together. A perfect team.

'I've referred her to the psych team and Social Services will be notified tomorrow.' Andy stopped talking and heaved a sigh as he closed his eyes. 'It wasn't pleasant. We do everything we can to keep parents and their kids together. Goes against the grain to start something that might break them up.'

He opened his eyes and looked straight at Gemma.

'Enough about me. You OK, Gem?'

His tone was so gentle. So caring. His face got a bit blurry as tears stung her eyes.

'He's always there, isn't he?' Andy went on in that same, soft voice. 'When you hear a baby cry in the distance. Or when you have to deal with someone who has a kid and they don't know how lucky they are.'

Gemma nodded. Yes. The memories of Max were always there.

'It doesn't hurt so much these days, though, does it?'

Gemma shook her head. It was true. Time might not heal things like that completely but the pain was…encapsulated somehow now.

'I find I can remember the good bits now and it doesn't automatically undo me,' Andy said. 'Do you?'

Gemma nodded again. Her voice seemed to have deserted her. Because she was afraid that by speaking she might break the spell that Andy's words were casting?

'Is there one thing that stands out for you?' Andy's question was gentle. She didn't have to go there if she didn't want to. 'A favourite memory?'

Gemma didn't have to take any time to think about the answer to that question.

'Holding him that first time,' she whispered. 'Feeling like…a mother.'

It wasn't the whole answer. Or the whole memory. Because a huge part of what had created the magic of that moment had been seeing Andy's big hands cradling his newborn son with such exquisitely gentle care and reverence. The way she had felt overwhelmed with love.

For both Andy and Max.

Andy was nodding. It felt like he was stroking the top of her head. 'For me, too. That extraordinary feeling of being more than a couple. Being…a family. Nothing prepares you for how different it feels. And you'd never really know if you hadn't been there yourself, would you?'

Gemma swallowed. Hard. 'No.'

Andy had harnessed that knowledge. Used it to become the kind of doctor who could relate to children and their parents. She had no doubt that his caring extended to the whole family of any of his young patients. It was far more than she had been brave enough to do.

His words were making her remember more than the magic of a new family being created. They had taken her back to older memories. To when they *were* just a couple. To when that had seemed too good to be improved on.

She needed to say something else. To try and move the conversation on. Could she do it without breaking the spell that seemed to have caught them both?

'The first time Max smiled,' she offered softly. 'That's a special memory. He…he looked so like you.'

A miniature version of the smile she loved so much. Had loved since the first time she'd seen it. When she'd been standing outside the door of little Jessica's room in the PICU, too scared to go inside and begin what she knew she had to do. When he'd offered to be her support person and he'd smiled in a way that made her feel more courageous all by itself. Not alone any more. Brave enough to cope with anything.

'I still remember how jealous I was when he spoke his first words. You remember what they were?'

Of course she did.

'Mum, mum, mum.'

Gemma's indrawn breath was a gulp. At the same moment her body decided to let her know how cold it really was out here by shuddering dramatically.

'Oh…Gem…' Andy pulled her close.

Gemma could feel herself snuggling closer to Andy and she didn't feel cold any more. How could she with his arms around her like this? So close she could feel the steady thump of his heart?

For a long moment they stood there in silence. Gemma could feel when Andy's head tipped so that his cheek was resting on the top of her head. It felt so familiar. So good.

As if she'd come home after far too long away.

'I'm so sorry.' Andy's voice was a rumble against her ear. 'I didn't mean to stir it all up again…'

'It's…OK…' Gemma sniffed and took a deep breath as she raised her face from the warmth and comfort of Andy's chest. 'Really,' she added, seeing the concern on his face. 'It's part of my life and I couldn't forget Max even if I wanted to. Which I don't. Ever. And…if I try and share those memories with anyone else, they…'

'They don't share them,' Andy continued for her. 'They can't possibly understand.'

No. The only people in the world who could still share Max were his parents. His mother and father. Andy and herself.

There was no way she could break the eye contact. It was intense and it held shared memories that were deeper than the 'snapshot' moments they'd had with their baby.

They were the memories of how much of a team they'd been. Andy had been the husband that most women would dream of. Rarely complaining about having to take his turn cooking or doing dishes. Happy to do the supermarket run and put the rubbish out and even clean the loo. They might have both felt they were doing more than their share at times but that's what it had taken to be young parents together so they had done it. Together. And it would have been enough if Max hadn't got sick.

It hadn't just been sharing all those household duties. They had both worked irregular and long hours, slotting in extra study when they'd been able to, juggling the days and nights so that Max would have one parent with him for as much time as was humanly possible.

Gemma remembered Andy bringing her a cup of coffee at some horribly early hour after they'd both been up half the night with a teething baby. She remembered him sitting on the side of her bed, stroking her hair until she woke up enough to drink it and then get ready for a day at work. She remembered the guilt she'd felt, knowing that Andy would probably get no sleep during the day and would then have to front up for a night shift and he'd make damn sure he was awake enough to do his job well.

Had she really secretly blamed him for falling asleep for so long on the day that Max died?

Oh…God…

Still the eye contact went on. She could see that a million thoughts were racing through Andy's mind as well.

Was he thinking the same thing? That, once, they had been such a great team? An amazing little family?

How could she have walked away from that?

Gemma's lips trembled. She willed herself not to cry but it was hard.

She had hurt them both so badly. The kind of hurt that could never be undone or even repaired. She had destroyed everything they'd tried to cling to in the wake of losing their child.

They couldn't go back.

Except...the way Andy was *looking* at her now...

It made Gemma think that some things hadn't changed at all. They'd been covered up, yes, but the love that had brought them together all those years ago was still there.

Was it possible she could ask Andy to forgive her?

Gemma's eyes had always been the most astonishing Andy had ever seen. It had been the colour that had struck him first, of course. Those gold flecks and the perfect, matching halos around the edge of the irises. But it hadn't taken very long to get caught by so much more.

They said that the eyes were the windows to the soul and, sure, Gemma had stained-glass beauties instead of plain glass but it was the light that shone through that made them so extraordinarily beautiful as far as he was concerned.

She'd asked him for some spare courage in that first exchange of words but he'd known she hadn't really needed it. The more he'd learned about her the more he'd realised how right he'd been.

Gemma had been courageous her entire life. She'd been a protector and mother figure for her baby sister. She'd fought for the chance to use her intelligence and perseverance to succeed in her dream career. She'd stepped up to the plate when she'd been faced with an unexpected pregnancy and she had loved Max as much as he had.

She still hurt, as much as he did. He could see it in her eyes now.

He couldn't look away. Because he could see more than the pain of the poignant memories they shared.

He could see the connection they'd always had.

The love?

Was it possible that Gemma…? The thought dissolved as the emotional response to what he could see tipped Andy into a place he hadn't been in for many, many years.

A place where passion ruled and everything else in the world ceased to exist.

The only muscles that moved in his body were the tiny ones that controlled his eyes but he felt them as his gaze finally left Gemma's and dropped to her mouth.

Maybe it was the trembling of her lips that tipped him over the edge of control. He was holding the woman he'd loved so much in his arms. He could feel the shape of her. The warmth of her body despite the sub-zero temperatures. His own heart was speeding up to match the thump of her pulse against his chest.

What man could have resisted that tremble? He needed to make it go away so that Gemma wouldn't be so unhappy. His hands were already in use, holding her against him, so the only part of his body that he had available was his mouth. Without thinking, Andy lowered his head and covered her lips with his own.

A light touch. Meant to be comforting. Broken almost as soon as it was made.

But then Andy raised his gaze to her eyes again.

And the world stopped.

They were both in that space now. Nothing else existed. It was just the two of them and the pull between them was a force that was overwhelming.

This time Gemma moved at the same time Andy did. Their mouths met with a pressure that was almost painful. Andy had to let go of Gemma's body and cradle her head to protect it, but he still felt the thump as her back came up against the wall. He felt her hands gripping his arms and then sliding up, touching the sides of his face before her fingers were buried in his hair.

It wasn't enough. It didn't matter how many times he changed the angle of the kiss or how hard he pressed or how often his tongue danced with Gemma's.

It just wasn't enough.

Maybe nothing could be.

They were both completely out of breath when they finally pulled apart. They stood there, shocked at what had just happened.

The evidence of the passion that they still shared.

As if driven by shared frustration, they both moved again but this time they both jerked back the instant before their lips touched.

There was confusion mixed with desire now.

Should they be giving in to this?

Could they go far enough to satisfy that desire?

And, if they did, would there be any point given that the way they'd parted had destroyed any possibility of a future relationship because a relationship had to be built on trust? It wasn't that he wouldn't *want* to trust her again. He just *couldn't*. That self-protection mechanism was too strong.

Andy could feel his physical response to Gemma closing down. Getting locked away. When their eye contact broke, they both moved apart. Turned away from each other.

What had just happened there?

Gemma barely heard Andy mutter something about needing to get back inside before they both froze to death.

Whatever it was that had just happened, it was over.

But there was no denying that it *had* happened. Dear Lord... She didn't even know whether Andy was single any more. Maybe he wasn't and that was why he'd pulled down the shutters and turned away.

Had it just been a response to being so close? Sharing memories that were theirs alone?

A blast from the past?

Andy wasn't even touching her now. There would be no hand-holding on the way back to the ward. He wasn't looking at her either as he held open the fire door for her to go back inside. He was staring up at the night sky.

'Santa's sleigh seems to be caught in a holding pattern,' he said. 'Let's hope he gets to land before morning.'

Gemma's quick smile was automatic but she said nothing.

Her brain was too busy thinking about something very different.

Another Christmas. The last one they had shared.

The final blow to their marriage that was now the barrier that could keep them apart for ever.

The year they'd lost Max had been the ultimate Christmas from hell. But that last one hadn't been so far behind, had it?

CHAPTER NINE

Christmas: four years ago

'So YOU'RE not working on Christmas Day this year, then?'

'No.' Gemma was glad the room she was in was too dark for her consultant to read the expression on her face. She knew it would be one of utter dread.

'Got family stuff on?'

'Mmm.' The oppressive weight of that dread intensified. She had known it would be like this. Why…oh, *why* had she let Laura bully her into it?

'Please, Gemma. I want this to be a real Christmas. A family one. You and Andy can't go through the rest of your lives avoiding every celebration that involves kids. It's not fair. On me or Ev or the children…' She'd been crying by now. *'Most of all it's not fair on you. You've got to start…I don't know…living again. Not just working. I know how hard it is but…please, Gem. Just try? Ev's already talked to Andy and he said he'll come. Please…'*

The radiology consultant cleared his throat. 'Anyway…let's get this tutorial out of the way, shall we? Tell me about case nine.'

The only source of light in this room was coming from the glass screens that had X-ray images clipped onto them.

'There's a focal shadow in the right lower lobe. Suggestive of pneumonia.'

'Differential diagnoses?'

'Carcinoma and lymphoma.'

'Good. Case ten?'

Gemma didn't have to look at the image for more than a few seconds. 'Classic evidence of left ventricular failure.'

'Such as?'

'Cardiomegaly, upper lobe and pulmonary vein diversion and…' Gemma had to grin. 'I can see sternotomy wires so it's highly likely this patient has had coronary bypass surgery.'

The older man chuckled. 'I don't think I've got anything in this lot that's going to trip you up. You pass, Gemma. Tutorials are over. You're perfectly competent in X-ray interpretation and you know when you need to call in a second opinion. Now…you going to come to the departmental Christmas party after work today?'

'No.'

There was a tiny silence in the dark. 'Nobody would ever call you a party animal, Gemma, but couldn't you make an exception just this once?'

Oh…great… There seemed to be a conspiracy going on, courtesy of the festive season. Did everybody see it as the perfect time to give her a bit of a push? Propel her back into the land of the living and the happy? Make everything all right again?

Fix things between Andy and herself even?

Gemma let her breath out in a long sigh. She hadn't even seen Andy that morning because he'd got up well before her. She'd known there was something he wanted to say to her because she'd sensed him standing there at the bedroom door, looking at her.

And she'd pretended to be still deeply asleep.

He'd simply let himself quietly out of the apartment without saying goodbye. Without even pausing long enough to have breakfast.

She would have to go and see him now. She'd been putting it off all day, letting her job fill her head. Telling herself she was too busy to think about anything else. Too busy to even answer when he'd texted her. Three times.

Staying inside her comfort zone. Not thinking about her reluctant agreement to visit Andy on the paediatric ward before she went home. A concession that had been dragged out of her at the end of their last, awful argument.

'It's where I work, Gem. Everybody's partners come to the Christmas party. I'm not even asking you to come to that, but, for God's sake, couldn't you just show your face on the ward? The staff up there think my wife is just a figment of my imagination. Sometimes it feels that way to me, too.'

'You know what they say...' The radiology consultant was on his feet, flicking off the X-ray screens. Any moment now he would turn on the main light and Gemma would have to be careful what showed on her face. 'All work and no play...'

'Yeah...yeah...' Gemma smiled to keep her tone light. 'The paper I want to get finished is interesting enough to count as play. I've got all the stats. I just need to write up the discussion bit.'

'The one about the false negatives in head injury with CT scans read by ED staff?'

'That's the one.'

'Sounds like work to me.'

Gemma shrugged. All work and no play was fine by her. It was pretty much what had kept her sane for the last two years.

Had her permit for staying in that safe place run out? Was that why she was aware of the increasing pressure to start behaving differently?

Was there more to Laura's passionate plea for a family Christmas than met the eye? When had Evan talked to Andy about it? Maybe he'd had a heart-to-heart with Laura as well. Maybe they'd all decided that if she could be surrounded by children and happy times she might decide that she was ready to try again.

The sensation of dread was suffocating now. Was that what Andy wanted to talk to her about?

Having another baby?

No. She wasn't going there. She couldn't. She couldn't even bring herself to talk about it.

'Well...have a great Christmas anyway.' The consultant was heading home. 'See you in the new year.'

'You, too.' Gemma could feel how tight her smile was. Every cell in her body seemed to be holding itself rigid.

Of course there was a conspiracy. Laura was pregnant again, wasn't she? And it wasn't enough to highlight the lack in Gemma and Andy's lives by simply having another baby. This time she was pregnant with *twins*.

The pressure was building. Something was going to snap and Gemma knew it was going to hurt someone. Herself? Of course. But what about the other people in her life?

Laura and Evan.

Cute three-year-old Hazel and her baby brother, Jamie.

Andy...

And hadn't she already hurt Andy enough?

Oh, yes...more than enough.

It was probably the understatement of the century that she hadn't been easy to live with for the past two years. She'd been perfectly well aware of how much it had hurt Andy to be shut out but she hadn't been capable of engaging with anyone on more than a professional level. The rest of her had become numb within days of losing Max. In the beginning she'd been grateful for that numbness. Clung to it, in fact, when anything threatened to penetrate. And then, when she'd been ready to try and feel again, she hadn't known how and that had been frightening. It had been so much easier to retreat back into the safe, numb space.

But the safety barriers of that comfort zone seemed to be crumbling and, yes, it was because it was Christmas. She'd been given a free pass to avoid all the emotional connotations last year but nothing came without a price tag eventually, did it?

She was going to have to pay this time.

And Gemma knew she was going to be dipping into an account that was still overdrawn.

'Hey, Dr Andy. D'ya know what day it is tomorrow?'

'Sure do, John Boy.' Andy dropped to a couch to put him at eye level with the seven-year-old boy he'd come to know very well during his time as a paediatric registrar. 'It's Christmas.'

John Boy's smile was enough to make you think that life was wonderful. This admission had been to try and correct a badly deformed bone in his lower leg to preserve his ability to walk a little longer. He had a complicated external fixation device from knee to ankle but he was up on crutches already and into mischief all over the ward. He got away with all sorts of things, from small misdemeanours like raiding the fridge in the staffroom to major naughtiness like going AWOL from the ward and ending up somewhere like the hospital laundry. It wasn't just because he'd spent his short life either in hospital or foster-care. It was because of that smile.

The one that said that, yes, life was full of hard stuff

but you could find good stuff, too, and if you didn't make the most of it, you were pretty stupid.

It was being around kids like John Boy that had given Andy a way forward in life.

If only Gemma could meet him. Or any of the other children that came through these doors on a regular basis. Or their families, who managed to stick together during the hard times and gain strength from each other.

'I'm gonna get presents.' John Boy's smile was still lighting up his small, dark face. 'I always do when I'm in here for Christmas. Santa comes.'

'I heard that.' More than heard it. He was lined up to don the costume and do it himself this year. He'd have to disguise his voice when he was handing out the gifts to the children. John Boy was probably too smart to get fooled for a moment but he'd probably go along with the pretence simply because it was fun. Andy hoped the gifts with this boy's name on them were special ones this year because he gave so much to others without even realising it.

'I'm gonna tell that new kid that came in today. He was crying.'

'Paul? He's not feeling so good today, John Boy. Why don't you just say hi and give him a smile?'

'Okey-dokey.' John Boy concentrated hard and moved his crutches. The short conversation had been enough to make him breathless so he waited for a moment before pushing his body into motion. 'See ya, Dr Andy.'

'See ya, John Boy.'

Andy watched the lad's slow movement down the corridor. He saw a nurse spot John Boy and smile as if her day had just brightened out of sight. He wished Gemma was here. If only she could receive that gift of knowing how good life could still be in the face of the difficult stuff. But how could she receive anything emotional like that when she'd shut herself off so completely?

Andy was at his wits' end. He'd tried everything he could think of. At first it had been easy to know what to do because they had both been so shattered by their grief. All they had been able to do had been to hold onto each other and cry.

He'd reached a point, after a few months of that desperately sad place, where he'd had to move forward to save himself. Gemma had agreed that it was the right thing to do but had simply refused to come with him. Worse than that. She had moved in the opposite direction. Andy had faced the tough stuff head on. It was hard to be around children and he couldn't let it grow into something that would destroy too much of him so he'd chosen paediatrics for his specialty.

Gemma had chosen not only to avoid children but to avoid people as much as she could. She'd chosen radiology as a specialty and spent most of her working life shut into a dark room, analysing the images that the technicians obtained from patients.

She'd hurled herself into postgraduate study as well so that when they were home together she was invariably on the computer or buried in a textbook. The care they had taken of each other in the early days after that dreadful Christmas had morphed into a relationship that felt like housemates. Polite housemates who had sex occasionally, sure, but something huge was missing. And it was something that had been there before they'd had Max so his absence from their lives wasn't enough to explain that massive hole.

Trying to push at all only led to fights but Andy was getting desperate. So was Laura.

'We've got to do something, Andy. I think she's lost and if we don't reach out and grab her, she'll disappear for ever. It's Christmas. The perfect time. Maybe the last chance we'll get.'

An hour or two with her sister's family for Christmas dinner wasn't going to be enough for Andy, however. He was desperate to get their professional lives to connect again, too. So he'd pushed and forced her to agree to come to the paediatric departmental party today.

And then he'd had second thoughts that morning when he'd stood there, watching her sleep. Feeling the gulf between them but knowing how much he still loved her. Wondering if she really *was* asleep or just avoiding him…again. He'd tried texting her a few times today, too. He just wanted to talk. If it was too much for her, she didn't have to go to the stupid party. They could go somewhere by themselves. Maybe, if he could show her that he was trying to understand, at least it could open the door to some real communication.

'You still here, Andy? Thought you'd be at the party by now.'

'I'll head off soon.' He'd give Gemma another ten minutes and if she hadn't arrived by then he'd go past Radiology and see if she was still at work. She'd said she'd text him but maybe things were really busy. Perhaps that was why she hadn't answered any of his messages. Why she hadn't turned up to visit his ward.

He used the ten minutes to wander around, seeing what everybody was up to. A Christmas movie was playing in the dayroom for the children who were well enough to be out of bed. A nurse who had angel wings pinned to the back of her uniform and a tinsel halo on her head was handing out ice-block treats. John Boy was using his like a sword to play with another small boy in a wheelchair. The Christmas tree had its lights flashing and there were spraypainted snowflakes on the windows.

A nurse was holding the door of a storage area open for a man Andy recognised as a patient's father. He grinned and took an armload of carrier bags into the private space. The nurse picked up one of the rolls of Christmas wrapping paper he'd dropped and handed it in before closing the door. She grinned at Andy, putting her finger to her lips.

Christmas carols were playing at the nurses' station and being sung along to with varying degrees of tunefulness. A tired-looking mother paused to listen and miraculously the crying baby in her arms became quiet. Her companion, probably her husband, was holding a toddler on his hip. The two parents exchanged a smile of pure relief as the baby settled.

Andy smiled, too.

And then he turned and his smile faded. Gemma was standing there, staring at the couple. At the baby the woman was holding?

No. It was the toddler that had caught her attention. Less than two years old, the little boy was wearing a Santa hat. Like Max had been in that last photograph of him that had ever been taken.

Oh…help.

'Gemma.' Andy pasted his smile back in place. 'I was just coming to find you.'

He could see how carefully she was holding herself. When he put his arm around her shoulders, he could feel a tension that made his heart plummet. She felt brittle enough to snap at any moment. She'd kept her promise but right now Andy wished she hadn't. It had been a bad idea to push her into this.

'You know what?' He began leading her out of the ward. 'I don't think I want to hang around here any longer today. Let me grab my jacket and we could head out for a drink. Dinner, maybe.'

'I…I'd rather just go home. I want to finish that paper I'm writing up for *Radiology Today*.' Gemma was walking just slightly ahead of Andy, taking her shoulders out of range for his arm. She was talking quickly. Sounding too bright. 'You know, the one about the false negatives for CT interpretation by ED staff?'

She was running again, Andy thought sadly. Avoiding anything that could be deemed too personal. Anything that required an emotional response.

He couldn't live like this any longer. He knew the Gemma he loved was still there somewhere but he was too bone tired of trying to coax her back.

'It's almost Christmas,' he said. 'It's time to stop thinking about work for a few days.' Taking a longer step, he got close enough to put his hand on Gemma's shoulder. 'It's the time people like to be with the people they care about. That's all I'm asking for...a bit of time with you. Is that too much to ask?'

'Of course not. Sorry.' Gemma's pace slowed. 'It's just...' She stopped and turned, looking up at him. 'It's Christmas, Andy. I can't...' She caught her bottom lip between her teeth. 'It's too...soon.'

The pain in her eyes cut into Andy. A rare glimpse of the real Gemma. But how long could he keep comforting her? Telling her that things would come right in time and that she would find a way through this? She thought she'd found the answer in burying herself in her career but she was so wrong. Not that he could suggest anything else. He'd tried to get her to go to professional counselling. He'd even once suggested that she might need antidepressant medication and that had led to a row that had lasted for weeks. She could cope, she'd yelled at him, but only if she was allowed to cope in her own way.

Just leave me alone. Why can't you leave me the hell alone?'

Laura could be right. Gemma was lost and something had to be done.

'It's been two years, Gem,' he said quietly. 'We *have* to move on.'

Her eyes widened with shock. '*We* have to move on? You did that a long time ago, Andy. This isn't *your* problem.'

'What do you mean?' They weren't far away from the office Andy shared with the other departmental registrars. He walked to the door and opened it, then turned and stared at Gemma.

This was it. They couldn't shove it all under the carpet any more. They had to confront this issue before it destroyed them, no matter how painful that might be.

Andy looked so *angry*.

Or was that desperate?

Gemma couldn't find any of that comforting numbness to pull around her as she forced her feet to move and take her into the office. She knew she couldn't brush this off by dismissing the conversation because she had something really important that had to be done. Like writing some totally irrelevant professional article.

This was what was important.

Their relationship.

Their future.

She was being dragged out of whatever safe place she had managed to create for herself, whether she was ready or not.

Because Andy couldn't wait any longer.

And fair enough.

Two years? It really had been that long, hadn't it?

Nothing like having an anniversary that coincided with something like Christmas to make sure you could never forget.

Gemma stopped as soon as Andy closed the office door behind her. The other registrars were not here. They were probably at the staff Christmas party. Someone had strung tinsel around the room and there was a miniature fir tree on one of the desks, decorated with boiled sweets tied to the branches. A gift from a patient? Christmas cards, some home-made, with children's drawings were pinned to the notice-board.

The room was small but Andy put as much distance between them as he could before turning to face her.

That hurt.

Were things really so bad that he didn't even want to be within touching distance right now?

'I don't know what to do, Gemma.' Andy's voice was low. And raw. 'I've been careful not to try and push you. I've given you all the support and space I know how to give. So has Laura. And Evan. We've *all* done everything we could to help you get through losing Max. You've got the career you always wanted but...' He pushed both his hands through his hair, making it stand up in spikes before holding his hands up in a gesture of surrender.

'But it's *all* you seem to want now. Your career. You don't have time for me. Or for your family. You won't have anything to do with children if you can help it. You won't even have anything to do with Christmas. And

Christmas comes around every year, Gemma.' Andy's voice was getting louder.

'Whether you're ready for it or not, it comes and you have to *deal* with it. You can't hide for ever.'

'I'm not hiding. I said I'd go to Laura's this year. I've…I've got presents for the kids. I'm *trying*, Andy.'

'You've refused to go to any Christmas parties here. You flat out refused to have a single decoration at home, let alone a Christmas tree.'

'You can't turn around without bumping into a Christmas tree around here.' Gemma waved her hand at the small version on the desk to emphasise her point. 'We don't *need* one at home.'

'I think we do.' Andy's voice was so controlled now. So vehement. Gemma had never heard him sound like this and it frightened her. 'I think it would be a symbol. That we've got past a tragedy. That we've still got some kind of future.'

Oh…God… Was this an ultimatum?

Andy was rubbing his forehead now. Clearly, he was finding this difficult but he couldn't stop. Something had been unleashed that couldn't be caught and locked away again. When he looked back at Gemma, his face was anguished.

'I just don't understand,' he said. 'Why can't you get past it? You never even wanted a baby in the first place.'

Something cold trickled down Gemma's spine. She couldn't deny that, could she? She couldn't say that things had changed the moment she'd held Max in her arms for the first time or that being a family had meant as much to her as it did to Andy.

She hadn't wanted to be pregnant. She'd wanted her career. To outward appearances, she had spent the last two years simply proving that. Looking as though she was relieved not to have the constraints of being a mother holding her back. Spending every waking hour working.

She'd thought Andy had understood that it was the only way she'd been able to get through each day. He'd done the same thing, hadn't he? Thrown himself into his work? He'd tried to be interested in the specialty she'd chosen but she hadn't been able to return that interest. Why hadn't she seen just how far it was pushing them apart?

Maybe she had but she'd put off trying to do anything about it because it was too hard. Too painful.

This was too painful. He was reminding her of something she'd felt ashamed of even thinking after Max's birth.

It reminded her of something else that had haunted her ever since.

'And you only married me because I was pregnant.'

A stunned silence fell. Andy looked as though she'd given him a physical blow. As though he had to stay very still for a moment to work out exactly where he'd been injured. When he spoke again, his voice was soft. Almost defeated.

'So why am I still here, Gem? For God's sake... I *love* you. All I want is for you to be happy because it's

becoming very obvious that nobody around you is going
to be happy unless you are.'

'It's…harder for me.'

'What is?'

The numb place had vanished completely. Gemma
felt like she had in those awful days before she'd discovered it. Her heart was breaking all over again.

'I…' I miss my baby, she wanted to cry. I miss holding him and hearing him laugh. I see his smile every
time *you* smile. I feel so empty. Like there's nothing
left…just a big, black hole…

The words wouldn't come out. Gemma was too
scared to break the dam because she knew the flood
would drown her.

'You think it's been *easy* for me?' Andy sounded incredulous. 'To get over losing our child?'

Gemma stared back at him helplessly. Of course he'd
coped better than she had. 'You *work* with children,'
she whispered.

'And you think it's been *easy*? That it doesn't remind
me of Max and break my heart every time something
goes wrong?' Gemma could see his Adam's apple bob
as he swallowed hard.

'I love kids. I always have. The *easy* thing to do
would have been to avoid them. Like you did. But I
knew that would have ended up being only half a life
so I took the hard road and jumped in the deep end. I
didn't know whether I'd sink or swim but I did know
that I understand how parents feel and that I'd do whatever it took to win the battle to save a child's life.'

Maybe that explained why Andy had gone off to work day after day, looking so grim. He'd had to find the strength to face his demons and he'd never told her because…because he'd been trying to protect her? Knowing she was facing her own demons in her own way? Oh…dear Lord…

'It's who I am now,' Andy continued. 'Who I'll be for the rest of my life.' His breath came out in a huff. 'Maybe it was meant to happen so that I would be this person. So I could spend my working life doing the best I can to keep families together. It doesn't mean I don't still want to have my *own* family. Can't you understand that?'

Gemma nodded, very slowly. Of course she could understand it. She'd always known that Andy wanted to have a family of his own. She'd watched the way he'd been drawn further into her sister's family over the last months. How much he loved being with Hazel and little Jamie. He didn't know about the twins yet but she could imagine the look on his face when he was given the news.

The longing she would see there.

She couldn't do it. She couldn't face being pregnant again and giving birth and holding an infant with the knowledge that it could all be ripped away. There wasn't enough of her heart left as it was. If any more got ripped out, it wouldn't be able to sustain life even.

Andy was walking towards her. He took her hands in his.

'I love you, Gem,' he said quietly.

'I…I love you, too,' she whispered.

'Then help me. Help *us*. We can't live like this for ever. It's been two years of hell. Isn't that long enough?'

Gemma could only nod. She had done this. Put Andy through months and months of hell because she hadn't been brave enough to even try putting her feet in the water, let alone jumping in at any deep end. This *was* all her fault. But she couldn't fix it, could she? Not if it meant having another baby.

Andy pulled her close and held her tightly. So tightly she couldn't breathe but that was OK. She didn't want to breathe because if she did, she'd have to think. And all she could think about was how she was destroying the person she loved most in the world.

'I need a drink,' she heard him say above her head. 'Come with me?'

Gemma shook her head this time. Somehow she found her voice and the words that might give her a brief reprieve.

'I think I need a bit of time on my own. To…think. Why don't you go to your Christmas party for a while and have a drink there?'

The pressure around her body eased a little too quickly. Andy knew he was being pushed away. He stepped back and Gemma knew he was watching her but she kept her head down. She couldn't face meeting his eyes just yet. Not with this new knowledge of how much she had failed their marriage. Would continue to fail it. After a long, silent moment Andy turned away and left, leaving only the echo of a sad sigh.

* * *

The apartment felt cold and empty.

Gemma couldn't stay there. Why on earth hadn't they moved somewhere else after Max had died? Made a fresh start?

Because she hadn't suggested it? They'd all been tiptoeing around her. Trying to protect her. Letting her build her defensive walls and use her career like a statement of denial about how deeply she'd been hurt.

She couldn't deny anything now.

And she couldn't stay here.

Gemma had no idea what she should do. She knew Andy loved her. If she told him she could never face the prospect of having another baby, he would take that on board and live with it.

And it would always be there as an undercurrent in their marriage. A resentment that would simmer away in dark corners ready to explode if tension built from any cause.

It was blindingly simple really.

Andy wanted a family. She didn't. *Couldn't.*

And, because she loved Andy with all the heart she had left, she had to set him free to get what he wanted from his life.

It might destroy her but she was broken anyway, wasn't she? At least Andy had the guts to face life and put the pieces back together again. To *live*. All she was doing was surviving.

But the decision was too big. Too terrifying. Maybe what she needed to do was give them both some space so that, when they saw each other again, they could talk about it.

Yes. That was the first step. Gemma pulled a suitcase from the storeroom that had once been a nursery. Mechanically, she began opening drawers and pulling out items that she might need for a few days. Underwear and tights. Nightwear and jeans. She moved to the wardrobe and pulled things off random hangers without even thinking, rolling the items of clothing and stuffing them into the suitcase.

Where would she go?

The obvious answer was to Laura and Evan's house but how would that help? Laura was just as worried about her as Andy was. She would want to see their marriage survive and she would try and convince Gemma that another baby was exactly what was needed. Of course she would. She was probably glowing with her own new pregnancy already.

And it was *Christmas*.

And Jamie was almost the same age as Max had been when…when…

Gemma almost couldn't see what she was stuffing into a toilet bag in the bathroom.

She was falling again.

Falling apart.

She couldn't go to Laura's. She'd leave the gifts for Andy to take. She would text Laura to say she was sorry but she needed some time on her own and then she'd turn her phone off so she couldn't receive a response.

She couldn't stay here.

She could go to a hotel but that wouldn't be far enough. If she was within reach of Andy she could never do what she had to do.

Set him free. Give him a 'get out of hell' card.

He could find someone else. Someone who would be able to be the mother to the children he wanted.

Could she stand seeing that happen? No. Even being in another city in England would be too close. She had to get further away. Maybe as far as the other side of the world?

Where was her passport?

It took some hunting down. It was in a desk drawer, along with all sorts of other bits and pieces. Lanyards with name tags from various conferences she and Andy had attended over the last couple of years. Some keys, the usefulness of which had been long forgotten. An old phone charger. Paper clips and even bits of rubbish.

No.

Gemma stared at the item in her hand. It wasn't rubbish exactly but why had this been shoved in a drawer and not thrown out when it had last been seen two years ago?

It was that piece of plastic mistletoe.

It was also the final straw because Gemma couldn't even remember when Andy had last kissed her.

She dropped the piece of mistletoe and picked up her passport. And her suitcase.

And left.

CHAPTER TEN

It was almost dawn.

Christmas Day.

Gemma hadn't seen Andy since she'd followed him down from the roof of the Queen Mary Infirmary.

'I have to duck home for a bit. I need to collect the Santa suit I'll be wearing in the morning.'

'You're the ward Santa this year?'

'It'll be my fifth time. It's become a tradition.'

The image stayed with Gemma as she returned to the children's room and settled herself in the armchair in the hope of catching at least a little sleep. She could picture Andy in the dayroom. Beside that Christmas tree. Handing out gifts to the small patients he spent his life caring for.

Five times? That meant the first time he'd played the role would have been the year that she'd walked out. He'd never mentioned that he was going to do it.

Why? Because he'd known that she wouldn't understand how he was even able to think of doing it?

How hard would it have been for him that first time? Even on its own, it would have been heart-breaking for a father who'd lost his own son but that year he would have still been reeling from going home to find an empty house the night before.

She'd tried to write Andy a note before she'd left but words had failed her. In the end, the scrap of tearstained paper had held only four words.

'I'm sorry. For everything.'

She'd left it on top of the desk. With her vision blurred by tears she had picked up the nearest available object to attract attention to the piece of paper in the centre of a bare desktop. And the way she'd been feeling, it had seemed appropriate to use that piece of plastic mistletoe.

Gemma heard a snuffle from one of the children and echoed it softly herself. Sleep was not going to release her any time soon, she realised. Her mind was too full. Of memories. Of Andy. Of that kiss on the rooftop with the lights of Santa's sleigh scribing slow circuits in the sky above them.

Her love for Andy hadn't diminished one little bit. Had she done the right thing by setting him free? If he hadn't moved on and found someone else to be the mother of his children, surely the answer was no. And, if the answer *was* no, did that mean there was still a chance for her to be with him?

The way he'd kissed her. Where would that kiss have gone if they hadn't been on a hospital roof in freezing weather?

A smile was competing with the threat of tears now. Gemma knew exactly where that kiss would have gone.

Other emotions were colliding inside her. Echoes of grief that had to come from those shared memories of Max. Guilt at the way she had been so self-obsessed with that grief. Had she really thought that her way of coping had been the right way? That Andy had found it all so much easier?

Sitting here in the dark, surrounded by sleeping children, Gemma was at last in a space where she could see a much bigger picture. It wasn't simply that there were more important things in life than a brilliant career. It was a combination of wisdom gained from isolation. From the devastating loss of a sister she had only stayed in touch with via phone and email for years. From having to step up to become a mother for her nieces and nephews.

Running away and burying herself in her career had been a successful device in hiding from the pain of losing Max but it was only now that she could see the full extent of the collateral damage.

She'd lost the place she thought of as her home.

She'd lost her family. Watching the precious early years of these children growing up.

She'd lost Andy.

Love. That's what she'd taken out of her life. People and places that she loved and people that she could be loved by.

Emotional safety was a very lonely place.

So lonely that a tiny whimper from Sophie had Gemma on her feet almost eagerly. She laid a gentle hand on the baby's forehead. Her temperature had obviously dropped and her skin felt soft and dry and healthy. Sophie stirred, bringing a small fist up to her mouth. The vigorous sucking noises made Gemma smile.

'You're getting ready to be hungry, darling, aren't you?' she whispered. Reaching into the bassinette, she picked up the bundle of baby and blanket, tucking it into her arms. 'Come on. We'll tiptoe down to the kitchen and see what we can find.'

The ward was beginning to stir. People arriving early for the day shift were quietly preparing to take over from the weary night staff. Fixing a bottle of formula for Sophie, Gemma was greeted by one of the day staff. A nurse called Carla.

'You'll stay for the Christmas breakfast, won't you?' she asked. 'The night nurses have labelled some spare gifts for the children.'

Could she stay and watch Andy do his thing as Santa? Heaven help her, but she wanted to so much. If she gave in to that desire, though, would it make it that much harder to walk away? It was what she would have to so. Or was it?

That kiss on the roof had done more than awaken too many memories of what being so close to Andy was like. It had planted a seed of hope.

Carla misinterpreted the hesitation she could see on Gemma's face.

'I could get one of the registrars to sign Sophie's discharge form but I'd rather Andy signed you off and... he's going to be a bit busy for a while. He got held up checking our little bone-marrow-transplant girl so he won't have much time to get changed when he gets back. Santa's supposed to make his big entrance at the end of breakfast-time.'

Gemma opened the microwave to rescue the bottle of warm milk. Sophie reached out for it and whimpered.

'I'll see how we go,' she told Carla. She smiled. 'It's never a quick job getting my lot organised.'

'I'm sure they'd want to stay.' Carla's gaze was frankly curious. 'I hear that Andy's their uncle?'

Gemma's nod was wary. The children didn't know that Andy was still their uncle. On paper, anyway. But of course they'd want to stay.

As much as she did?

Back in the room, Gemma settled into the armchair to feed Sophie, grateful that she still had some time before the other children were likely to wake up. She had to decide what the best thing to do for the children was and she couldn't let that decision be influenced by all the memories and feelings that had been stirred into life for her again. What if the children found out about Andy's relationship to them but he wanted nothing more to do with them? They had suffered the loss of too many adults in their lives already.

The last of the bottle had been hungrily guzzled and Gemma was holding Sophie up against her shoulder to burp her when Hazel woke up. There was enough light in the room for her to see the way her niece's eyes snapped open fully as she registered her unfamiliar surroundings. She heard the sharp, fearful intake of breath.

'It's OK, hon,' she said softly. 'You're safe. Everything's fine.'

Hazel's gasp turned into a sigh of relief as she scrambled into a sitting position.

'I need to wee,' she informed Gemma.

'Can you wait for a sec?' Gemma made faster circles on Sophie's back and patted it a few times. 'Soph will get grumpy if she doesn't have a burp.' She sniffed. 'And I think she's overdue for a nappy change, too, but I can do that after I show you where the bathroom is.'

'I can go to the loo by myself,' Hazel said with some indignation. 'I'm *seven*.'

'I know. I just thought...being in a strange place...'

'I can manage.' But Hazel hesitated when she got to the door. 'Which way do I go?'

'Left.' Gemma tilted her head for emphasis because both her hands were full of baby. 'If you can't see a door that has a sign saying "Bathroom", just go a bit further and you'll find a nurse you can ask. They're all very nice.'

Hazel nodded, went outside the door and looked up and down the corridor. She couldn't see anybody in either direction.

Which way was left again?

Andy eyed the big, plastic rubbish sack on the chair. He needed to go and find a spare pillow or two to stuff under the red jacket of the Santa suit the sack contained. And was that special glue still in the smaller bag containing the fake beard? It had taken some time to find that glue again. Why on earth had he put it in his desk drawer?

Andy opened the sack, lifting out the red hat with white trim on the top to have a look but then he paused, hat in hand, turning his head very slowly. An odd prickle on the back of his neck suggested he wasn't alone.

Glancing over his shoulder, he found his instincts hadn't deceived him. A small girl was standing, framed by the office doorway. She was wearing hospital-issue pyjamas but she wasn't a patient.

'Hazel.' A beat of alarm pulsed through Andy. Had Gemma sent her oldest niece to find him? Why couldn't she come herself? 'What's up, chicken?'

Hazel's bottom lip quivered. 'I went to find the loo,' she said, 'and...I got lost.'

'Oh, no...' Andy's smile was sympathetic. He dropped the hat he was still holding onto the top of the bag and held his hand out towards Hazel. He could fix this. He could show her where the toilet was.

But, with a sob, Hazel launched herself at him and Andy found himself scooping the small girl into his arms to give her a cuddle.

'Hey...it's not that bad. You didn't really get lost cos you found me.'

'That's not why I'm crying,' Hazel sobbed.

'What is it, then?' Andy wasn't used to holding distressed children. He might be in the same room but there were always parents or nurses to do the cuddling. He'd almost forgotten what it was like to have small arms entwined around his neck as though he was some kind of giant lifesaver.

'It's…' Hazel unfurled one arm to point at the Santa hat that had slid from the top of the sack to land on the floor. 'It's *Christmas*.'

Andy nodded. 'So it is. But…it's supposed to be a happy day, you know.'

'Not…not when you don't have a mummy or daddy any more.'

'No.' Andy closed his eyes for a moment and held Hazel closer. This was the first Christmas for these children since they had become orphans. As the oldest, Hazel would have the clearest memories of their parents and she would be missing them most. 'I'm sorry about that, chicken. It's really sad, isn't it?'

'Mmm.' Hazel snuffled and then sniffed loudly.

'Would you like a tissue?'

'No…' She ducked her head and wiped her nose on her pyjama sleeve. 'S'okay.'

'But you'd like to go to the toilet?'

'Yes.'

'Come on, then.' Andy put her down. Hazel's fingers caught on his name badge as he lowered her to the floor. Then she took his hand and let him lead her out into the corridor and down towards the bathroom.

'My last name is Gillespie,' she told him.

'I know.'

'Your name's on your badge.'

'It is.'

'Why have you got the same name as Aunty Gemma?'

'Because...' Oh, help. Andy's respect for children meant that he always tried to be as honest as he could within the limits of their understanding. How much did Hazel know? Or remember? 'Gemma's got the same name as me because we got married.'

'When?'

'A long time ago. Before you were born even. Here's the bathroom. I'll wait out here for you and make sure you don't get lost going back to your room.'

Hazel was back in a commendably short time. She slipped her hand into Andy's without hesitation and the trusting gesture was heart-melting.

'Gemma's Mummy's sister,' she told Andy.

'I know.'

'Are you mummy's brother, then?'

'Kind of. I married your mummy's sister so that made me something called a brother-in-law to your mummy.'

Hazel looked confused.

'I'm...I was your uncle,' he added.

Hazel looked even more confused. 'Why did you stop being my uncle?'

'I...didn't.' Whatever had melted inside him moments before had congealed into something hard now. He'd missed these children far more than he'd realised. They had been part of his family. The closest thing he'd had to children of his own after losing Max.

'So I can still call you "Uncle"?'

'Sure.'

Hazel tried it out. 'Uncle…Andy…'

Could she remember using the name? He could remember. He could actually hear an echo of a three-year-old's gleeful shriek as he came through the front door of that wonderful old, converted barn.

'If you're still our uncle, how come you never come to visit us, then?'

A fair question but he couldn't tell a seven-year-old it was because it had been simply too painful. That the children were part of Gemma and if she didn't want him in her life any more, he'd felt that maybe he had no right to keep any part of her family.

'I don't know, chicken. I'm sorry. I should have.'

If he'd kept up contact with Gemma's family, he would have known about the tragedy. He could have been there for Gemma. He might have been able to re-establish contact with her and not have had to live with the awful silence of the last four years. But that was exactly why he'd let the contact lapse in the first place.

It had been Gemma's choice to leave and she'd ignored his attempts to track her down by phone. She hadn't wanted to live with him any more. Not even in the same country. She hadn't wanted to talk to him. She'd wanted space and he'd given it to her. And the weeks had turned into months and he had kept putting off making contact that would probably deal another blow of rejection. And then the months had turned into years. How on earth had he let that happen?

'So why did you stop being married to Aunty

Gemma?' Hazel asked as they neared the door to her room.

Tricky question. How could Andy answer that without getting into a complicated discussion about divorce laws?

'We haven't stopped being married, exactly,' he said awkwardly. 'We just haven't been living together.'

'Why not? Aunty Gemma's nice.' Hazel stopped outside the door to their room and gave Andy a very steady glance. 'Aunty Gemma's our mummy now.'

'I know. You're very lucky. She *is* nice.'

Hazel opened the door. Jamie was getting dressed. The twins were standing up in the cot, blinking sleepily. Chloe had her thumb in her mouth. Ben was holding Digger under his arm.

Gemma was changing Sophie's nappy. 'You've been gone a long time, hon,' she said, without looking up. 'I was getting worried.' Sticking the last piece of tape into place, she looked up to see Andy standing beside Hazel and she stilled.

'Oh…hi…'

'Hey…' Andy responded.

They both seemed to be at a complete loss for words. Standing there staring at each other like embarrassed teenagers on a first date. Was Gemma's head suddenly filled with that kiss? Like his was?

Hazel looked at Gemma and then at Andy. Then at Gemma again.

'Uncle Andy says you're still married.'

'O…' Gemma bit her lip. 'That's…true, I guess.'

'And you're our mummy now.'

'Also true.'

Hazel nodded as though she had finally sorted out something important in her mind. She turned back and looked up at Andy.

'That means you're our daddy now, doesn't it?'

Oh...no...

Gemma saw the way the colour drained out of Andy's face. He looked around at all the children in the room and then opened his mouth to say something but didn't get the chance because a nurse appeared beside him.

'I just came to see if you guys needed a hand with anything in here,' the nurse said cheerfully.

Andy muttered something completely unintelligible, stepped back, turned and strode away.

Gemma could feel every step of his increasing the distance between them and something finally snapped. She couldn't let him walk out like this. Not after the bombshell that Hazel had just dropped.

'Yes,' she told the nurse. She handed Sophie over. 'Please watch the children for a few minutes. I have to...'

She didn't know quite *what* she had to do.

She just knew she had to do *something* and it could possibly be the most important thing she was ever going to do in her life.

Right at this moment, it felt like her life depended on it.

Her sentence didn't need to be finished in any case because she was already outside the room. She could see Andy at some distance down the corridor. Already past where his office was. Where was he going?

Gemma started running.

'Andy….*wait for me…*'

CHAPTER ELEVEN

ANDY was heading for the stairs.

An escape route. To the roof, maybe, for some more fresh air?

He heard the sound of Gemma's voice behind him.

'Andy....*please* wait.'

No. Not the roof. Not when the last time he'd been there was still so fresh in his memory. He could feel that kiss, all over again, in every cell of his body.

He could feel the desire.

And the confusion.

The wanting to open himself up to Gemma again.

The fear that came with knowing how much pain that could cause. Was he strong enough to go through that again? Did he want to even go there?

He didn't really have a choice. Not when he could sense the speed and urgency with which Gemma was approaching him. When he could hear the desperate plea in her voice.

Andy stopped and turned to face Gemma.

She almost skidded to a halt just a few feet away from him. She must have run all the way from the children's room because she needed to catch her breath for a moment. At least it gave Andy the chance to say something first, instead of waiting for the axe to fall.

'I'm sorry,' he said. 'I shouldn't have said anything to Hazel. But she noticed that our names were still the same. We *are* still married…legally, anyway…and…I like to be honest with kids if I can be.'

Gemma nodded. She opened her mouth and then closed it again. She took in a great gulp of air.

'Why?' The word came out in a kind of croak.

Andy raised his eyebrows. 'Don't you think it's a good thing to be honest?'

Gemma shook her head with a sharp movement. 'No…*why* are we still married?'

Here it came, Andy thought. The axe. There was no reason for them to still be married so Gemma was about to ask him to set divorce proceedings in place.

Her eyes were searching his face. 'I've been waiting to hear from you. I thought you would have found someone else long before this. Someone who could give you the baby you wanted. Someone who…who could make you happy.'

Her voice broke.

Andy stared at her. Behind them, kitchen staff were pushing the breakfast trolleys into the ward and the smell of bacon and eggs and other breakfast treats filled the air. The trolleys had strings of bells attached to them and the kitchen staff were singing 'Jingle Bells' with great enthusiasm for so early in the morning.

Andy barely heard them and was only vaguely aware

of the smell of hot food. His focus was on Gemma. On what she was saying, of course, but more the look on her face.

'Was that really what you thought would happen when you left?'

Gemma nodded. She had a tear rolling down the side of her nose. 'You wanted to start again. You wanted a Christmas tree and...and you wanted a baby. I couldn't give you anything you wanted but...I wanted you to be happy because...because I love you so much.'

Love?

Not *loved*?

Andy shook his head. He let his breath out in a huff that was almost laughter. 'How the hell did you expect me to be *happy* when I didn't have you?'

'Because...you weren't happy with me.'

The statement was so simple.

But so huge.

'I'm sorry.' The words came from somewhere very deep inside Andy. A space he had tried to stay away from for a very long time. 'I've wanted to say it a million times but I thought it was far too late.'

'What are *you* sorry for? It's me that messed things up in the end.'

'I'm sorry I couldn't help you. I knew you were hurting but there seemed to be nothing I could do that would help. In the end, I guess I gave up trying.'

'You were hurting just as much. *I'm* sorry.' Gemma sniffed and rubbed at her nose. 'I know I made it harder for you...'

'I think we made it harder for each other, even if it was the last thing we wanted to do.'

'But you tried to help me. I just made your life hell. You *said* that.'

He had. He couldn't deny it. The echo was right there.

'It's been two years of hell...'

'I'm sorry. I—'

'I couldn't understand,' Gemma cut in, 'the way you were dealing with it all. I couldn't see what you got out of being near other children. Maybe I never would have if I hadn't been thrown into being a mother figure.'

Andy felt his lips twist at the irony of the cards fate had chosen to deal. 'It was the last thing you ever wanted to be, wasn't it? A stay-at-home mum to a big bunch of kids?'

Gemma's voice was soft. 'Losing someone as precious as a person is a very fast way of learning what's really important in life. I should have learned that way back when we lost Max. Maybe I would have if I hadn't been so completely numb for so long.'

'I'm so sorry you had to learn it the way you did. Laura was very special.'

Gemma's nod was jerky. 'She was. But she's not the only person I love that I lost.'

'No. Evan was great, too.'

'I wasn't talking about Ev either.'

The way Gemma was looking at him was…heartbreaking. He'd never seen her looking so forlorn. So vulnerable.

And then it hit him.

She was talking about *him*.

Andy could feel that glow again. The one he'd felt when he'd gone into the reception area in the emergency department and seen her again for the first time in so long. Shafts of it were coming from beneath the lid he'd slammed over the hole it lived in. If he let it out, was it possible that the light would be bright enough to blind him to the pain?

Was it really true that she'd left him because she wanted him to be happy? And she thought he'd be happier *without* her?

How stupid was that?

If Gemma kept looking at him like that, the glow couldn't do anything but get stronger. It was so strong already that it was pushing up that lid without any conscious effort on his part.

Andy took a deep, deep breath.

'You haven't lost me, Gem,' he said quietly.

'You haven't found someone else?'

'I tried,' Andy admitted. He gave his head a small, sad shake. 'But they weren't you.'

Somehow, without either of them taking a noticeable step, they had come closer together. Within touching distance but only their eyes were holding each other's.

'I can't ask you to take on a ready-made family.' Gemma's smile wobbled. 'I've got five kids. *Five*.'

'They're already part of my family,' Andy said. 'They always have been. I've just been...absent from *their* lives.'

'You and me both.'

'You've made up for it now.'

'I'm trying. But I don't want to put any pressure on you. We don't have to rush anything, Andy.' Gemma's smile was still wobbling. 'It's enough to know that you don't hate me. That…there might still be a chance…'

'Hate you? As if I could.' Andy was watching her lips. They'd been trembling like that up on the roof, hadn't they? He'd cured that by kissing her.

He could do it again.

He moved closer.

'Andy?' The call was urgent. 'Thank goodness…I've found you.' Carla sounded anxious. 'Breakfast is nearly finished. Why aren't you in the Santa suit?'

The dayroom was packed as full as a can of sardines.

Beds lined the walls for the children who weren't mobile. There were wheelchairs tucked into corners, adults holding small children in their arms and a group of children, nurses and parents sitting cross-legged on the floor.

Christmas music was playing, the lights on the Christmas tree were sparkling and Santa was sitting in all his red and white glory on a throne that looked suspiciously like an adult-sized wheelchair covered by an old red velvet curtain.

Gemma was standing just inside the door. She had Sophie in her arms, who was sleeping like a little angel. Hazel was pressed to one side and she had a twin clutching each of her legs. Jamie had edged closer to the children sitting on the carpet. Gemma was very proud of how well her little family was behaving. And she was selfishly delighted as well because it gave her the chance to simply stand there and enjoy looking at Andy.

She was loving seeing how much pleasure he was getting playing his part in giving so many children a happy day. And every so often, when he was waiting for a new parcel to appear from the sack or another child to come and share centre stage, his gaze would stray toward the door.

To where Gemma was standing.

As if he wanted to reassure himself that she was still here.

That he hadn't imagined the urgent, whispered exchange of plans for the rest of today as Carla had supervised his attention to important Christmas duties.

He would go home with Gemma and the children after he was finished here. They could all have some time together. All of them.

And later, when the children were in bed, they would be able to talk.

Really talk.

The way they had all those years ago? Before they had carried such a burden of grief? Before they had been tired and stressed new parents even?

The way they had when they had been starting out perhaps. So very much in love, with a future in which almost anything had seemed possible.

They were both older and wiser now.

If they still loved each other enough, surely anything *was* possible.

Every time Andy's gaze found hers, Gemma found herself feeling more and more hopeful.

The touch of eye contact was like a physical caress that became steadily easier. More familiar. Touching a little deeper every time. Trusting a little more every time. How crazy was it that they could be so far apart in a crowded room and be getting closer with every passing minute?

It was magic.

Christmas magic.

'Ho, ho, ho,' Santa boomed. 'Do I have another present in my sack?'

A young nurse wearing a very cute elf costume reached into the sack and produced both a parcel and a very wide smile.

'It's for John Boy,' she announced.

Santa peered over his gold-rimmed spectacles. 'Is there a John Boy here?'

'It's *me*.' John Boy looked around the whole room to make sure everybody had heard the exciting news and his smile was enough to create a ripple of laughter.

The parcel for John Boy was the largest one yet and he couldn't wait to rip the wrapping paper off.

'It's a box of magic tricks,' he said in awe.

'Better than jokes.' Santa nodded. 'You won't find any plastic vomit in there, lad.'

John Boy grinned. 'How do you know about that?'

Santa wasn't disconcerted in the least. The fluffy

beard moved as he grinned and he tapped the side of his nose with a white-gloved hand. The lights on the tree made his spectacles shine as he looked up. Gemma was close enough to see the crinkles at the corners of his eyes as he smiled at her.

He'd been about to kiss her before, when Carla had interrupted them, but it didn't matter. There would be plenty of time for that later.

Nothing needed to be rushed.

As corny as she knew it was to even think it, Gemma couldn't help reminding herself that today was the first day of the rest of her life.

Of their lives.

And it was Christmas. Having Andy back in her life would be the most priceless gift she could ever receive.

Her eyes were misty as she led the twins up to receive the gifts Santa's elf had found near the bottom of the sack with their names on.

How priceless a gift would it be to these children if they could have Andy as a father?

The sack seemed to be bottomless.

Gift after gift had been distributed. There was a sea of wrapping paper on the floor. His elf had trotted back and forth to give parcels to the children in their beds and she'd even put on a special elf mask to give Ruthie her present on the other side of the glass windows where she was standing with her parents to watch. The extras in attendance, like siblings of patients and all the

Gillespie children, had been given small presents to let them feel included.

Surely, surely it was almost over.

He could take off this astonishingly hot outfit and he could leave work. He could go with Gemma and the children and find the time and space they needed to... to put things right?

To start again?

Andy had no idea what the immediate future held. What he did know was that he was feeling more alive than he had done for years. Bursting with it, in fact. He couldn't wait to step into that future.

Because Gemma would be there.

And the children.

His family.

The elf produced yet another parcel. It looked like a late entry. The size and shape suggested a very generic bar of chocolate.

'It's for Gemma.' Even the elf was losing a little of her enthusiasm.

John Boy hadn't pushed his wheelchair very far away after receiving his gift. He was inspecting a black bag and a plastic egg that were clearly the components of a magic trick but he looked up at the announcement.

'Who's Gemma?'

Carla had taken Sophie, and Gemma was picking her way towards him through the crowd, looking embarrassed at being included.

Andy smiled. 'Gemma's...'

What could he say? There were more people than

John Boy who seemed to be interested in his response. Carla's eyebrows were very high. His elf had her mouth open.

Who was Gemma indeed? Could he call her his wife? No. It was too soon. It would be making assumptions that he had no right to make no matter how much he might want to believe in them.

But then his gaze caught Gemma's as she came closer.

And he knew. He just knew that everything was going to be all right. He could see a reflection of love that was every bit as strong as the love he was feeling for her.

'Gemma's my wife,' he told John Boy.

It felt *so* good to say that.

So right.

Gemma seemed to think so, too, because she was smiling. And crying? She certainly wasn't looking where she was going, which was probably why she tripped on the footplate of John Boy's wheelchair.

Andy leapt off the Christmas throne to catch her before she fell.

John Boy was grinning from ear to ear.

'That makes her Mrs Santa,' he said loudly.

The world seemed to stop spinning for a moment. Was it really all right for this to be happening so fast? So publicly?

'Hmm…' Andy needed to let Gemma know she wasn't under pressure here. 'I guess it might.'

Gemma was laughing.

'I think it does,' she said.

Andy caught his breath. 'Do you want to be Mrs Santa?'

She was looking up at him, those amazing eyes dancing with joy. 'If you're Santa, then yes…of course I want to be Mrs Santa.'

'That's good.' Andy finally remembered to use his Santa voice again. 'Because I have a present for you.'

'It's chocolate,' John Boy said.

'Maybe I have another present for Gemma,' Santa said.

'What is it?'

The question came from John Boy but when Andy hesitated he could suddenly feel way too many pairs of eyes on him.

'Where is it?' John Boy demanded.

'In my pocket,' Andy admitted. He was talking to Gemma now. Only Gemma. He dropped his voice to a whisper that none of the children could overhear. 'I found it in the desk drawer this morning when I was looking for the beard glue.'

Gemma knew what it was.

He'd kept it? After all these years?

That scrappy little piece of plastic mistletoe?

Yes. There it was. He was holding it above her head.

And Santa was kissing her. Amongst the tickle of all that white fluff, she could feel the warmth of Andy's lips. The strength of his love.

The promise of the future.

'Eww.' John Boy was joyously disgusted by the display.

But everyone else seemed to think it was a bonus gift. Gemma could hear clapping. Cheers even.

Nothing to compare with what she could see in Andy's eyes, though.

The joy.

The hope.

'Let's go home,' Andy said softly. 'I have a sleigh that's not far away.'

Gemma held his gaze. 'Does it have room for a few kids?'

'It was made for kids. And you. Especially you.'

'Oi...' John Boy's voice was stern. 'You're not going to start that kissing stuff again, are you?'

Gemma and Andy looked at each other. And smiled.

Of course they were. But not yet. Not here.

'Yes, please, Santa,' Gemma whispered. 'Let's go home.'

* * * * *

A DOCTOR, A FLING
& A WEDDING RING

BY
FIONA McARTHUR

MILLS
BOON

To Rosie, my shipmate, who made it possible.

First published in Great Britain 2012
by Mills & Boon, an imprint of Harlequin (UK) Limited.
Harlequin (UK) Limited, Eton House, 18-24 Paradise Road,
Richmond, Surrey TW9 1SR

© Fiona McArthur 2012

ISBN: 978 0 263 89206 2

Harlequin (UK) policy is to use papers that are natural, renewable and recyclable products and made from wood grown in sustainable forests. The logging and manufacturing process conform to the legal environmental regulations of the country of origin.

Printed and bound in Spain
by Blackprint CPI, Barcelona

Dear Reader

Have you ever been on a sea voyage? Or imagined being on one? Had moments when you lean on the rail and gaze out over an ocean that stretches away to the horizon?

I've always wanted to write a cruise ship love story, and have been fascinated by the staff who work in those mini-hospitals below decks. There was even a handsome single doc on my cruise, who showed us around, and I've been itching to write his story.

So meet my two shipboard doctors: Nick and Tara.

Tara has been working as an aid doctor under primitive conditions in the Sudan and is being forced to have a break. She just doesn't expect to end up as a doctor on a cruise liner.

Nick Fender loves to party. He was the only man in the house with four fabulous sisters, and he has no wish to settle down. Nick's on holiday at the moment, but working as a cocktail waiter on the *Sea Goddessa*, filling in for his youngest sis Kiki, who has pneumonia. It's a job he did himself once, when he took a break from medicine. (Watch out for Kiki's story coming soon!)

Our voyage sails Nick and Tara around the magnificent Mediterranean, and they discover each other's strengths as they pass the Greek Isles, the coast of Italy, Croatia and finally Venice. Venice... Ahh... I hope you have fun as we sail away on the fantasy of the *Sea Goddessa* and the emotional journey of Nick and Tara.

With warmest wishes

Fiona

Also by Fiona McArthur:

SYDNEY HARBOUR HOSPITAL:
  MARCO'S TEMPTATION**
FALLING FOR THE SHEIKH SHE SHOULDN'T
SURVIVAL GUIDE TO DATING YOUR BOSS
HARRY ST CLAIR: ROGUE OR DOCTOR?
MIDWIFE, MOTHER...ITALIAN'S WIFE*
MIDWIFE IN THE FAMILY WAY*
THE MIDWIFE AND THE MILLIONAIRE
MIDWIFE IN A MILLION

*Lyrebird Lake Maternity
**Sydney Harbour Hospital

Praise for
Fiona McArthur:

'McArthur does full justice to an
intensely emotional scene of the delivery of a
stillborn baby—one that marks a turning point in both the
characters' outlooks. The entire story is liberally spiced
with drama, heartfelt emotion and just a touch of humour.'
—*RT Book Reviews* on
SURVIVAL GUIDE TO DATING YOUR BOSS

**These books are also available in eBook format
from www.millsandboon.co.uk**

CHAPTER ONE

TARA MCWILLIAMS walked away from the tent but the whispering sobs of grief from the widower followed her like the relentless harshness of Africa followed her clients. The sound of heartbreak. Losing a young wife and child because by the time they'd walked here it had been too late for Tara to be able to help.

A tiny insect flew into her eye and as she brushed it away she wished she could summon up some tears. Doug's hand rested gently on her shoulder and she reached up to cover the wrinkled skin, offering comfort. Just to feel life beneath her fingers.

Douglas Curlew squeezed her shoulder. 'You're done, Tara. No more.'

Tara pushed the limp hair off her forehead and sighed as Doug's fingers fell away. 'I'm fine.'

Doug glanced back over his shoulder towards the tent. 'You're not fine, you're mentally exhausted, physically frail and need to get away from here for at least six months, if not permanently. Two years battling to save lives here is enough. Vander wouldn't have expected it.'

'We both know he would have.' She glanced around

at the grimy greyness of the tent city. The harsh sun beat down on them from overhead and she shielded her eyes. 'And I'm not the one who's left crying.'

'Maybe you should be. When was the last time you let yourself go?'

A trickle of sweat rolled between her breasts and skittered down to her belly. Not much cleavage there to stop it any more. She lifted her head wearily. 'I haven't cried since he died. No time for useless emotion here, is there?' Tara thought about that and sighed again.

For the first time she glimpsed the truth in Doug's words. Her body ached with the lethargy of deep exhaustion. She had no doubt she could sleep where she fell.

She almost couldn't remember why she stayed here. 'You know as well as I do, Doug, we're critically understaffed. Who would do my job if I didn't? That's why Vander wanted me to stay.'

Doug shrugged philosophically. 'Vander died eighteen months ago.' He was more grounded to reality than Tara. 'Who did the job before you both came?' He shrugged. 'The same person who'll do your job if you burn out completely. The fact is, you're different from the vibrant young woman you used to be.'

Her chief patted her shoulder and gestured to the sea of tents in the refugee evacuation camp. 'You've done an incredible job for too long. This place has grown from five thousand to eighty thousand. The emergency birth procedures you've taught are saving countless lives that would have been lost. The staff you trained will carry on, but they love you and they're worried, and they're entitled to care enough to ask you to rest.'

It was almost too much effort to lift her shoulders in a shrug. 'Okay. I'll rest.'

Doug's dog-with-a-bone worrying became even more tenacious. 'Have a decent holiday at least. A total change of scene.'

'And do what?' Tara threw out her hands. 'I've seen so many tragedies here I don't think I could stop and just sit. Images of all those brave women who've died would revolve in my head like a horror film.'

'That's exactly what I mean.' He lowered his thick white Scottish brows and his brogue softened and shifted like the sand beneath their feet. 'Time to go, Tara. Find a little light relief. I've seen staff crash and burn and you're close. I don't want that for you.'

And do what? she thought again. Her parents were gone. No significant other. That was a laugh. 'I can't just sit. Do nothing. My house is rented, I don't have a job, there's nothing in Australia for me.' Sure, she was different from the wanting-to-do-good and eager-to-learn young woman of two years ago. You couldn't stay enthusiastic and fresh when you saw birthing women stoically accept they would die because they lived in the wrong part of the world.

'You don't have to go all the way home.' He rubbed his chin. 'Been thinking about that. I've a friend who captains a cruise liner due to sail in three days from Rome. Twelve days at a time and their junior doctor broke his leg. He's willing to rush the paperwork.'

For the first time in a long time Tara felt like laughing but the tinge of hysteria she could feel in her throat gave her pause. Shakily she gathered her control, like grasping at the string of a kite that almost got away. 'You're not talking change, Doug, you're talking a different planet.'

Tara grimaced and tried to imagine herself caring for pampered cruise-line passengers after the horrors she'd seen here in the Sudan. 'You know how many women out of every thousand women die having babies here, Doug. How could I move to a luxury liner?'

'It's the quickest option I can think of. The cruise is less than two weeks long. Then they'll drop you off in Venice, where they can replace the crew doctor and you can fly home or wherever you want. Or you could stay on and have a working holiday.'

Venice? She'd always wanted to see Venice.

She shook her head. Incomprehensible.

'And you wouldn't be treating the passengers as your main priority—the unfortunate guy was the junior and you'd be caring for the crew. The senior would do most of the passenger liaison.'

Still. A luxury liner? After this? 'I don't think so.'

Doug stared her down. Not something he would've been able to do a year ago. 'It's not a suggestion, Tara.'

'Are you ordering me to leave?' She raised her brows but her voice wasn't as steady as she would have liked.

'Yes. And if I could, I'd order you to indulge in a random dalliance with a cocktail waiter or gym instructor and really let your hair down.' Doug had one hand on his hips and the other in the air, admonishing.

Now she did laugh and it sounded almost natural. 'And I always thought of you as a father figure. I can't ever imagine my father telling me to get laid.'

His finger dropped. 'I didn't say that.' He smiled as he continued, 'But maybe treating yourself to a bit of pampering, indulging yourself for a week or two, go all out on the massage and happy hour when you're off duty. I would love to picture that when you drive away.'

'I'll think about it.' Nice dream. Last thing she could imagine but she could pretend.

But Tara's world shifted as Doug laid down the law. 'Your driver will be here in the Jeep in four hours to take you to the airport. You fly to Rome, sleep for an extra day, and pick up the ship there. You should have enough time to pack and say goodbye.'

Tara felt the cold wash of reality, of change, and a little of the trepidation new places caused in a woman who just might have forgotten how to be a woman. And just a tiny whisper of relief. She really was getting close to the edge. 'I can't leave just like that.'

He looked at her kindly. 'Can I tell you, in my experience, when you've invested as much as you have into this place and with these people, it's the only way to leave?'

CHAPTER TWO

Two DAYS later at eleven a.m. Tara stood on the dock in Civitavecchia, Rome's nearby port for cruise ships. Apart from the blinding white cruise liner that dominated the dock, it wasn't a romantic place, more a service centre with cranes and cargo ships and a semi-deserted building more reminiscent of a warehouse than a cruise-liner departure hall. Well, that was good. She wasn't feeling in the least romantic.

The officer in white asked her business and she handed over the papers Doug had given her.

'Welcome to the *Sea Goddess*, Dr McWilliams. I'll page Dr Hobson to meet you as soon as you board. If you would move through to check in via Security, please.'

'Thank you.' What the heck was she doing here?

Nick Fender, temporary bar manager for the Sea Goddess, decided the hardship of holding his sister's job for her wasn't so bad.

The sounds and subtle shift of the moored cruise ship soaked into his smile. It had been a while since he'd done a stint on a ship, as ship's doctor last time. It had been even longer since the early days when he'd had a year off from med school after his parents had died and worked as the cocktail waiter everyone had loved. That's when he'd laid the foundations for the life-of-the-party persona he'd grown very comfortable with.

So here he was back behind the bar, selling cocktails and holding down Kiki's job while she fought off pneumonia. Wilhelm, the current ship's doctor, had thought Nick's retro-vocation hilarious and Nick was starting to see the funny side of it too.

And then there were the women. Some men could develop an ease with the opposite sex and Nick was one of them. He loved women. No favouritism.

That was until he glimpsed the tall, fine-boned dolly bird arrive late to the briefing room, and judging by her uniform she was the ship's new junior doctor.

An uneasy prickle of déjà vu kept his eyes on her but he'd remember if he'd seen her before. But something was there. Something about her that tweaked at all the protective instincts he hadn't known he had, at some gut level of awareness.

Nick loved the female gender. His doting sisters probably had something to do with that, and Nick liked to dip and dally, like the seagulls he could see outside the porthole, because he wasn't falling for the have-and-hold dream. His parents' early deaths and the letter he could tell no one about had seen to that.

Nick laughed his way through life with like-minded friends, and there were a lot of those working cruise liners. It was all about avoiding the horror of being left with just one person for ever.

Until she walked in. What the hell was that? He dragged his eyes away and concentrated on his watch to work out when the first passengers would arrive, when the ship would sail out the harbour, and when the bar would open. He didn't have time for some random woman to explode unexpectedly like fine champagne on his frothy beer life.

He was the good-time guy.

Tara glanced around the small room filled with chairs and smiling crew members and started towards a seat in front of the hunky guy in the back row. He had those laughing black eyes all the best pirate actors had, the ones who could crook their little fingers at buxom wenches who'd come running.

Well, nobody would call her buxom. She'd lost so much weight she'd left her breasts in the Sudan and now for the first time she almost missed them.

He looked away as she caught his eye and she thought of her boss, Doug, and for the first time today a small smile tugged at her mouth. The smile broadened as she got closer, read his badge and realised he was actually a bar manager. Doug had said find a cocktail waiter so she was going up in the world.

Not that she really wanted to have an affair. Being the merry widow wasn't her style but she did need to relearn how to talk to people. How to talk to men. That was, men who weren't relatives of women who'd died or Doug.

She'd grown up enough not to expect to find 'romantic love'. Vander had laughed at that. Still, maybe she could practise her smiles and small talk and become a normal socially acceptable human being again.

She'd at least managed to have her cracked and broken nails attended to and her hair cut this morning at the hotel. She really would try to lighten up for a week or two as ordered because even with the twenty-four hours' sleep she'd had she was starting to feel better.

Maybe Doug had been right and she did need to touch the other world out there.

Her immediate superior on ship, Wilhelm Hobson, had met her at the gangplank and given her a quick orientation tour. Big ship! No doubt she'd be hopelessly lost for a few more days and planned on sticking to the crew areas and the medical centre to keep her bearings.

She certainly didn't want to flirt with Wilhelm. The last thing Tara needed was to discuss work socially, apart from the fact doctors and death went together in her mind at the moment. She didn't want to flirt with anyone but she would like to meet people she could talk with and, heaven forbid, even laugh with after the uneven fight she'd been waging for the last two years.

She sighed and wrenched her mind away from the camp. Concentrate on the here and now, she reminded herself.

The ship's medical centre, much larger than she'd expected, seemed almost obscenely stocked with equipment after her workplace at the camp. Apart from three consulting rooms and ten observation inpatient beds, the centre even had its own X-ray machine. And morgue. She frowned at herself.

There were ECGs, defibrillators, minor surgical equipment and orthopaedic immobilisation gear. No doubt all would be useful, along with the myriad general-practice skills that would be needed in this isolated community far from land.

It actually did promise to be interesting the more she blocked her mind from her desertion of the refugee camp. In fact, perhaps not a bad way to ease back into the general-practice headspace she'd need to revisit for the next six months. That was how long Doug had stipulated before he would even consider her return.

The dashing young South African physician in charge was sweet, and obviously a bit of a player, but if she wanted to learn people skills, she wanted light, frivolously very far from medicine, and definitely short term. Just so she could show Doug she was fine.

So here she was and she resisted the evil urge to sneak another peek at the heady masculine brew behind her. Way out of her league but maybe she could make up a drink name for him. Unfortunately the ones that popped into her head tinged on the Curacao blue side and she mentally backed away.

What had got into her?

She hadn't expected to leap onto Doug's idea with a vengeance. Bizarre when she hadn't looked at a man since med school and look where that had left her. A widow in a refugee camp with shoulders full of guilt for being the one who'd survived.

She'd never even been a necessary part of her parents' lives, and Vander had said he needed her. Actually, as a missionary he'd needed her skills, so she'd flown off with her new husband filled with the warm and fuzzy idea that he'd loved her. Reality had left her bewildered but before she'd been able to get too angry at him for not being interested in love and sex, apparently the last thing he needed after a fifteen-hour day, he'd died of cholera.

So two years down the track was that what she wanted? Sex? Would that fix her? Make her human again?

Because she certainly felt robotic with years of bounding out of bed after ten minutes' sleep, crash Caesareans with one eye open, triplets before breakfast, and massive post-partum haemorrhages at least once a night.

She'd have to stay awake for it, of course. Sex. She'd never really had the chance to figure what all the fuss was about. But one glance behind at corded muscles and mile-wide shoulders and she was contemplating caffeine to help keep her eyes open.

Good grief. She was seriously unstable and maybe Doug had it right. She chewed her lip to stop the smile. She felt decidedly immoral just thinking about it, and as a blush stole up her neck she glanced at her watch, willing the safety lecture to get going.

Safety seemed like a good thing to dwell on. That, and removing her mind from the gutter.

A shift in air currents and a sudden blocking of light

was probably what had caused her breath to catch. That
or the fact the intoxicating man behind had shifted and
sat down beside her. Suddenly the room was two degrees hotter and filled with a crackling tension. So
there really were men out there where that pheromone
antenna thing actually happened and you got goose-
bumps?

'Hello, there. You're new here?' Deep, skin-tingling
voice that raised the hairs on the back of her neck and
a whiff of some expensive cologne the price of which
would probably feed a Sudanese family for a month.
Pleeease. Tara fought the blush from her cheeks.

Nick had specifically told his legs no when they'd
wanted to shift him forward one row and sit beside the
too-thin brunette, but the force of nature was not to be
reckoned with and by the time he'd settled in next to her
he'd already accepted it. Just a conversation.

She raised thick brown eyebrows that disdained fashion. In fact, he smiled to himself as he thought of the
women he knew and their fetish for perfect dyed and
primped arches, he doubted these had ever seen a pair
of tweezers. 'Do I look that new?'

He waggled his forehead. 'New. Lost. And very
new....'

She glanced away. 'Thanks.'

'You're welcome.' She looked at him again and he
grinned to show he was only kidding, but she didn't
smile back. Crashed and burned, old boy, he mocked
himself. 'And on that auspicious beginning perhaps we
could introduce ourselves.'

He held out his hand and he'd have to say gingerly she put her fingers briefly in his. Maybe he should have assured her his were clean, judging by her reluctance.

'I'm Tara McWilliams.'

'Tara.' *The star-ar.* He always rhymed names to remember. First rule of attracting women. Remember their names. Nick had never noticed hands during a handshake before. Not what you did, really, but hers… fingers, bone-slender, too cold. She looked a little anaemic, her hand so workworn that he had the bizarre impulse to rub it warm and shelter it between his palms.

Instead, he continued the conversation as if he hadn't noticed her pull herself free quickly. 'Nick. Bar manager for the Casablanca Bar.'

'Appropriate.'

He scratched his head comically and shook it. 'Don't get it?'

'Humphrey Bogart. Casablanca. His name was Nick in the movie.'

He grinned. 'Actually, it was Rick. Sorry. I have four sisters who love romantic movies but will henceforth think of Bogart every time I see my name now.'

She narrowed her eyes at him but not enough to distract him from noticing the colour. Honey brown. Or toffee. Like her skin. Like her gorgeous legs and arms. Edible. And yet incredibly weary.

She folded her arms across her chest. 'Do you always correct people?' She was cross. And still looked good with it. Damn good.

He blinked and opened his eyes wide. 'Only when they're wrong.'

Tara had to laugh. Or be hurt because she wasn't used to people correcting her. It had all been life and death for the last two years with very little light relief and this barman had probably seen just the opposite. In fact, maybe she should cultivate him and relearn her humour and fluff from the fantasy world of shipboard existence. Good candidate.

'Don't worry. You'll have fun.' Could he read her mind?

She tasted the word. Rolled it around in her mouth and nibbled at it. Fun. Imagine. She grimaced. Boy, was she out of practice.

This guy looked like he rolled in good times. Most likely shimmied in sex. 'I'll try.' She had no doubt he could provide her with more fun than even Doug would want for her if she made any effort at all. Scary thought but she'd been a reasonably fun person before she'd grown up.

The emergency drill session at the front of the room started and she sat up straight.

Nick watched her concentrate as the senior safety officer began to speak. So a serious pupil, determined to pay attention and learn all she could before the new influx of passengers arrived that afternoon. That was good.

He was interested too, had had a private introduction as a manager that had been more in-depth and he'd come along to see if his staff were attending, but there was no doubt he'd become distracted by the intensity that Tara gave to her own process of learning.

He sat forward and concentrated. Had to admit he was keen to see where she'd be deployed compared to him. He might just have to keep an eye on her.

He guessed he had the advantage, having worked on ships before. After he'd qualified he'd done a year as junior doctor on board the sister ship to this one, and had actually been instrumental in Wilhelm deciding to try the life. So his old friend owed him and he'd called in that favour to put a word in for his sister when she'd gone down with pneumonia.

But all they'd been able to manage was Nick replacing Kiki for the two weeks or her bar manager's job would go. Luckily for Kiki, he didn't mind. He'd been due for a holiday anyway.

His ex-girlfriend, Jasmin, had been getting way too serious and not been pleased to jet off from Rome to New York on her own. Hence the relief in his newly single status. Family came first and he made no apologies. Especially when it suited him.

His attention flicked back to the lecture. The safety officer discussed the routine of a compulsory muster for all passengers before they sailed and outlined the crew's duties as emergency officers. Not much had changed and he was glad to see he was on the same station as Tara.

With over three thousand passengers and one thousand crew members the ship would give enough opportunities for her to slip out of sight. He couldn't remember when he'd last been so aware of planning to 'bump into' a woman.

Usually it just happened—or not. Funny how he didn't feel the same relaxed acceptance of fate with this slip of a medic beside him. Must be because she looked so frail—in an I-can-look-after-myself way that dared him to mention it. He wasn't saying a thing but he'd be watching for her.

But as the middle child and only male in the family, it was his job to make everyone smile. After his parents had died it had been even more reason to be the entertainer. He was still the entertainer. He could show this Tara a very good time.

Tara walked away from Nick Fender. Fender? She could imagine the guy with an air guitar, thrusting his hips and pretending.

She blinked. What? Had she left her brain back in that room? She concentrated on the directions to the hospital pinned to the wall in front of her.

She had to keep reminding herself she was at work. It was so strange without the need to rush from one emergency to the next.

With the help of the occasional map, Tara navigated two stairwells and a corridor and found her way back to the hospital where Marie, the head nurse, was shifting boxes of supplies.

'Let me help with that.' Tara hurried forward and helped lift the other side of an awkwardly shaped parcel Marie wanted on the desk.

The nurse brushed the hair out of her eyes when the parcel was safely stowed. 'Thanks, Tara. It's the new ECG machine. It wasn't heavy but, boy, was it awkward.'

'So what else can I do for you?' Tara glanced around. Boxes everywhere.

Marie grinned at her. 'Seriously, I'm just unpacking. First day is all about unpacking and stowing.'

Tara rubbed her hands. Activity would be excellent. 'Then I'll help. It's the best way to find where things live anyway. Can't be asking you where everything is all the time.'

The two women smiled at each other and Tara felt like she'd gone the first step to making at least one friend. 'Always happy to have help. Though you'll have to go through the crew's notes before we leave this afternoon. Those with illnesses they've notified us of, anyway.'

She gestured Tara through to the ward area and a sterile supply room. 'Reckon this will be the place that confuses you most.'

The storeroom was wall-to-wall shelves. She glanced around and Tara wondered if she'd get back to being as easy to talk to as Marie was. Her own conversation skills needed repolishing—just those few exchanges with air-guitar Nick had shown her that—and she wanted to fit in. Drop her doom-and-gloom mantle that had grown since she'd married and try at least to pretend to join in with 'normal' people.

The day passed swiftly, especially when the passengers came on board. Most of them looked as lost as Tara had been when she'd been out of the hospital but the mood was high and excited and totally different from the world Tara had just left.

Tara stood with Marie on the deck and watched the lines being cast off, then they eased away from the dock and maybe she could adjust to the sway of the ship and the routines on board. It was all so different from the hectic rush from one dire patient to the next.

Normally the clinic for passengers opened three times a day for two hours. The crew phoned down for quick access most of the time.

Today the passenger clinic would open once except for emergencies—most of which Wilhelm would deal with. Lovely change. She only dealt with occupational mishaps of the crew, minor illnesses among them, and passenger cabin calls when Wilhelm couldn't attend.

Even her cabin on the crew deck seemed outrageously luxurious compared to her tent at the camp. Air-conditioning and hot and cold running water and a porthole that was much larger than she'd expected and afforded an amazing view across the water. She just might be in heaven.

CHAPTER THREE

When Tara woke on her first morning they weren't even at sea. They'd docked at six a.m. She'd never got around to really studying the itinerary before she'd boarded, had been so busy finding routes and equipment that when she opened the blinds, pleasure craft and even a castle on a mountain seemed surreal. Here she was, peering out of her window at the glorious bay of Monte Carlo.

Another good night's sleep had lightened her step and she found herself smiling as passengers oohed and ahhed over the rich and famous playground off which they'd anchored. There was something amazingly special about sitting at anchor on a floating hotel adjacent to a charming principality.

When Tara walked into the clinic waiting room she found it surprisingly busy for a day in port until she realised that most passengers wanted their tests and injections before they left on the tenders heading for shore.

When she offered to help with the backlog, Marie sent her in a young mother and her small son.

The woman was petite, perfectly coiffed and immaculately dressed. 'I'm Gwen, and this is my son, Tommy.' The woman patted his head and touched her son's forehead. 'I'm so worried. He's got spots. He's not contagious, is he?'

I sincerely hope not, Tara thought as she looked down at the little boy. 'Hello, Tommy.' Tara bent down and the little boy held out his hand for Tara to shake. His skin wasn't hot or dry and his eyes were clear.

'Is he getting German measles? He has spots,' his mother said again, clasping and unclasping her hands, and Tara felt the pull of sympathy for Tommy and his obviously distressed mum.

'You poor thing. Imagine that on the first day of your holiday. But I think he's fine. It may be a heat rash. Does he seem unwell to you?' She looked at the reading from the digital thermometer she'd just used in Tommy's ear.

Tara had seen more than enough German measles to be fairly certain this wasn't a case. The rash wasn't typical, barely visible and mildly pink, and the little boy didn't present as being unwell, but she gave the mother a list of other signs and suggested she bring him back if they manifested.

The mother nodded her head with concern. 'He's normally a little terror. Are you sure the spots are okay?'

'Yes, but you did the right thing bringing him in to check. Especially if he's going into the child activity centre.'

Gwen shook her head vehemently. 'Oh, no. I'd never do that. There's just the two of us. His dad left us, you see, and we're visiting my sister in Mykonos on holiday. Sometimes he's not a well little boy and on the ship I don't have to travel without being safe. It's Tommy's holiday too.'

Tara smiled at the pair. 'He's very lucky to have you. Bring him back if you're worried, Gwen.'

Tara showed them out and Marie sent in an older lady who wanted her ear looked at for wax. Marie was chewing her lip, trying not to laugh, and Tara pretended to frown at her. This was not life-threatening stuff at all but the waiting room was emptying. Still no crew and at this rate they'd be clear of patients before the two hours was up.

Wilhelm was still sequestered with his previous patient so Tara took the older lady in with her.

Wilhelm and Tara had planned to catch up on the in-service needed with the new ECG machine, as well as go through the cases from the day before, and Marie planned to venture ashore to peep into the casino in Monaco.

Tara couldn't help but wonder what a certain bar-staff member was doing because most of the bars were shut when the cruise ship was in port. No doubt by the end of the cruise she'd have a fair idea. She even toyed with the idea of looking for him after tea, she'd seen the bar on the wall directions, but a swell came up and the hospital was inundated with motion-sickness sufferers and that put paid to that. Good thing too.

On the second morning when Tara woke they were tied to the wharf at Livorno, the gateway to Florence, the leaning tower of Pisa and Tuscany, none of which she'd seen. Or would.

But Tara was off duty later in the morning and quite happy to explore the less-crowded ship.

She ventured through the main passenger areas in civilian clothes and gazed around at the surprising throng of passengers foregoing the shore excursions.

Up in the sunlight, at one of the few open bars on board, Nick lorded it behind the Casablanca Bar like a sheikh in a harem. Tara stepped back behind one of the ship's columns on the swimming-pool deck and watched him work.

She had to admit he filled his blue T-shirt admirably and the muscles in his chest and those arms were blatantly provocative as he shook his cocktail shaker and grinned at the world.

Why weren't these women off visiting the city where they were docked? The rattle of ice carried across the hum of conversations that floated above the deckchairs and his teeth flashed as he theatrically poured the contents into a glass from a great height without a splash.

Well, she guessed Nick was one reason. She had to cover her mouth to stop herself laughing out loud, which kind of surprised her because the little bubble of excitement that surfaced just by seeing him was totally unexpected.

She frowned and looked away but there was nothing quite as much fun to look at. She couldn't dispute she was feeling better than she had been when she'd stepped on board but this guy was nobody to her. And she was certainly a nobody to him.

Her gaze drifted back to Nick as he scooped up a decorative skewer of pineapple and cherry and garnished a creation with a flamboyant wave.

He was so confident, Tara could feel her lips tug again, so clearly a showman and ladies' man, she probably didn't have a hope of practising her extremely rusty wiles on him, but if she got the chance, at least it meant he couldn't be hurt if she did get to first base with him.

Still she hung back. Watched the woman he'd served walk away with an exaggerated wiggle, and noted with approval Nick's attention was on cleaning his cocktail equipment, not on her bikini bottom. So he took the rules for consorting with passengers seriously. She'd been surprised how severely intimacy with passengers was dealt with on the ship. No doubt instant dismissal wouldn't look good on his résumé.

Or maybe he just wasn't interested. He didn't look gay. At all. She smiled to herself. She wondered how he would look at her if she asked for one of those non-alcoholic 'mocktails' they served to teetotallers? She'd never been much of a drinker, most alcohol gave her a headache, and during college she'd usually offered to be the designated driver if she'd gone out.

Maybe that was what Vander had liked about her. She'd often wondered because she'd certainly felt she'd let him down in some way, though he'd never said.

Nick glanced up, saw her skulking behind the pillar, and gestured her over. Well, maybe he wasn't totally disinterested.

She straightened away from the column and smiled shyly. Funny how that little tug in her stomach made her mouth curve. Her feet seemed pretty eager to move his way too and she tried not to wiggle like the last woman had.

He gestured to a stool at the side of the bar. 'Hello, there, Dr Tara. Fancy a drink?'

She smiled back. 'Non-alcoholic?'

'Sure.' He gestured to his makings. 'I'll have you know there is just as much skill needed for a really top mocktail, if not more.'

'You reckon you're pretty good at these, do you?'

'The best.'

'I see you lack in confidence.'

'I know. Sad really. How about a *No*-jito?' His white teeth flashed and she had to grin and the extraneous noises faded until it was as if the two of them were in a private little bubble. She bet all the girls behind her at the pool felt like that too. He went on to explain. 'Crushed mint, loads of limes, sugar syrup and soda?'

'Sounds great.' She shook off her absorption of him and glanced around. 'How's the bar-manager gig going?'

He smiled at the half-naked women on loungers spread out in a fan in front of him. 'Always fun.'

She shook her head sadly. 'Tsk, tsk. Men.'

He leaned towards her. 'Perhaps it should be "Tsk

tsk, women"? Though I don't mean that. I love women.
I have sisters I adore and a new girlfriend every month.'

Tara wondered if he was warning her. Temporary.
Don't plan a wedding. Nice if he was. Because that
suited her down to the ground!

Nick wondered if he was warning her. Bit of an exag-
geration, that monthly girlfriend thing, but he certainly
wasn't into permanence. Had discovered long ago that
even the most likely couple would stretch to find eter-
nal happy-ever-after. But to warn about his preference
for the short term was not his usual tactic when he was
trying to chat up a woman.

What made this one different? He'd kept an eye out
for her but had been unexpectedly busy with his duties
and he'd have much preferred it if his sister had decided
on a position with less responsibilities.

Dr Tara had intruded into his thoughts persistently
last night when the sea had played games. He'd bet there
were a few seasick passengers and some crew not used
to the sway of the ship yet. 'Did the swell bother you
last night?'

'No.' She shrugged. 'I have a cast-iron stomach.' He
pushed the peanuts her way but she wasn't interested.
'A few of the new beauty staff were a little queasy and
we doled out some anti-emetics.'

Nick shoved the cheese and crackers across and
she ignored them too. She glanced at the women and
changed the subject away from medicine. 'What about
your patrons?'

'It was pretty quiet for a second night.' Lord, he just wanted to feed her. He used his tongs to put two hulled strawberries in a dish in front of her. She couldn't miss them. To his delight she picked one up absently and bit into it. Gorgeous lips, white little teeth… Nick's stomach kicked as he tried not to mimic her.

He glanced at his watch for a bit of control. 'So, what time are you off duty?'

'Apart from being on call?' She patted her lips with a paper towel he gave her. 'I'm off now till lunch. Then off again at eight. Why?'

Maybe he shouldn't do this. He'd always listened to his instincts before so why was this so difficult? 'Care to join me for dinner about eight-thirty?'

She narrowed her eyes at him and then glanced away. 'I guess so.'

Had he sounded too eager? She certainly hadn't. But he'd seen a few other crew members eyeing her and it hadn't sat well with him. Another out-of-character trait she seemed to bring out in him. Maybe he just needed to demystify her attraction and then he'd understand what drew her to him.

CHAPTER FOUR

AT TWENTY-THIRTY hours they sat in a quiet corner of the crew dining room, or middle mess as they called it, because it was common ground.

Nick was aware she'd normally eat in the first mess because that was where the officers congregated, and on this gig he ate with the auxiliary and admin staff.

The largest staff dining area catered for the seven hundred domestic and deckhand staff but there was always a little mix and match that went on with the dalliances.

It was after the usual time for dinner and before late supper so nobody came near them.

Unobtrusively Nick had been studying the fine veins in her hands. She was so frail when he really looked. There was that stupid protectiveness again. 'So what made you go to the Sudan?'

He pushed a bread stick her way but she ignored it. Two years? Nick was still flabbergasted. No wonder she looked like a strong wind would blow her over. One of his friends had lasted three months. He wanted to draw her into his arms and protect her. That was a serious worry. Apart from his sisters, he'd avoided the whole emotional responsibility thing.

'I went with my husband. We wanted to do something worthwhile, use our training, and after he died it was too hard to leave.'

The impact of her statement sat heavily in his chest. He wouldn't have picked her for a widow. There was a certain naive vulnerability he couldn't miss. 'I'm sorry. How did your husband die?'

She glanced away. 'Cholera.'

Ouch. 'Nasty.'

She looked back at him. 'Very.' Succinct.

'So why the Sudan?'

She shrugged. 'We'd both finished our internships and he met a midwife who'd worked in the displaced person refugee camps. She told him how they were crying out for GPs with obstetric training and he enquired. The next thing I knew we were there and I didn't lift my head up until a week ago when my boss said I needed to take a break.'

Nick shook his head. 'After two years. I'll bet.' He glanced at her hands again. She didn't wear a ring. Why was that? Almost ruminatively he said, 'What were they thinking of to leave you there so long?'

She blinked and for a horrible moment he thought she was going to cry and he wanted to kick himself. It brought home just how close to the edge she was and he vowed to himself he'd keep a close eye on her. Might even have a word to Wilhelm about her work hours.

'You don't want to talk about it?' He could see her

squirming. He wanted her to eat something. He picked up the strawberry he'd kept for last and put it on her plate.

She shook her head. 'Not particularly.' But at least she absently ate the fruit. He was ridiculously relieved.

So she didn't want to talk about it. Good. Neither did he. Especially about her husband. 'Fine.'

She glanced away but he couldn't tell if she was upset from her voice when she spoke again.

Such a bright and cheery voice that said back off. 'Hey, I'm tougher than I look.' She turned to him and he decided her smile was only just forced. 'And here I am...' she spread her arms '...talking to a bar manager, on a ship cruising the Mediterranean, and very glad I don't have to think about anything disastrous.' She put down her fork.

'So, talk to me about something light and frivolous. That's why I'm cultivating you.'

So she was cultivating him, eh? Sounded promising and damn straight he could be frivolous. Well, he guessed that summed him up. Compared to her anyway.

It didn't seem the time to tell her he was a doctor too. Not frivolous enough. Or about his own transition through med school and rotation to learn the lot, anaesthetics, obstetrics and surgery. He'd had his moments requiring skill and dedication but compared to what he could imagine she'd been through, his world was a cinch.

Though frivolously speaking, he never had to get involved with patients and their real lives because he would only be there for a weekend or a month at the most because he was locum man. So no talk of medicine and he told her what he thought she wanted to hear.

'I haven't been on a ship for a while but worked my way up from barman to cocktail master.' He puffed out his chest theatrically. 'Took out a medal at the world cocktail championships with a friend.'

He didn't usually tell people that, it had been years ago, but he guessed the title would sound playful enough for her, and he wanted to see that smile he knew was in there.

'So what do you do?'

'I mix drinks when the bar staff are on their breaks, make sure all the behind counter orders are filled and we don't run out of Margarita mix. I fill in when staff are sick and just try to keep everyone happy.' He shrugged. 'Apparently I'm pretty good at that.'

'I can see you are.' Now she smiled and it had been worth waiting for. He felt a flicker of satisfaction from lightening her mood and more than a flicker of awareness, as though the moon had just peeked through a bank of clouds outside. Bizarre how good she made him feel.

He leaned towards her and a tendril of hair fell across her face, making his finger itch to push it back. 'Been for a swim yet?' He fancied seeing her in a bikini.

'No. I'm very boring. Just getting used to things and finding my way around. I bet you use all the amenities.'

'Every single one.' He flashed his teeth at her and she smiled again. 'I like a good game of table tennis.'

'Do you? I used to have a very competitive streak for ball games.'

'Aha! That sounds like a challenge.'

Tara almost laughed out loud. The fizzing in her stomach was getting stronger. And was it all about a ball game? Was she challenging him? Maybe she wasn't as bad at this as she'd thought she'd be. 'We'll see.'

He went on like a tour guide and she could feel herself relax more every minute. He was like her own personal cruise director. 'Then there's Movies Under The Stars, with deckchairs, checked blankets and popcorn, and of course the latest flicks.'

'Checked blankets, eh? Very observant for a man.'

He shrugged. 'My sisters have this thing for tablecloths under trees for picnics. So I have a soft spot for checks.'

The image of cuddling up with Nick and a blanket under Mediterranean stars was almost tangible. 'I'll watch out for those blankets.' Though she wasn't quite sure now just what she was watching out for.

'So why don't you let me show you around when we anchor off Naples? Maybe hire a convertible. We could take a drive down to Amalfi, check out Praiano and Positano.'

His chest tightened and he realised he was actually holding his breath. This was crazier by the minute. Her toffee gaze slid over his face thoughtfully and he could almost taste her sweetness. Something whispered sweet was dangerous.

'Sounds good. I've always wanted to see the Italian

coastline from those windy roads.' She opened her eyes wide and he had an epiphany as to what they meant by 'almost fell in'. Was that a come-on? He sure as hell hoped so because he could feel his body stir like leaves in a breeze at that hint of promise.

'The roads have to be seen to be believed,' he warned with a grin. 'And they appeal to the frustrated Ferrari driver in me.'

'A Ferrari?' She pretended to frown. 'They must pay good wages where you work.'

He guessed he could hire one if he wanted to but he'd be too worried he'd scratch it. Not many cars were dent free on Italian roads. 'No. But maybe a little sports number so we can put the roof down.' He grinned. 'You know, feel the whoosh of air as the buses push us up against the cliff.' He watched her. Deliberately painting the picture to make sure she knew what she was getting into. To his delight, if anything her eyes sparkled more.

'Oh, yeah. I've heard about that. A little danger that's not blood-product related would be a great way to re-member life is for living.'

Not blood-product related. He wanted to hug her. Felt the rapport. Medical people laughed at the odd-est things and he was feeling a little more alive than usual himself.

Tara couldn't believe she was flirting like this. And had made an infectious-disease joke that he probably hadn't got. He might think she was loony but the idea of capturing a few hours of wind in her face and amazing views was enticing. Cathartic even. And she couldn't hide the fact the idea of spending time with someone light and mischievous like Nick wasn't a big plus too.

'So tell me about your morning,' Nick said. 'Any interesting cases?'

Did he really want to know? She doubted it. Probably the whole 'I'm paying attention to everything you say' persona he had down pat. 'It was fine. A few bouts of nausea and a fractured forearm.'

'They have an X-ray machine here, don't they?' Interest shone from his eyes and she enlarged slightly to explain.

'Yes.' She smiled at him for humouring her. 'Not something I've had to do personally before and interesting to learn how simple taking an X-ray really is. The patient's views are emailed away to a large centre to be reported on, and the results are emailed back.'

She shook her head, still bemused by the speed of reporting. 'Wilhelm had the results within two hours, which was even faster than my training hospital in Sydney.'

'Which hospital was that?' She saw his eyes sharpen and she frowned. Warning bells rang.

'In the south.' But she didn't go into more detail. She quite liked the fact he didn't know where she came from. 'A long way from here. But, of course, at the refugee camp we had nothing except our hands to decide if a bone was broken.'

She saw him accept she wasn't about to give out her home address and her relief expanded. She wasn't sure why she was so keen on keeping distance from the real world with him but it was better to err on the side of caution.

This whole Nick exercise was designed as a holiday flingette, just a tentative fling, and the idea of the future or anything or anyone serious made her cringe. Like Saint Vitus's dance. A full-body shudder. She knew for a fact she wasn't mentally ready for any kind of normal relationship.

'So the last two years will always have an impact on your work?'

Not just my work, she thought with sudden insight and a flash of her late husband's face. 'Of course.' Images from their work flooded back, some of them uplifting but most of them tragic, and she winced. 'Another thing I don't want to talk about. Tell me about the world cocktail championships. I love the sound of that.' Blunt, but she hoped, effective.

He studied her for a moment and saw him nod with understanding but there was no way this man would have any idea what she'd seen. 'You mean the place where all the movers and shakers go?'

Effective communication, then. She smiled. 'That would be the place.'

'Vegas.' He spread his arms. 'You gotta think big. And sparkly. We were dressed in black with blue sequins, my sisters had a ball making the outfits, and our drink was a Morrocan Marguarettaville.'

'Sounds deadly.' She couldn't keep the smile from her face and she was suddenly conscious of how big

and handsome this man was. This man, who was paying intense attention to her. Quite a heady experience
really for a girl from tent city.

He spread his hands self-deprecatingly. 'A cocktail
that carries a decent kick. Made for slow sipping at
sunset.'

The picture of the two of them sipping drinks on
some beach seemed ridiculously easy to imagine.
'You'll have to make me one.' She laughed. 'One sunset when I can sleep in the next day.'

He put his finger to his lips and her gaze followed
his finger. 'As long as you don't tell anyone the recipe.'

'My lips are sealed.' She'd said it and shouldn't have
been surprised he glanced at her mouth in return. But
she felt the heat.

For a woman who had minimal experience of se-
duction she had no trouble recognising his ability to
turn it on.

Zap! Almost as if he'd touched her, and suddenly the
making of drinks in competitions was ludicrously un-
important. His eyes darkened, his gaze locked on hers,
the air thickened with his intention so that she knew he
needed her alone, in the dark, locked in an embrace.
And soon. Whoa, there. Her imagination was working
overtime here.

Then he glanced down at the food they'd only picked
at and she let out her breath. Felt like a fanciful idiot.
'Would you like to go outside? I'll share the rest while
we walk. It's nice on deck at this time of night.'

Her stomach kicked. She hoped he hadn't read her

mind again. He stood up and moved around to help pull out her chair and she stared at the tablecloth thoughtfully. He could be quite smooth at getting his own way when he wanted, but knowing it didn't stop her feet from shifting, standing, moving beside him with a little beat of anticipation fluttering in her throat.

When they stepped out onto the walkway around the ship he tucked her hand into his arm and after the initial shock she let her hand relax and just enjoyed the sensation of being close to a man she had to admit she fancied. She even had to fight down the heat in her cheeks like a schoolgirl. The concept made her grin. Her hip brushed his solid thigh as they walked and when they passed two female crew members walking together she even enjoyed the envious look they cast her.

A little devil of satisfaction made her fingers curl more tightly into his arm and his skin warmed her fingers. He must have felt her approval because he looked down at her and smiled.

She hurried into speech in case he read too much into her involuntary action. 'Maybe I could get used to forgetting the world on a cruise ship because it's all an illusion that only lasts twelve days.'

He tilted his head and studied her. 'Not everything is an illusion.'

That was a laugh. 'What's not an illusion?'

She watched him search for an example that was amusing and backed up her statement. This guy's life was an illusion. Which was why she liked him.

'I imagine the person with the broken arm is steeped in reality at the moment.'

She dug in her chin, refused to be deflected from her common-sense *aide memoire* that they had no future. Light, frivolous, she reminded herself again. 'I prescribed decent analgesia. Checked the cast wasn't too tight. I'd say she's floating along quite nicely despite it.'

She felt his glance brush over her again, felt it physically because her skin prickled, and she hurried into speech. 'You were going to tell how you became the world cocktail champion.'

'Well, I boasted a little. There were two of us. And we had an idea for a drink that resembled a boat and tasted like an island. To be sipped, as I said, at sunset.' He grinned. 'Lots of rum.'

He stopped beside a little tuck in the deck that created an alcove and she stopped beside him. The waves were quietly relentless, insistently slapping the side of the ship as the big white hull sliced its way through the swell. The breeze was cool and laden with the tang of salt as they sped to their next port.

At the bow of the ship, to the side, the wheelhouse hung out over the sea and she could just discern figures on duty.

They both turned to look out over the ocean as they leant on the cool lacquered rail and the intensity of the moment that had sprung from nowhere eased. The tension she'd picked up slowly dissipated from her neck as, in the distance, tiny flickers of light twinkled on the horizon from the nearest land.

'Gotta love the Italian coastline.' His hand swept along the land mass.

'Where do you think that is?'

He shrugged. 'There's so many cliff hewn townships plastered onto the side of Italy, I'd be guessing.' Then he moved his hip until it was firm alongside hers and she forgot the lights as his solid thigh imparted insidious heat like a warm current through a cold sea.

The slow slide of awareness seeped up her body until she couldn't resist her own lean to increase the pressure.

His hand tightened on hers and slowly but surely he drew her into his arms.

Nick's head bent closer, close but not all the way, and his voice rumbled in her ear. 'I'd really like to kiss you.'

It wasn't a question but it wasn't a demand either. Just a statement of how he felt and one she could whole-heartedly agree with.

She could do this—be brave enough to say what she'd been thinking, out loud. 'I think that would be nice.'

A flash of teeth in the dimness at her less than smooth answer but the result was good. His head bent and his mouth came down to stop just a breath away from hers until she leaned in and made the link. He re-turned with a gentle brush of those gorgeous lips that pressed against her mouth with a little fizz of connec-tion she hadn't expected.

She'd actually assumed it was going to be hard work to learn to kiss again, not that she'd ever been remark-ably good at it before, because there hadn't been much of it, but lessons and ratings and thoughts of her own ability seemed to slip away from her consciousness, like trying to catch the breeze in her fingertips.

Drifting into sensation.

Drifting into Nick. Nick's mouth, his breath mingled with hers, the wash of the waves against the side of the ship a distant accompaniment to the feel of his mouth moving over hers.

Then the slide of his other hand as he sought and found her free fingers and linked with them too. Dimly she admitted she liked that bond, just their mouths and their fingers joined and her breasts firm against his solid chest.

When his tongue touched hers gently she inhaled sharply and unconsciously flattened herself against him to deepen the sensation until unexpectedly she was lost to time and place and everything except the silent mating of mouths in this corner of the deck under the moonlight.

She'd never offered herself like this before or maybe she had offered but had never shared as an equal—been a part of the experience instead of the outsider not meeting some rigorous standard. The thought drifted. She winced at the disloyalty that still bit but, boy, imagine if it had been Vander missing the ingredients, not her. Heretic thought.

But there was no doubt this man ignited a slow burn inside her that she'd never expected so that she could feel herself almost glow incandescently.

'Stop thinking,' she murmured to herself against his mouth.

He said, 'Mmm' back, and suddenly it wasn't so hard to let go of all thought, revel in the moment, explore it, until dimly she realised he was moving backwards, drawing away, squeezing her fingers downwards as if to help her return her feet to the deck.

'Oh, my.' Tara stood back and compressed her lips as she slowly withdrew her fingers from his. 'Oh, my,' she said again, and he pulled her into his chest until her face was pressed against his shirt and his mouth rested on her hair. She could feel the thumping away under her cheek and there was no doubt his heart rate had picked up. So he wasn't immune either.

Nick squeezed her for a moment, they both sighed, and he spoke into her hair. 'I think you'd better go to bed.'

She stepped back, cast one glance into his unsmiling face and turned, pretending her heart wasn't thumping like the ship's engines below her feet.

She walked away. Oh, my. What the heck had happened there? One kiss. Or a series of kisses that had made her head spin.

She put her hand out for the rail and used it as a support to get her back to the doorway that led inside. She could feel her lips tingling and when the ocean breeze caught her hair and spread it across her face she couldn't help touching her mouth as she dragged it away. Apart from being sensitive, her lips felt no different—she couldn't say the same for the thumping in her chest. Either the guy was seriously charismatic or she was seriously at risk of being a pushover. Not what she'd planned.

Nick watched her go and he inhaled a big breath in through his nose as he tried to quieten the boys in the basement, who'd wanted to break out and conquer. It had been let go then or who knew where they'd end up? And this he didn't want to rush.

Since when? Innocence causing his undoing? And why did her untrained mouth seem more erotic than the most practised women he'd been with while her fluttering fingers left trails on his skin that still glowed with angel dust? He rubbed his hands over his arms as if to break her spell as he took another breath.

He could still sense her perfume. Nothing he'd come across before—violets? Tara was like a violet. Hiding at the side of life, doing her job, easily bruised, overshadowed by the showy roses yet surprisingly beautiful when you took the time to look.

She wore a top note of spring that blended with her warm skin like the kiss of an angel and complemented her lack of artifice. A little old-fashioned. Like he wanted to be when he held her. Whoa.

Stop! He had good reasons why he wanted to keep his relationships super-casual. He did not want to be another man who broke Tara's heart. Even in the brief mention she'd made of her departed husband he'd sensed it had been a less than perfect marriage. She deserved a good man, not a good-time guy like him.

Nick took off for the crew's mess and hopefully some diversion at a sharp pace. Maybe find a woman he could chat up and go dancing with. Someone who was here for the fun to take his mind off what he really wanted to do. Like search out a certain young medic and lose himself despite the danger?

CHAPTER FIVE

WHEN Tara woke two days later their cruise had docked at Naples and she decided she liked this business of going to bed in one city and waking in the next. There were even a few inklings she could settle into the routine of the ship's obsession with the clock. Begin to enjoy this slice of time that didn't belong to the real world.

Her shore day as a tourist promised the first frivolous—there was that word again—excitement in a long while. She couldn't help the little jump in her pulse rate at the thought of spending the day with the heady cocktail that was Nick.

The feeling was amplified by the fact she hadn't seen him at all during the preceding twenty-four hours despite several attempts during her breaks to nonchalantly pass the Casablanca bar.

Where had this light-hearted woman come from? She couldn't believe only a few days ago she'd been working under primitive conditions in a tent city of eighty thousand people with round-the-clock disasters.

Sickeningly, her mood plunged and she dragged herself back from the abyss with a determination borne of need, to another world, a different world she was only just discovering, the here and now of lighter responsibility.

Focus on yesterday where her work in the ship's medical centre was like a walk in the park compared to the Sudan. And the best thing was she couldn't lose a baby or a mother because the rules for travel on board excluded women over twenty weeks pregnant and infants less than six months old.

Non-critical diagnostics that required routine action were a breeze. They'd had two crew members with unexplained high temperatures, whom they'd isolated and were transferring off the ship today, and a few muscle strains and headaches, but apart from that the staff seemed a healthy lot.

Wilhelm had been a little busier with a series of minor complaints and two asthmatic children. Gwen had brought Tommy back with a temperature, which had settled with paracetamol.

The most serious case had been the dehydrated woman with deep-vein thrombosis who'd needed heparin and transfer.

Tara was so well used to finding venous access in very ill women she had no trouble at all when asked to help out. The hardest part was not to keep comparing the patient load to the last two years.

But that was work and today was play.

Most of the passengers would be off on shore tours and Wilhelm had assured her she could have the whole day free as long as they were back by six-thirty before the ship sailed.

The anticipation built as she walked sedately down the stairs to the disembarkation deck in her new blue T-shirt she'd bought from the on-board boutique.

Nick looked especially debonair in an open-necked white shirt and fawn shorts, his strong legs deeply tanned all the way down to his sandalled feet. He waited for her in front of the gangway and they swiped their crew cards to record their absence.

Security waved them on with a grin and suddenly she was on solid ground. Just the two of them.

The tarmac of the pier shifted unexpectedly under her feet and she wobbled a little.

Nick laughed and put out a hand. 'You just need your land legs.'

The ground steadied and he let go to retrieve the keys from the attendant.

Tara hesitated before she started walking again. Maybe she was still unsteady or maybe it was realising she was suddenly on her own and getting into a little red sports car with a man she barely knew.

Nick must have noticed her falter because he stopped and looked as he held open her door to the rental car that waited on the pier for them. 'You okay?'

She didn't say anything, couldn't actually, was just having a private little panic attack about why he'd possibly want to spend time with her. She had no social skills, was skin and bone and downright boring. She conveniently forgot it had been Nick who'd asked her along.

He let go of the doorhandle and put his hand over his heart. 'It's okay. We'll have fun.' He shrugged. 'Just reminding you, while I don't have a written reference, we have to work together on the ship. You know in my other life I have sisters I adore and can promise have never frightened a woman in my life.'

It wasn't because she was scared. Tara mentally shook herself. He'd asked her. If they didn't prove compatible there'd be tons of gorgeous scenery to ease the conversational burden. And she doubted making conversation was a problem Nick had any issues with.

She didn't know why she was having cold feet, unless it was because she was more worried they'd be too compatible. And that was ridiculous.

Nick noted the tension in her face. So he wasn't the only one unsure if they were playing with fire. Though he doubted she had enough experience to know what it was she was feeling nervous about.

She shook her head, more at herself than at him. 'Sorry. Just out of practice.'

He cursed himself. He'd suspected she was fragile and still he'd gone steaming in like a bozo on steroids.

'It's me who should apologise. I did railroad you into this.' And shouldn't have if he'd had any sense, but it was too late now.

He glanced towards the city. 'If you like, we can just drive into town, have a coffee and come back. I didn't think you needed Pompeii today so wasn't going here. Though we could zip up to the top of Vesuvius and admire the bay. It's spectacular from up there. We don't have to make a day of it. I keep forgetting you'll still be tired from your work.'

She lifted her pretty little chin. 'I'm fine. Let's go.'

Yes! He'd offered and she'd declined. The relief was ridiculous. He told himself he wasn't suddenly feeling like he'd won the lottery. That was just because he was looking forward to taking the car for a spin. Any company would have been good.

An hour later, on the cliff road coming into Amalfi, Tara wasn't so sure she was cut out for this type of excitement.

'How can you drive here?' Tara's fingers whitened unobtrusively as she gripped the edge of the seat beside her leg and tried not to look at the rocks in the ocean below.

When he took his eyes off the tarmac to smile her way she gripped tighter. 'For goodness' sake, keep your eyes on the road.'

Nick laughed but complied. 'I have an aunt who owns a hotel in Praiano, a little town on the cliff between Amalfi and Positano. We used to come down here for holidays. Learnt to drive on motorbikes here and progressed to cars.'

He didn't sound Italian. 'So you grew up in Italy?'

'Between here and Sydney. My mum was Italian and moved to Australia when she married my dad. We spent a lot of holidays here.' He grinned at her quickly then returned his attention back to the road.

Tara frowned. It all sounded very breezy and humorous but there was something underlying that suggested to Tara it hadn't been as smoothly transitional as he made out.

Another scooter with a death-wish pillion passenger slipped between them, a bus and the sheer drop to the ocean five hundred feet below. She let the subject drop. 'Those guys are crazy!'

He flashed his teeth and dared her to live dangerously. Somehow it was infectious. She'd wanted to know she was alive. Her fingers loosened. What the heck. Hanging on wouldn't save her anyway. She grinned back with determination. She was going to enjoy today. If it killed her. 'Do your worst, then.'

They scooted down the mountain, zipping around coaches as incredibly skilled bus drivers pulled over to stop the backlog of cars and the cheeky motorcycles ran around both of them.

To the side, the cliff fell sheer to the sea hundreds of feet below, and on the azure water cruise ships dotted the horizon while charter boats left trails of whitewash across the ocean.

They coiled their way into Amalfi and the vibrancy of the little Italian seaside town made Tara's eyes widen and her breath ease out in a sigh. 'It's so pretty. And look at the shops!'

Her eyes flicked between gaily decorated windows like an addict in a chocolate factory and she frowned at herself. 'Do you know how long it is since I saw shops like these?'

Pretty dresses fluttered on hangers outside doorways and she could feel herself lean towards them.

She was so shallow. How materialistic could you get? Apart from her new T-shirt it had been years since she'd bought clothes. Vander had been very scornful of fashion. 'They make me feel guilty. An indulgence when so many people don't have food.'

Nick sniffed. 'As Kiki, my youngest sister, would say, piffle!' He pulled into a tiny parking spot as if their bumper bar wasn't less than an inch from the car in front and she shook her head incredulously.

'How on earth did you do that?'

He shrugged. 'Parking in Italy is an art form. Not much car space so use it to the max.' He turned to face her. 'As for not buying clothes, guilt is self-indulgent— so you may as well use real self-indulgence and go shopping.'

She wrinkled her forehead as she replayed his words in her head. How could guilt be self-indulgent? Was she wallowing in it? She didn't think so but maybe she could shop a little, try the experience out, and see how it went. 'You'll be sorry. I feel like I could hunt bargains all day.'

He waggled his brows. 'Do your worst. I'm an experienced bag carrier.'

She blinked. Didn't shopping made men frown? 'You sure? You could meet me at a bar.'

He grinned. 'I really do enjoy watching women disappear into change rooms and twirl and frown and dither.' He shrugged. 'Sick, I know, but it amuses me.'

She glanced longingly at the fluttering frocks and scarves. 'A little walk around wouldn't hurt.'

He glanced up the street, found what he was looking for and drew her forward. 'Try this one. My sisters come here all the time and there's a chair for me to enjoy the show.'

She shrugged, happy to be steered, and Nick watched her disappear into the shop before he followed at a leisurely pace. When Tara had slipped into the little change room Nick engaged the owner in conversation, and when Tara came out without finding anything she really liked Nick stood up and handed her a new selection.

'The saleslady suggested these with your colouring.' He watched the confusion in her face as she warred with the idea he'd actually selected clothes for her and the fact that she'd already been in there ten minutes.

He sat down again in the chair and raised his bottle of water. 'Go.' She glanced at her watch and dithered. He could see she wanted to try more.

He grinned at her. 'And this time can I please see the ones you fancy?' He held out his hands. 'Not bored. Honest!'

Watching Tara was as enjoyable as he'd imagined once she started to venture out with each new outfit.

Shy, face pink, she did the fastest twirl in history when he gestured for her to show him the back, with a quick glance at his face to see if he thought she looked okay. This was the part he loved about women. Nick could feel it expand in his chest. See her confidence grow as each new outfit appeared. Loved the little frown when she disagreed with his verdict.

An hour later Tara was over it. Nick could have spent the day watching, but hoarded the bags and seemed to find a new delight in every corner of the shop for her to try. Already she had three dresses, three shorts and shirt sets, and two new bikinis she hadn't let him see. 'Enough,' she said.

He dropped his lip. 'Shame,' he replied, then grinned. 'But fine. We'll put these in the boot and take a run up to Praiano to my aunt's hotel for lunch. The view from there's incredible.'

He opened the door to their zippy little sports car and as she bent to climb in she caught a woman watching her enviously from the side of the road. Her face warmed as Nick stowed the bags in the back. Tara felt like shaking her head but then realised she really was living a fun life. She just needed to remember not to apologise for it.

Consciously she relaxed her hands and lifted her face to the breeze. As they took off she reminded herself this leg also involved another hair-raising ride along the coast road but she did trust Nick's driving to get them there safely. They'd be fine.

Fifteen minutes later they zoomed into the cliff-hugging town of Praiano, where finally Nick pulled in front of the white facade of a hotel.

Tara read the sign: 'Hotel Tramonto d'Oro'. A bus squeezed past and she wondered why a hotel would be built so close to the road.

As soon as they stepped inside the foyer she could see the vista that stretched right across the cerulean sea. 'Well, that explains it,' she murmured as her nose itched to press up against the glass on the other side of the room. Before she could move to the windows a stylish Italian woman appeared from the office and swooped on Nick.

'Nico!' She glanced at Tara and smiled. 'So my nephew has brought you to see me.' She glanced at them both and threw her hands into the air with Gallic drama. 'So finally he has fallen in love.'

Tara blushed and shook her head. 'No.' Good grief, no. 'We're just friends.'

Nick sent her an apologetic look but appeared unperturbed while Tara wanted to crawl under one of the big plush lounges in front of the window and hide.

In Italian Nick did his own gesticulating until his aunt laughed. '*Sì, sì.* Just friends.' She laughed again. 'But you are hungry? No?'

Tara lifted her head as her stomach rumbled. She could answer that one. '*Sì.*'

'Then you shall have the best table. The view is good today. No haze.'

Angelica shooed them in front of her and Tara's mouth opened at the view across the Mediterranean Sea from the lounges. A gelato-hued town in the distance hung on the cliffs like different flavours in an ice-cream shop and island smudges dotted the expanse into the distance.

When they sat at a wrought-iron table on the long outside veranda Tara couldn't drag her eyes from the vista. 'I can't believe I didn't bring a camera.'

'Neither can I.' But Nick wasn't looking over the rail as he spoke.

She pointed to the postcard village in the distance. 'So is that Positano?'

'Yep. Pretty place, great shops.' He didn't glance at it. Just watched her as if trying to work something out that puzzled him. Tara screwed up her face at him. 'Stop it.'

He blinked, shook his head and turned his attention to the seascape. 'Sorry. I was somewhere else.'

Just the sort of thing Vander would say. She winced. Well, that wasn't very flattering, she thought perversely, and now she wished he'd look at her again. How contrary could you get? She'd never been any good at this girl-boy thing.

Nick's mind surely was somewhere else. Vivid visions of some of the activities they could do there, like get a room, spend the day there, distracted him and he glanced down at the menu and tried to concentrate. 'We'll go down to Positano after lunch and maybe catch a ferry across to Capri. It's a beautiful trip. Or at least see some boats come in if we run out of time.'

Her beautiful eyes narrowed and he knew, no idea how, what she was thinking. Conscientious and paranoid they'd be late back. She'd brought it up on the car already on the way here. He wished he hadn't mentioned the word 'late'.

'What time do we need to leave?'

'Relax if you can.' He put his hand over her hers and squeezed it. She tensed and he smiled ruefully. Well, that hadn't worked. 'I'm a responsible guy and I'd want to be back in Amalfi by three to give us enough leeway. I get the impression you don't want to miss the ship on our first shore excursion.'

Her eyes widened with distress and he cursed himself for his flip reply.

'There's no chance of that, is there?' She began to look seriously worried and he backpedalled to make up lost ground.

He'd never been so conscious of a woman's moods. So concerned that she would worry. 'We'll give ourselves loads of time.'

She glanced at her watch again and he lifted his hand and pressed her arm back to the table. 'It's okay. Enjoy the view. Life is short.'

'Family saying?'

'My saying.'

Tara drew a breath and forced her eyes to the horizon. Once there it was hard to look away. She really needed to stop being so tense. Nick had done all this before and she was supposed to be having F.U.N.

She savoured the calamari, adored the insalata Caprese, and sipped a limoncello, the lemon liqueur made by Nick's uncle from their own lemon orchard. By the time they'd finished their lunch and waved goodbye to Nick's aunt she was feeling much more relaxed.

So relaxed that she didn't even blink when they proceeded past cliff-hugging mansions and through mountain tunnels and over bridges with pylons planted hundreds of feet below in the rock. At last they drove down the mountain into the postcard-perfect Positano with its colourful buildings and deckchair-strewn beaches.

The shops were even more enticing than those in Amalfi but Tara was eager to swim in the salty Mediterranean. Cool her cheeks and her thoughts because Nick was making her smile and laugh more than she could remember ever smiling and laughing.

Nick decided the day was going well and was looking ahead to the new bikini he hadn't been allowed to see, but he didn't say that to Tara. Instead he indulged her, hired a change shed, and waited with bated breath for her to reappear.

CHAPTER SIX

Nick whistled. It had been worth the wait.

Tara tugged at the side of the bikini bra as she opened the door of the change shed and Nick chewed hard on his lip so he didn't smile.

'I think I must have picked up the wrong one. Is this bikini too small?' Tugging the sides did incredible things to the front of the small scrap of material but he wasn't saying anything that would jeopardise the beauty of the moment.

'No. It's fine.' He forced himself to turn and glance at the inviting blue of the Mediterranean. He'd need a cool shower soon if they didn't get in. 'Looks good. Ready?'

He risked another look. A tiny, unconvinced frown marred her brow, but as far as he was concerned she looked hot. Maybe too hot. He glanced around to see who else was looking. The fact that she could do with a few more pounds just made him want to hug her more. She still did a delightful job of filling out the swimwear.

Tara tugged again at the edge of the bra cup and Nick smiled at her. 'Leave it. You look gorgeous. Now, come into the water before I have to carry you in there just so I can get my hands on you.'

She froze, glanced at him, and to his relief began to giggle. He decided she had a seriously cute laugh. 'I won't need you. I hear the water round here is especially buoyant.'

He enjoyed the view some more and decided now was the time to submerge. Once in the water he felt way more relaxed and the angle was good for watching Tara edge in gingerly across the pebbles.

'Don't they have sand at the beach in Italy?'

He grinned. 'Lots of volcanoes make lots of pebbled beaches.'

She sank under the water on her back. As she took the weight off her feet and savoured the coolness of the water he watched her lips part in a blissful sigh and tried not to stare at her breasts poking up. 'Oh, my.'

He remembered the last time she'd said that. He sank lower in the water. Her little feet floated to the surface and she lay there suspended without effort.

Her eyes shut. 'This is so cool.'

'You mean the temperature or the fact that you can float without trying?'

'Both.' She sighed again and drifted with her lashes on her cheeks, which meant he could drink in the sight of her to his heart's content. 'The sea is glorious. To think I've watched it for days and I've only just touched it.'

Nick drifted closer until he could brush her hand. 'Hmm. I feel the same.'

She opened her eyes lazily and paddled with her hands until she bumped into his chest. 'Oops. Sorry.'

'Don't be.' His hands captured her shoulders and pulled her slowly into his chest so that she was anchored on his lap in the water. 'I'm a sea god. You have to pay a tax when you bump into me.'

She closed one eye. 'Well, I'm a mermaid. Do you have any idea how dangerous I am?'

Oh, yes. She was dangerous all right, much more than a woman who knew the rules, but he still turned her to face him.

'I laugh at danger,' he said, and she giggled again.

So he kissed her, which was what he'd wanted to do since she'd met him at the gangplank this morning. Time stood still and her skin felt like silk under the water as she twined her arms around his neck.

When she returned his kiss with such an innocent ardour it tore at his heart and tightened his chest. He couldn't remember when it had been like this. Holding Tara was precious, yet terrifying, and some of that fear was residual warning of becoming too fond of someone.

Of the risks that he didn't take or believe in. His friends would roll around on the floor at the suave Nick mentally sweating like a nervous teenager at where to put his hands.

The kiss dissolved into a hot and lustful memory and she snuggled into him with ridiculous faith that she was safe, and he felt his chest swell at her trust. He vowed to earn it, though he wasn't sure why this was a necessary part now when it wasn't usually, and he worried at the thought of the one tiny untruth between them.

His fingers, of their own volition, began to gently knead her shoulders, gently massage her neck and the tightness within. To his further discomfort the slide of his hand across her skin was torture, especially when she purred and stretched under his fingers like a satisfied kitten.

He felt his lips curve with the warmth of satisfaction as knots softened and dissolved the more he stroked until he closed his eyes, stroking her by an unknown instinct, time forgotten, and she was soft as liquid in his arms, as if they had both become one with the waves lapping against them.

'Mmm. Your skin.'

He dropped a kiss and she sighed into him just as a family arrived to swim.

They both opened their eyes, saw the tiny baby cradled in his father's arms, helpless and mewling, and she stiffened in his arms. He felt the tension soak into her like ink into chalk as she slid out of his arms.

When she turned to face him, despite the smile on her face, the darkness of memories in her eyes made him want to hug her to him but she didn't give him the chance.

'I think I'll get out. Let's go down to the wharf, see the ferries come in. And I want to look at one of those shops I saw that only sell white clothes.'

That forced bright voice and a protective wall back

in place around her was so high and strong he knew he wasn't getting back in there for a while.

'Sure.' He stood up and faced the shore. 'Maybe we'll manage one more swim before we go.'

'You're on.' She waded from the water and he watched her tread gingerly across the pebbled beach.

He wished. But he'd rally and maybe that was half the draw. Capturing and connecting with a reluctant mermaid. He tried not to listen to the warning voice that wondered if it was more than that.

In the end the afternoon passed as a series of cameo moments of a beautiful woman and gorgeous surroundings and lots of promise. Nick didn't want it to end but he knew it had to.

Tara kept going back in her mind to that drugged relaxation when Nick had massaged her shoulders in the water. His gentle strength had miraculously soothed months of neck tension and shoulder aches and there in the water she'd felt like she'd stepped into a fantasy resort with her very own gigolo.

Before she'd seen the baby. The sight should have made her smile, any normal woman would have, but, no, she had plunged back into darkness, it had all come back and she wondered if the memories would ever go so she could be the sort of woman a man would want to stay with.

She glanced to the horizon where islands were dotted below the blue sky and the day was drawing to an end. For the last few hours she'd almost banished the last of the spectres that had tried to ruin her morning with Nick.

Briefly reality surfaced as they sat next to each other on sun loungers and she said, 'You sure we have enough time to get back to the ship?'

'Tons.'

Tara sighed and rested back in the chair. She did trust him. 'If you say so.'

Two hours later Tara glanced anxiously at her watch as they slowed to a halt. This was taking too long. She didn't care how much fun they'd had or how beautiful the beaches were. She'd never been late for work in her life, responsible doctors weren't, and she'd bet this irresponsible cocktail waiter thrived on it.

Nick could feel the waves of distress beating across the space between them in the car like heat waves across the sand they'd not long left. He had factored in extra time but obviously something was up as they rolled to a stop.

Because of the winding road he couldn't tell if the trouble was a hundred yards ahead or ten miles.

He pulled on the handbrake and turned to face her. After a second of observation he lowered his voice in the face of her turmoil. 'I'm just going to talk to the bus driver behind us. He'll have spoken to other drivers on his mobile and might know why we've stopped.'

She nodded and turned to look out her window. Nick winced and opened his door. She was such a serious little thing and he hoped they did make it back in time because he doubted she'd trust him in a hurry again if he let her down here.

'*Buon giorno,*' he said as he leant against the side of the bus at the driver's window. After a thirty-second conversation he nodded and sprinted back to the car.

'A motorcyclist and his girlfriend have come off his bike around the next corner. Come on. We're needed.'

He saw her swallow. 'Oh. A young woman?'

He saw the panic before she clamped down on it, glanced ahead and then back. 'Look. You don't have to come. Seriously. They'd have it in hand and I can do the muscle bits.'

Not the right thing to say because he saw her stiffen her shoulders. 'Don't be ridiculous. Of course a doctor can help. At least I'm used to dealing without equipment.'

Tara pushed back the dread that had hit her out of nowhere. She'd let herself relax today. Let down her guard. Fool. Of course death and disaster followed her. Now she needed to kick herself into gear and do what she always did. Toughen up. Cope. Work. Save.

The heat beat off the black tarmac of the road as she rounded the bend and the first thing she saw was the wheel of the motorbike poking out from under the bus.

As she walked swiftly towards it she could make out the pale faces of the passengers staring out the window and in some distant space in her mind she hoped none of them had a heart condition.

But her eyes were on the girl and suddenly she was back in the Sudan. The tang of blood thick in the air, the beat of fear and shock and urgency from those around, and over all the slowing of time as someone's life drained away.

The young woman lay on her back on a spine board ready to move to the waiting ambulance with her rounded belly pointing to the sky and her pretty white shirt damply crimson.

For a second Tara's mind recoiled at the farce she would be safe from losing mothers and babies.

The young woman's terrified eyes were fixed on the anxious female ambulance officer who bent over her as she attempted to tape a line for urgent replacement fluids.

Tara crossed swiftly with Nick beside her and they spoke simultaneously. 'Pregnant. Tilt the uterus.'

They looked at each other and Nick broke into Italian as they bent down, and as soon as the paramedic understood, Tara supported the neck brace as Nick and the paramedic tilted the board to shift the weight of the heavy uterus to the side off the young woman's major blood vessels.

As they repositioned the woman he explained to the paramedic that while on her back the weight of the baby would be dangerously slowing the mother's reduced blood flow to her heart and brain. The woman's thin backpack was beside her and he packed it in under the board on the right side as Tara supported her, but just as they did so their patient gasped once and then her eyes glazed.

Tara blinked. She'd seen this too many times when a

heart stopped, and unless they could give a huge trans-
fusion this woman and her baby would die, regardless
of how good the bag ventilation and cardiac massage
the paramedics had begun was.

She'd performed too many of these crash Caesareans
over the last two years at cardiac arrest but the concept remained the same. Thirty per cent of the injured
mother's blood volume was being diverted to the pla-
centa and the baby and was taking from her vital or-
gans. With not enough blood to go around, they would
both die. They had four minutes for the baby without
maternal circulation.

She snapped the order at Nick. 'Find a scalpel and
big sponges in case they can't get her heart going in
time. And get people here to face the other way and
form a human screen.' She turned back and began to
open the buttons to the woman's chest around the working paramedics until Nick could return, and she prayed
she wouldn't have to do what was rapidly becoming the
patient's last hope.

Nick understood immediately. He knew of doctors
who had been faced with difficult decisions and had
acted. He admired them. Once he might have been one,
but not now. Caesarean on a dead or dying woman. No
theatre operating staff or sterile conditions. But who
cared about germs if the patient was dead? Infection
could be treated later—death couldn't.

No anaesthetic but, then, the woman was deeply unconscious, technically dead as her heart wasn't beating

by itself from the lack of blood. Which ironically helped with blood loss from the splash-and-slash surgery.

The most direct route to the baby was down the midline of the mother, scoop baby out before it too died from lack of circulation, pack the uterus with sponges to stop bleeding and resume cardiac massage more efficiently with the patient now flat on her back again.

Great theory if you had the courage, Nick thought savagely as he fired orders at the paramedics. Why couldn't he speak up and tell Tara he knew what she was thinking and it was a good idea?

He flicked his medical identification, and hurried back to Tara with the minimal equipment. Brave strategy—but he'd never seen a good outcome. She didn't let that frighten her. He thrust sterile gloves at her. 'Please put the gloves on.'

'Don't worry. Where I've been working we're very careful about protection.' She donned them swiftly and took the scalpel. He saw her close her eyes briefly and then she opened them and narrowed her gaze.

Nick watched in awe as the fastest and boldest operative retrieval he'd ever seen in his life was performed by this slip of a woman he hadn't realised possessed such single-minded determination.

'Nearly there. Are you right with the baby?' she said tersely.

He'd have to be. He wouldn't let her down. Tara clamped and cut the cord and Nick held out his gloved hands covered by a small rug retrieved from the ambulance.

The baby girl was white and floppy and Nick took her and rubbed her little face and chest, and to his delight she whimpered feebly and even began to flex her legs weakly as he placed the small resus bag over her tiny mouth and nose. He puffed three breaths from the bag through the mask and watched the little chest rise.

Incredibly the baby began to cry, then with increasing loudness she wailed, and Nick felt the sting of unfamiliar tears burn in his throat. He hadn't even cried when his parents had died.

He looked across at Tara and they shared a searing moment of joint relief before Tara turned back to the mother. In some corner of his mind he wouldn't have been surprised to see tears in Tara's eyes but there were none. Her face stayed frozen with determination to save this woman.

'Baby's okay,' he said unnecessarily, and then a bossy grandmother pushed through the throng. 'Give to me. I am nurse. Save the mother.'

Nick nodded, handed the squirming baby over to competent arms and turned back to Tara. 'Removing tilt now.' Then he changed places with the flagging paramedic, who'd been doing cardiac massage grimly throughout the operation, her stunned eyes incredulously trying not to watch the macabre events.

'I've found the torn femoral artery and I'm tying it off now,' Tara said. 'They can fix it later.'

Within a minute, with the mother's blood supply now bypassing the uterus, there was enough blood to fill her heart's chambers and help the cardiac massage achieve its goal of restarting the heart.

Nick saw the flicker of a beat in her neck and the paramedic listened quickly with the stethoscope and nodded. 'Got a pulse,' Nick said to Tara.

Tara sank back as she packed the wound with the last sponge. 'Right. Let's load and go. They can stitch her up at the hospital if she makes it.' She glanced at Nick, still totally focused. 'I'll go with her—you follow.'

Nick looked then he nodded. One of them had to go and Tara needed to see this through, but he'd be there for her at the door of the hospital.

All the way there as he followed the ambulance his heart beat with post-adrenalin rush and a sizzle of pride in Tara. She'd been amazing. Incredible. He'd never forget her slight body performing rapid surgery under the most primitive conditions.

Her actions shook his conception of self. Would he have coped as well if he'd had to call it?

Should he be out there learning more and not coasting like he was? Avoiding the difficult decisions by flying in and out. Doing stints on cruise ships. Sure, he stepped into different short-staffed situations and managed to be the one they wanted back next time, but he hadn't stretched himself like Tara had stretched herself.

Early in his career, not long after his parents had died, the one time he'd become involved and stuck his neck out, he'd almost left it too late. Told himself his suspicions were ungrounded, because the truth was too horrific for a playboy to grasp, and had almost caused

the death of a child. Since then he'd shied away from
responsibility because he still hadn't forgiven himself
for that. Didn't deserve forgiveness.

But Tara made him want to be more and he'd never
felt that before today. Never considered forgiving himself and stepping up to the plate again.

An hour later, he met her at the entry to Emergency
and helped her climb wearily into their hire car. He
closed her door and walked swiftly around to the other
side. When he was back at the wheel he looked across
and her thick lashes were resting on her cheeks again
but in repose it was a different face from the one in the
water that day.

Lines of strain and dark shadows under her eyes
proclaimed the toll that had been taken. 'You okay?'

Her lashes lifted. 'A day with a difference.' She
sighed and then grimaced. 'But then again not very
different from last week.'

Nick turned the key in the ignition. 'When I spoke
to the nurse she said the baby is perfect. Mum is still
critical.'

She made no move to do up her seat belt and Nick
glanced at her unfocused gaze as she stared at the am-
bulances parked in front of them. He leaned across and
buckled her belt.

'You did well, Tara. We'll be back at the ship soon.'
She did that blinking thing with her eyes that he was beginning to recognise was Tara marshalling her thoughts,
cute in a getting-to-know-her kind of way, and turned
her head to face him.

'So were you. Amazing.' She shook her head, then frowned as if she was trying to work out what niggled. 'Too amazing?'

It certainly wasn't the time now for coming clean. 'I wasn't the one who did a crash Caesarean on the side of the road.'

She winced. 'Another memory to add to the batch—but I must admit I've done a few in my time.' She sighed. 'I just want to sleep now the panic is over.'

'Then sleep. We won't be back at the ship for an hour or more. Plenty of time for a nap.'

'That's not very polite of me.' She almost smiled. 'Were we on a date or was that in another century?'

'Any of my dates who do surgery while we're out is allowed to rest. Close your eyes.'

So she did but Tara had no thought that she would really go to sleep.

When she woke up her mouth was dry and she hoped to heck she hadn't been dribbling because her neck was cricked from drooping.

Nick pulled onto the wharf and to her relief the ship was still there. They hadn't missed it but suddenly it wasn't so overwhelmingly important. But maybe she'd think twice before she rushed to go on a car tour again.

Nick opened her door and helped her out before he handed the keys over to a young man who'd hurried over. One of the officers at the bottom of the gangway waved to hurry them up.

Tara quickened her pace. 'Will we get into trouble for being late?'

Nick smiled. 'I think the excuse makes up for it.'

Still she frowned. 'I should see Wilhelm and tell him I'm back.'

Nick almost laughed out loud. She didn't get it. They both looked like they'd been in a massacre. 'I'd have a shower first, Tara.'

Tara glanced down at her blood-speckled shorts. Then she looked at him. He was smiling but there were some suspicious marks on him too and she thought again of all he'd seen today. Pretty horrific for a cocktail waiter. The tears in his eyes when the baby had cried. Lucky guy.

Her mind shifted. And the way he'd dominated the CPR and resuscitated the baby. Her brow puckered and she opened her mouth to ask but they'd reached the gangway.

'Go. I have to get scrubbed and check my staff. We'll meet later.'

Then he was gone and she stared thoughtfully after him. 'Scrubbed?' Odd choice of words. There was more here, she mused in sudden exhaustion as she began to climb the stairs. A passenger looked at her strangely as she passed and she picked up her pace.

Nick was right. So much had happened. She needed a shower. And maybe a long cool drink to think about the last eight hours and the man she'd shared them with.

CHAPTER SEVEN

WHEN Tara walked into the mess that night there was rumble of chairs being pushed out and everyone stood up and applauded.

She frowned, turned and glanced over her shoulder to see who else had come in but then the captain came across with a huge bouquet of flowers and shook her hand.

'It is for you. This applause. For your amazing skill today and the brilliant outcome.'

It took a moment to sink in. Then all she could think of was that she'd kill Nick for telling and she glanced around until she found him. He was shaking his head.

Something must have shown on her face because the captain chuckled. 'It is not Mr Fender's fault. I have had the girl's parents on the telephone. They ordered the flowers and send their gratitude for saving their daughter and grandchild's lives.'

'Oh. Thank you.' That meant their patient was still okay. Tara felt relief well inside her and she smiled. She'd been going to call but had decided that tomorrow would be a better indication of the woman's stability. 'So I'm not in trouble for being back late?'

The captain shook his head solemnly, tongue in cheek. 'This one time we will forgive you both.'

Her gaze flicked across to Nick, standing beside Wilhelm, and she realised these two were friends. Wilhelm said something to tease Nick and Nick punched Wilhelm's arm. Good friends?

A suspicion began to form in her mind and the events of today and Nick's confident behaviour in the medical crisis meant that suddenly the crazy idea in her head wasn't a suspicion but blinding truth.

She was about to confirm that with the captain when Nick appeared at her side. 'May I borrow the good doctor, sir?'

The captain waved them away good-naturedly. 'Off you go.'

Tara opened her mouth but before the words tumbled out Nick had steered her to the corner of the room. 'You've guessed my secret?'

He glanced firmly towards the door. Maybe a bit of privacy wouldn't be a bad idea. She didn't know why she was so angry, shattered even, but maybe blurting it out while she was the centre of attention would be a little indiscreet.

Nick read her mind as usual. 'I know you have questions and I'll give my reasons, but please remember I'm not working as a doctor on this cruise.'

She narrowed her eyes at him, nodded and headed

for the door. 'I think I'm too angry to eat right now anyway.'

The breeze off the ocean as she hit the deck was a welcome relief to the heat in her cheeks and she didn't stop at the first rail. Nick caught up and kept pace with her easily as she began to stride towards the bow of the ship.

He glanced down at her. 'I'm sorry.'

She continued to stare straight ahead and walk at a clipping pace. 'That's fine, then.'

He kept beside her. Wondered if she was really trying to walk away from him. 'Never picked you for sarcasm, Tara.'

She stopped. Drilled him with two hard toffee eyes. 'And yet I wondered if you were a liar!'

So she did have a hard streak inside. He guessed she'd have to be or she'd never have survived that long. He liked the idea, though he wasn't sure why, then bit back a smile because if he laughed he'd be really dead. 'Nasty.'

When she looked like taking off again he held up his hand. 'Stop. For a minute. Then you can walk away if you want and I won't follow you.'

She crossed her arms. Not the best listening pose he'd seen but he guessed he deserved it.

Here goes. 'I'm here to substitute for my youngest sister, who fell ill at the last moment. The bar manager gig is her job, a break after med school. And I was a cocktail waiter many moons ago on board the sister ship to this.'

She raised her brows. 'Before med school?'

He sort of nodded. 'Well, after med school. After my parents died I took a break from medicine. I suggested Kiki have one too because I thought she'd lost her cute chuckle. She's got a great one. Usually.'

'What's wrong with your sister?' It was as if she needed to catch him out again.

'Pneumonia.' He hoped she could see there was no hesitation. 'She hid it until the last, which was why there was such a rush to replace her.'

Another toffee glance. 'Aren't you worried about her?'

'My eldest sister is a respiratory physician. She's with her.'

'Close-knit family. All doctors.' Tara would have loved to have sisters. Or even a brother who cared. One who thought she had a cute chuckle. Or maybe parents who cared. She could feel herself soften towards him and it made her cross again. He had lied to her.

She started to walk on but he could come if he wanted to keep up. 'That doesn't excuse you saying you were good at first aid. Not telling me the truth. I feel like a fool.'

He stopped and she slowed. 'I never intended you to feel that way.' She looked back at him.

'Well, you did.'

'I'm sorry.' He caught up. 'You were in the zone at the accident, you have more experience than me at crash Caesareans, so I was happy to be back-up and explain later when less important things were going on.'

He crinkled his eyes at her. That was a play. She was sure of it. Shame it worked. 'You said you liked the frivolous cocktail waiter. I didn't think I could stay light and frothy if I was an MD in your eyes.'

There might be just a hint of truth in that. 'So you admit you were dishonest for a reason.'

He raised his brows. 'I got the message you didn't want a constant reminder of what you'd been doing for the last two years.' She couldn't dispute that.

He shrugged but there was a wicked glint in his dark eyes that almost made her smile. 'I was happy to help you relax.'

'Oh. Relax. Is that what we were doing?'

He shrugged and his exposure to Italian charm was obvious. 'Sì.'

'Well, I haven't forgiven you.'

'Early days yet. It's more important you accept my apology.'

She screwed her face up at him. Why was she so cross anyway? Because he was a doctor or because he wasn't a cocktail waiter?

Or was she scared because they did have more in common that she'd planned? Because the man who'd worked beside her today occupied a whole lot more of her thoughts than she was comfortable with, and this trip was about rebuilding her confidence in society, not finding new angst.

'So are you still tired or should we sneak up and grab a couple of deckchairs and check out the movie?'

That sounded so brainless and attractive. She was

in no rush to lie on her bed and relive today's events in gory detail, and she had the idea he knew that. See, she shouldn't be second guessing his intentions all the time. Why couldn't she just breeze along and not worry about the what-ifs and subtext? Mentally she folded her arms. She wasn't going to! 'Deckchairs under the stars with checked blankets?'

'One each.' Snapshot of Nick wearing virtue. She couldn't help but smile. He was the guy for amusement all right.

'Do you know what's on?'

'*Titanic*?' He pulled a serious face. 'Could be good practice.'

She so didn't believe him. She was learning. 'Very funny.'

He grinned. 'I think it's a romantic comedy.' He held out his hand suggestively.

She tucked her hand into her side and ignored his offer. She ticked the conditions off on her fingers. 'My own blanket, if you can guarantee no blood, no guts, no death. I'm in.'

The movie hadn't started when they arrived, rows of tucked-up passengers munched on popcorn as they lay back and watched the big screen on the top deck. The ocean sloshed against the hull seventeen floors below, the stars shone above, and rows of lanterns beside the huge screen gave it a carnival feel.

The Casablanca Bar was doing a roaring trade in Irish coffee and hot toddies and after he'd settled her

Nick went across and returned with two cappuccinos and a bag of popcorn.

He wanted to feed her again. When he'd put their mugs down on the little tables he nudged his chair closer to hers. He avoided her eyes and wasn't quite whistling innocently.

He could tell Tara was pretending not to notice behind a wall of indifference but he'd bet her mouth ached from trying not to smile.

Insidiously, he could almost see the stress from the day begin to fade away, even as the introductory credits faded away from the screen.

Nick settled beside her and offered her popcorn from a striped yellow bag he kept hold of. Okay, he was like a big kid, but he wanted her to lean over him. As if he'd said, *Mine*.

She reached and he drew it towards him, she leaned over further and he watched her frown and narrow her eyes at him. She was getting cross.

She sat back. 'Did you have to pay for the popcorn?'

'Nope. It's free.'

'So why didn't you get two?' More glaring and he struggled to keep his smile tucked behind his teeth.

'Because I'm a control freak. Did I tell you that?' The grin escaped. 'Besides, if I got two you wouldn't have to lean over and get some. Think what I would have missed out on.'

'I'll get my own.' She went to stand and he put out his hand to stop her. She avoided his touch because she knew he was laughing. That was a shame. Now he felt bad.

'Seriously, I don't eat popcorn. This is yours.' And he gave it to her with a flourish until she smiled back.

She opened her mouth to say something but he turned to her with a mock admonishing finger. 'Shh. The movie's starting.'

She narrowed her eyes at him and subsided, and he could tell she'd totally forgotten about the stresses of the afternoon.

Tara sighed and had to admit he amused her in an annoying way. Finally she was learning not to take him seriously. Something she'd never practised with Vander. Everything had been serious with him and she wondered why she hadn't seen that before she'd married him.

By the third mouthful of popcorn she'd recovered her good humour and was absorbed in the film.

Tara really enjoyed the movie. Sitting here with Nick was companionable and low key. She didn't have to do anything or be anyone. Just another humped blanket in the dark. Finally. It was amazing how good that felt.

When Nick stopped teasing she really did relax. And there wasn't a drop of blood or hint of violence in the whole ninety minutes, as he'd promised. Or any sinking ships.

Watching a movie with Nick was a hoot. When an unexpected or pivotal moment came, he'd glance across at her as if to check she was enjoying it, she'd glance back and smile. Satisfied mutual enjoyment was there and they'd move on to the next scene.

When she laughed, he'd look across and smile with what looked like real pleasure, and Tara didn't get why he cared but it warmed her that he did. It was the most relaxed she'd ever been, watching a movie with someone. Her parents had thought television an unnecessary evil and she'd been pushed towards reading. In fact, she couldn't really remember the last time she'd watched a movie with someone who was in tune with her like this.

Towards the final scenes Tara knew she didn't want it to end. This whole ambient slice of time. This bubble of fantasy after the horrors of the day. They'd go soon. And Nick would help her up, they'd fold their blankets and she'd trot off to her lonely cabin and lie awake.

Her mood flattened and she wondered why a guy like Nick would want to hang with someone damaged like her anyway.

The hero kissed the heroine and they both shone with the promise of new life together. She could hear the lady next to them sniffing, and someone behind her blew her nose, and Tara just wanted to get out of there before the credits rolled and she had to think again why it was she could never cry. She couldn't even cry when someone was happy, let alone when someone died.

That was never going to happen to her. Too many moments like this and she'd be just setting herself up for a fall. She needed to keep her eye on reality.

Six months recuperating and she'd go back. Take up

where she'd left off. A life-saving machine meeting a need someone had to meet.

That's what Vander would have wanted. What she was good at. What her parents would have anticipated for her. She tried to imagine her husband's face but his features were much harder to remember than she expected. She could remember promising she'd keep up his work as he died, though, and she tried not to sigh. Already she knew it was going to be hard to go back.

For some stupid reason she wished she could just explode into noisy sobs.

Enough angst. She faked a yawn and thrust the yellow striped bag at him. 'Sorry, Nick. I'm out of here or I'll fall asleep.' As she looked at him the weariness really caught up with her and she could feel herself droop.

Nick had been thinking of taking Tara's hand for a while now, in fact, but he'd been waiting for the schmoozy part of the film because she could be dangerous to push too quickly. Then they could walk back to her cabin hand in hand and who knew where that might lead?

He'd blown that one well and truly. Not something he could remember doing for a while. He couldn't quite grasp she'd gone before he could even stand up.

Funny how sitting here in the dark, alone, he could remember in vivid detail the feel of her hand in his earlier today. Something simple like that should not have been so memorable, or so desirable.

He watched her walk away, knowing there was no

use following, glanced at her empty seat and his hand holding the popcorn.

Unpredictable. Her middle name.

Nick didn't sleep well. He couldn't get the picture of Tara's exhaustion as she'd walked away from him out of his mind. Or the fact that he had been responsible for putting her in the position they'd stumbled on.

He understood why she'd been angry he'd kept his medical background a secret and he'd surprised himself how much it mattered she forgive him for a stupid lie he'd so carelessly started.

Why had he started that? Random bad choice or un-adulterated deceit to get into her good graces? Maybe he wasn't such a nice guy after all when he wanted something badly.

The thing was, it was turning out he'd never felt like this before and that came with a whole boatload of concerns. Like he needed to remember that a good time didn't equate with happily-ever-after. Ever.

The weariness in Tara's face should not haunt him and he shouldn't blame himself for making it worse for her. Bringing it all back.

He should have listened to instinct and started with a small morning trip instead of the full day extravaganza he'd planned like the big show-off he was. Then they wouldn't have been anywhere near the scene of the drama.

But then the young mother and her baby would most certainly have died. No way could he wish that.

And there were other things he couldn't wish away.

Memories of Tara's golden eyes gazing raptly from their lunch table at Praiano, her mouth laughing at him from the waves at Positano, and her hand in his as they'd strolled the streets of Amalfi.

Nope, wouldn't give that away either.

It seriously shouldn't have mattered that much if his profession had alienated her.

And why the big rush to show her off to his aunt, or show those places so special to him on the Amalfi coast to Tara? He'd never felt the need to share that with anyone except his sisters, let alone a first date.

What the hell was he thinking? Longer term? Life term? For a woman he'd known a few days who only wanted superficial escape from the horrors of her past? Before she went back?

What if he'd been lying to himself all this time and had been secretly longing to find his deeper soul mate. He laughed out loud and it sounded way too bitter even to him. He'd long ago decided he had no faith in soul mates.

Lord, no. Next he'd be fantasising about baby brunettes and breastfeeding in the family home. That definitely wasn't his style. He wasn't going there and the best way of making sure of that was to steer clear of the whole intense relationship thing like the plague.

To be sensible, today needed to be the first day of avoidance week for him.

So back to happy-clappy flirting in non-specific directions. For safety's sake maybe that should be in directions that pointed anywhere but at the ship's hospital and its junior doctor.

He should listen to his own advice. And just let it all flow. Life was too short to wallow in a might-have-been relationship. Enjoy the view—but don't touch it. Don't touch Tara.

In the corner of his mind a little voice whispered so quietly he barely noticed. The voice wondered what her husband had been like.

The night stretched ahead of him and hopefully the crew's bar would be extra-busy because he missed her on hour one of avoidance week.

At Sea

The next morning Tara decided dodging Nick was a great idea because a fling wasn't a fling when it started to take over your life. When your life started to grow tendrils of excitement with each new facet you discovered of the flingee. That sounded like an obsession.

Or if you couldn't clearly remember your late husband's face.

Of course, avoiding Nick would prove less difficult if the darned man would stop appearing in her dreams. Surely Technicolor reverie was not the only reason she'd woken up with a smile on her face that morning.

The little voice went on to suggest dreams of a tanned and muscular cocktail waiter were immeasurably better than nightmares of the medical dramas and disasters of the last two years, but the jury was out on that idea too.

The cruise only lasted another week and no way was she getting close enough to expose her seeping wounds or open her dark soul for Nick's perusal. Caring involved way too many emotions. She still had such a rock of collected grief and a bitter well of anger from the last two years that it was a wonder she could drag her feet, carrying the weight.

Work. Work would keep her mind where it should be, pleasantly busy, not too close to her patients so she wouldn't get involved, pleasantly distant from her work colleagues so they wouldn't ask about her past or start a discussion about the crash Caesarean at the side of the road that had brought it all back just when she'd been getting some perspective.

For the rest of her time off she would avoid the pool deck and bars. And Nick. That would help.

Tara had a late start today and somehow at breakfast got dragged into auditions by the beauty girls for the final-night crew pageant. She suspected she still looked a fright, though, because one of the girls in the beauty spa she'd treated for a stomach bug/hangover offered a free beauty treatment and under protest Tara now sported new designer eyebrows and a sultry lash tint.

Every time she passed a mirror she couldn't help glancing at the stranger she saw and even though the last thing she wanted to do was appear on stage, even she could see her face was filling out, the lines of strain were easing and there was a new lightness in her step that she hadn't felt for a long time.

It was only a spotlight dance and she could manage that. She'd once been a good dancer but Vander had had no time for frivolous things like dancing or parties.

She was beginning to think that if they'd structured in some down time, maybe the rest of the time in the camp would have been more balanced. Pretty strange that it had taken a cocktail waiter to show her that.

CHAPTER EIGHT

ONE of Nick's bar staff, George, had burned his hand on the cappuccino machine and even though Nick hadn't started work yet he accompanied him down to the sick bay to assure himself George got there safely. Seemed the responsible thing to do—him being manager.

Nick glanced around the waiting room as they waited, peered behind the desk to see who was in the obs ward and leaned back nonchalantly when Marie arrived to log the new patient.

The door to the consulting room opened and he started to smile but it dimmed a little when Wilhelm appeared to direct the barman into his office. His friend raised his eyebrows at Nick as he hovered, lifted his hand in a sardonic wave, and when Nick continued to stand there he came out.

'She's not here.' Wilhelm shrugged and pretended his ignorance of Tara's whereabouts. 'Not due for another couple of hours.' He lowered his voice.

'You sure she's for you? Don't know if she's your party girl, Nick. Very serious, aloof, you sure you guys are from the same planet? I wouldn't like to see her hurt.'

Since when was Wilhem Tara's new protector? Nick avoided Will's eyes. He'd already seen a side different from serious and aloof. Heck, he'd had her giggling in her seat of the little sports car, before they'd been held up in the traffic.

'She has some issues. But you're right. I don't want to add to them.' He shrugged. 'Just wanted to make sure she's okay after yesterday.'

'Seemed fine when she dropped in for a minute this morning.'

'So she's been in?'

Wilhelm tapped his head as if it all suddenly came back. 'Gone to the crew auditions, I think.'

'Just remembered that, did you?'

'Need to get rid of you so I can do my work.' Wilhelm raised his brows as if to say, *So why are you still here?*

'Thanks.' Nick moved to the door and crossed to the stairway. A sudden excess of energy had him jogging up them two at a time to the next level, where he could cross to the cavernous stage theatre.

They'd been nagging him all week to do a baritone spotlight at the crew pageant and at the time he hadn't been in the mood but the cruise director had hinted about setting an example to his staff and finally he'd agreed. So he had the excuse.

To his delight the first person he saw there was Tara, under her own spotlight on the stage, though less delightful was that she was dancing with Miko, Nick's counterpart on the restaurant side and the suavest man on the ship. They were leaning together to the strains of a sexy salsa.

Tara yelped and the music halted. Miko stepped back off her foot with an apologetic shuffle while Tara rubbed her toes. Even better, as far as Nick was concerned, one of the directors came across and pointed the senior catering officer to the phone. They all knew what that meant.

Nick vaulted over the seats in front of him and disappeared up the side steps into the wings before Tara had a chance to back away. So much for avoidance—it was more like a golden opportunity and he couldn't have stopped his forward momentum if he'd tried.

'I'll take over until Miko comes back,' Nick said nonchalantly as he walked across the stage. The musical director nodded and started the music again.

Nick loved to salsa. He loved it even more with Tara, even if she was still a little stiff in his arms, but she couldn't hide her relief she'd found someone she could dance with.

'Miko's normally a pretty good dancer,' Nick said, to open the conversation.

She raised her eyebrows and he noticed how her eyes seemed bigger and darker. Something was different.

'I heard that.' She shrugged. 'It's probably me. He's a bit macho.' She mimicked, '"I vill lead this time."' She shrugged. 'I kept getting the steps wrong and I don't like being told what to do. Just couldn't get his rhythm.'

He was happy with that, Nick thought with an internal smile. 'Imagine you not taking orders.' That was supposed to have come out under his breath and Nick glanced again at her face to see if she'd heard.

The brows went up again and he got the change. New and darker brows. He loved the way women did things like that. No way would he allow someone to reef out his facial hairs for the sake of fashion but she looked even more divine now.

His hands remembered her from when they'd been in the water yesterday as his fingers slid down her arm. Like toffee-coloured silk.

'And whose rhythm am I supposed to get?' she said.

They bumped hips perfectly in time as long as he steered decisively and she agreed to be directed. It seemed she did.

They both knew she fitted into his embrace like a missing link and floated across the stage in unison because she let him lead.

'You tell me.' He spun her away and back again, and she tilted her neck and smiled.

'Nope. Your head will swell again.'

The music came to an end and reluctantly their hands parted. The musical director came across and grinned at them. 'Guess that's a wrap.' She winked at Nick. 'You want her on stage while you sing to her too?'

Tara's hands still tingled from touching Nick but at that suggestion she looked up. If she wasn't mistaken, Nick even looked a little embarrassed. 'You're singing?' She walked across to the wings. 'I want a good seat for this one.' As far back as possible.

In fact, she needed space because dancing with Nick was like lying in the ocean with him, a journey into sensory overload, every cell aware, recognising, communicating, warning her she'd want more. Like the memory of their skin-to-skin frolic in the Mediterranean, dancing was like being wrapped in a warm buzzing blanket, and she needed to fan her face and get the heck away from him.

So much for avoidance. Tara sincerely hoped he was a terrible singer. She didn't think she could take any more attraction and any chance for their light and breezy relationship had been further weakened when she didn't have the barrier of their professions to protect her.

No way was she ready to be trapped into a love affair. A lust affair had seemed possible for a woman who had a block of ice where her heart was and just needed it warmed a little.

But being with Nick was having a blowtorch applied to her block of ice and the speed with which she was melting absolutely terrified her. She knew she couldn't risk allowing herself to get close to someone in case they saw how closed she was, or, God forbid, wanted to help her, because if more than the edges of her heart thawed she was at dire risk of drowning in emotion and she didn't know if she'd come out the other side.

With feelings came pain, and regret, then came the kaleidoscope of memories of all those she'd lost and all the guilt and shame and desolation she'd bottled up so long that her tears had withered and died and dried for ever.

If she couldn't be honest and open with herself, no way was she ready to be honest with anyone else—least of all a light-hearted, good-time guy like Nick. No man deserved that.

Nick stepped across to the front of the stage and her turmoil of thoughts froze like a speech bubble in front of her.

Nick began to sing, not loudly without the microphone but somehow the notes drifted to the edges of the huge room in a liquid-chocolate baritone that should be outlawed, especially in a tall black-haired pirate who promised every woman there he would protect and comfort them until the end of the world.

Tara rubbed the goose-bumps that rose on her skin and peripherally she saw others stop, turn, listen, while the women in the audience sort of drifted en masse towards the front of the auditorium.

Tara could feel the flutter of panic as her body responded to the call and she stood shakily and edged her way to the exit. At the last moment she broke into a trot, and as the doors shut behind, her shoulders slumped as if released by a giant hand.

She fought the emotion that clenched like a fist in her chest, something she'd become very good at in the Sudan, and within minutes she had her control back.

No wonder her instinct had told her to run from this man.

Nick saw Tara leave the auditorium and as he finished the song he knew it was no use seeking her out. Even though he'd been singing for her. The applause came out of the dark unexpectedly and he blinked, remembered there were others there, and his mask slipped into place.

'That was amazing, Nick.'

The female director came up and patted his arm. Very friendly woman, this, Nick thought sardonically, and flashed a smile at her.

'I hope you can do a couple of numbers for us. And I think you should be the second last song of the night. Right before the finale with everyone.'

Nick just wanted to get out of here. 'Just the one, Delores. I don't care where it is. I have to get back to work now.'

She touched his arm again and now there was a little group of women hovering and the moment didn't have the usual fillip of amusement he would normally have got out of the attention.

'I'll have to see about that,' she purred, and Nick put his hand in his pocket, ostensibly to retrieve his phone, so her arm fell away.

'Just the one,' he said, and smiled as he glanced at the blank screen. 'Gotta go. Have a good day, everyone.'

A chorus of 'Bye, Nick' floated after him but already his mind was back on Tara.

Waking up the next morning with Santorini above her porthole was like looking at someone else's travel brochure. She couldn't believe it was real.

Cliff faces soared from the brilliant blue of the Aegean Sea, layered in sedimentary colours from eruption after eruption until you reached the top where the white-painted town sprawled along the ridge and down the sides like white icing dribbling on a cake.

Twenty minutes later, after a visit to the crew's dining room, she still couldn't stop looking. She shook her head and dug her spoon into her breakfast yoghurt. She'd taken to eating at the rail, at the bow of the ship, because it made sure she at least spent some time outside the ship in the sun.

In front of her today were volcanic islands, pieces left from a once whole volcanic island. She'd never seen so many cruise ships together at once as Santorini was serenaded by the brilliant flotilla of liners anchored off the cliffs.

Snub-nosed tenders ferried passengers from ship to shore, where their gaily garbed passengers could make for the cliff-climbing mules or the cages of the cablecar and the town of Fira.

Tara was rostered on late today, and could have had early shore leave, but she couldn't dredge enthusiasm for shore forays after the last one. The problem was she hated spare time and found it too slow waiting for her shifts to start.

It felt like she spent half her time dressed and watching the clock, waiting for work. No doubt Nick would think she was sick, then she grinned, but Wilhelm seemed to appreciate it.

She leant on the rail but she could sigh at the beauty

of the view for a while yet. She drew another deep breath, inhaled the promise of a beautiful day, something she was only just learning again how to do. It felt tentatively good and she vowed one day she'd come back and explore this coastline, and even that tiny step to admitting there was a future out there somewhere lifted her spirits.

She owed Doug for getting her away when he had because she shuddered to think what she'd be like if she'd spent another year buried in disaster. As long as she kept perspective she could thank Nick too for helping her take the first few steps to letting go. She just had to remember he had a twelve-day expiry date.

After half an hour she gave up and headed for the ship's hospital. To heck with waiting, she needed work and maybe there was something she could do before she started her shift.

Maybe she could relieve Will so he could go and do something at the rehearsal. He and Marie had a hoot of a comic act they'd practised.

When she walked in the door she wondered if she'd jinxed herself.

The clinic was overflowing and Tara frowned as she squeezed past two pale-looking young women at the desk. Marie looked up wearily but when she saw who it was her eyes brightened.

'Boy, am I glad to see you. Glad someone caught you. We thought we'd have to page. As you can see, Will's snowed under with this bug that's taken over on level ten. Huge family group and it's spreading like wildfire.'

'Gastro bug? Nasty.' She thought about that in an enclosed space like the ship and winced. 'Have they despatched a cleaning crew to the cabins?'

'The barrier team has gone in to disinfect everything and has isolated the passengers involved.' She looked around the room. 'It all started a couple of hours ago and we have twelve already.'

'Is this a common thing?'

Marie wiped her damp brow. 'No. Thank God. We do drills in case it happens but this is the real thing with a vengeance. The captain wants hourly updates.'

Tara nodded. She had a bad feeling about this. 'I'll find Will and see where he wants me to start.'

Just then the consulting-room door opened and Will showed a passenger out. Tara followed Will into his room when he waved her his way.

Will fanned his face. 'We're in trouble, Tara. This virus is exploding exponentially, and that's the good news.'

Crikey. 'What's the bad news?'

Will slapped his hand over his mouth and threw himself at the handbasin, which he reached just in time before he was ingloriously ill.

When he'd finished Tara handed him a damp sponge and he mopped his lips. No prizes there. 'I'm guessing that's the bad news?'

There was a knock at the door and Marie stumbled in and shut the door hastily behind her, blocking out the sea of anxious faces in the waiting room. She looked even paler than before. 'I'm sorry I have to go off duty,' she mumbled, and bolted past them into the sluice room, where she was similarly affected to Will.

Will sat wearily on the empty patient's bed and Tara glanced around the room until she tracked the disposable masks. She washed her hands and pulled on a pair of gloves and a mask. Looked at the disposable gowns and pulled one of those on too. 'So I'm going to have to be aware it's incredibly infectious?'

Will sucked in a breath and spoke rapidly through gritted teeth. 'Not something we realised when the first person stumbled in. And it's fast-acting. That was only two hours ago. And I was careful.' He cast an agonised glance at Tara, shook his head, and followed Marie into the sluice room.

Tara picked up the phone and dialled the bridge. No medals for thinking the captain needed to know this was bad before the hour was up. The captain wanted the names of the nurses off duty and promised her help as soon as he had them tracked. Another disinfecting team would be dispatched and she was to use a different consulting room from the one Wilhelm had been using and seal the area until it could be cleaned.

When he suggested additional medical help she knew what was coming. 'But there are no other doctors on board, are there, sir?'

'Just Mr Fender. I'll send him down.'

Nothing else she could say. 'Thank you, sir.'

The captain summoned Nick to the bridge. 'The hospital is in crisis. I know you intended remaining incognito with your staff but it's too much work for the two nurses and one doctor I have left. Hopefully it's a twelve-hour virus and not a longer one.'

Nick nodded. He'd seen it happen once before on a ship and containment was everything. So much for avoiding Tara. Not his fault, though. There was no way out. His salute was crisp. 'Yes, sir.'

When Nick entered the hospital in his white officer's uniform he couldn't be sorry he'd been called in. Tara looked calm and confident but there was no doubting the relief he saw in her face when she met his eyes.

Tara had segregated the clinic between those with gastrointestinal symptoms and the others. Already exposed, she turned the incidental medical problems, and any liaison with complainers over to Nick.

She pointed to the smallest consulting room and he nodded and got on with it. That was the last Tara thought for the next few hours as a new wave of sufferers arrived.

Gina, the replacement nurse, began to triage the waiting room until the usual clientele were cleared and then between them they began to make headway in the chaos.

Those mildly affected were sent to their rooms and checked on hourly by the remaining roving nurse, and the more severely affected were sent through to Tara, who medicated, cannulated and pushed intravenous fluids through. As each patient became more stable and were discharged to their cabins, the next would be ushered through and processed.

Tara meticulously washed her hands, changed her masks and gloves and gowns between patients and steadily worked through the list until finally, towards evening, when the loudspeaker announced they were leaving port, the waiting room was nearly empty. The nurse assigned to follow up reported those from earlier in the day were improving and even Wilhelm phoned to say he'd settled to lethargy as opposed to violent spasms.

By ten p.m. it was over. Tara and Nick looked at each other as the last patient was ushered to the door.

Nick shook his head and began to clap slowly. Tara frowned and then accepted her due with as good a grace as she could.

'End of shift,' Nick said.

She was almost too tired to return the favour but dredged up the energy to offer a reluctant smile then inclined her head and put her hands together and slow-clapped him back.

The nurses peered out to see what was happening and Nick and Tara applauded them too. They all smiled at the empty room and groaned collectively. That made them all smile again, wearily.

'Bags first shower,' Tara said with a feeble attempt at a joke, and there was a chorus of agreement. 'You were all amazing. What a team. Thank you so much.'

'I'll finish tidying up here,' Nick said. 'You ladies deserve to go.' The nurses grinned and bolted before he could change his mind.

'I'll stay too.' Tara couldn't leave him to do that. She was the medical officer in charge.

'I'll do it, Tara. Go.'

There he was again. That bossy person she'd glimpsed before. And she hated taking orders. But it did sound temptingly attractive. To hell with being territorial, she felt like a wreck. A possibly infectious wreck. He could win this one, bugs and all. 'Fine. Thanks.'

Nick waved her away with a suspiciously straight face and it seemed a long way up the three flights of stairs to her cabin because her legs reminded her she'd been on them non-stop for twelve hours.

Ten minutes later the steamy water was cascading over her scalp and face and she sighed as she leant her forehead against the shower wall. The wall was solid. Like Nick.

In fact, he was a bit of hero, staying back so she could be here.

The water ran down her shoulders and between her breasts and the heat soaked in, and as she lathered with her favourite violet soap, the tension from the day seeped away down the plughole with the suds.

Nick sure was a hero with his unfailing good humour today under trying circumstances. Some of the passengers had been very unhappy and determined to blame the ship's food. Nick had very gently but clearly explained that apart from one family and friends no others were sick, which meant one of their members had brought the virus on board and spread it between them.

Yep, a hero. Her mind drifted back to that dance in

the auditorium—where she'd somehow forgotten those fifty eyes watching them—and how she'd spun in his arms and in sync like no other dance she'd ever had, and she still blushed at the thought.

Then his song in the dark, his deep, dark voice steeling around her heart with velvet fingers until she'd had to flee. The guy had some serious mojo going on there.

Even after the twelve exhausting hours of exposure today, his infallible good humour and caring expertise all made her feel good. And that was what she was looking for.

Right? Just to start feeling good for a change.

So meeting Nick had been a good thing. He made her forget the horror of the last two years.

Made her smile. Made her want him to smile. Glimpses she'd caught of him ushering in the next patient, his compassionate dealings with the children and the way he'd lifted spirits when the nurses had become stressed, and even the occasional wink he'd sent her way as they'd passed in the waiting room had made her giggle.

Crazily, she thought with a sigh, even the back of his neck as he'd passed her by left a good feeling in the pit of her stomach.

The shower spray cascaded over her and she sighed with the bliss of it. She was *not* going to think about his backside because she'd very recently discovered a previously unknown fetish for slim male hips and taut backsides. It seems they turned her on. When had she become a voyeur?

She lifted her head and let the water run over her face as if she could wash away the growing awareness of everything about Nick Fender that persisted despite her feeble attempts at denial.

Very feeble because that reaction to thinking about Nick twirled a baton in her belly like that of a drum majorette and she shifted her feet on the tiles as if she could step away from it.

'Get out of my head.' The words echoed in the bathroom and she ducked her face out of the stream. So now she was going barking mad. And her legs even wobbled as her knees seemed to soften when pictures of Nick sashayed into her mind. Now, bizarrely, her stomach had started to tremble with the fantasy sensation of Nick rubbing the tension from her shoulders like he had that day in the ocean.

Her breasts were suddenly too receptive to the rush of sensation, too responsive to the heat, too reactive to the thought of Nick's long fingers rolling her suddenly aching tips.

She snapped the shower onto cold, then off, and grabbed for a towel. Her face felt as red as the floral arrangement in the bowl on the table.

The distant sound of the doorbell penetrated from the room beyond.

She tilted her head and heard it again. How long had that been ringing? Tara wrapped her hair in the towel and grabbed the white robe from the back of the door, and as she crossed the room she could see the missed-call light on the phone beside the bed.

She quickened her step. Hoped it wasn't a dire medical emergency. At this time of the night it could be little else.

Nick stepped back as Tara opened the door and his breath hissed out with relief that she looked fine. More than fine, really, with her honey-gold neck exposed like a swan and a towel holding her hair high on her forehead.

Damned if she wasn't naked under the robe. And wet. His gaze skimmed down to the trickles of water running down her legs. A diffusing trail of soapy steam stretched out behind her, laden with the elusive scent of violets, and he tried not to lean towards her to inhale.

His gut kicked and he couldn't regret what had obviously been a dumb impulse. He'd tried to ring her after his shower and let her know he'd do the early shift in the hospital so she could come in later.

When she hadn't answered he'd got it into his brain she'd come down with the bug and was lying miserably ill alone in her room.

He lifted his gaze to her face because that was a lot safer than imagining what was on display under the white robe she was hastily tying. 'So you're okay!' he said.

He loved the way her forehead puckered when she frowned. 'Yes, I'm okay. Why wouldn't I be?'

He was a fool. Now a turned-on fool. And he'd disturbed her when she needed her rest more than anyone. He needed his fantasies back in their box.

'Sorry I bothered you. Maggot in the head.' He turned away, cursing himself so hard he almost missed her soft reply.

'Nick?'

He jerked to a stop as if she'd pulled a string taped to his back. Turned to see a whimsical little smile that lifted his spirits miraculously as she leaned towards him with her foot in the doorway to stop the door shutting her out in the hallway with him. 'Can you come here for a sec? Please?'

He finished the turn and took a couple of steps until he was right beside her, could smell her skin again, and then, to his delight, she leant up and kissed him on his cheek. A feather-light brush of lips that reverberated through his psyche way out of proportion to the pressure.

'Thanks for today. You were wonderful,' she said softly.

The last thing he'd expected. She'd been the amazing one. He jammed his hands into his pockets to stop himself pulling her into his arms and kissing her thoroughly and then some, then blurted out the first thing that came into his head. 'I didn't see you flagging.'

'I would have if I'd had to manage on my own.' She pushed herself back against the doorframe. 'Anyway, see you tomorrow.'

Tomorrow. He breathed. Pulled his hands from his pockets and pushed then down the outside of his legs. Relaxed his fingers and kept them there. 'That's what I came to say. The captain's rostered me in the hospital another day. I'll do the early clinic and you can come later. Sleep in.'

She nodded. 'I'll be back after breakfast.'

'Make it lunch. I'm good for it.' His words hung in the air and he wondered how something so innocent could create such double meaning.

'I'll see if I sleep.' More hidden meanings? He wished.

'Stay in bed anyway.' Banished that thought from his brain. White sheets, Tara's hair spilled across the pillow, honey skin bare and silken soft under his hands.

She opened her mouth to argue but he was ready for her if she did. Maybe she knew that because all she said was, 'Then you'd better go to bed.'

That was when the devil stepped in. Made short work of the restraints he'd placed on himself, pushed him in the back so that he was propelled into saying it out loud. 'Don't suppose you'd like to invite me in?'

He couldn't banish the vision of him walking in and closing the door with both of them inside. To stand behind that door and feel the length of her against him, backing slowly towards the bed they both wanted.

Tara saw Nick's eyes darken. This was her fault. The kiss! As soon as she'd done it Tara had known she shouldn't have kissed him. Well, it had rocked her just as much. Even that feather-light caress across his raspy cheek had made her knees weaken and turn to jelly, like she was standing back in the shower. Naked. Wet. Imagining him.

Now she really could taste him. Inhale that aftershave that she'd forever associate with Nick. She passed her tongue over her lips and drank in the sight of the real thing. Here he was. Fantasy Nick.

Her new favourite scent. When had that happened? Her body still thrummed with wicked fantasies that surely you were allowed in the privacy of your own shower stall, for goodness' sake. How was she to know he was going to turn up at her door, his hair still damp from his own shower, the half-open shirt exposing his strong chest and throat so that she wanted to bury her nose in him.

Her suddenly rapt gaze hovered over that throat. She saw him swallow and she followed the movement. Drifted down over his abs, taut against the material of his shirt, his black jeans snug on his slim hips, the un-mistakable tightness across the front tweaking the cen-tre of her with just the thought.

She'd been quietly excited about what she would share with Vander after their marriage, but sex had been such a small part of their relationship she'd tried not to be disappointed. All she knew was she'd never wanted a man like she wanted this one right here, right now.

Please.

If she asked him, he'd stay. She was sure of it. Did she want that? She should feel ashamed, thinking that. A one night stand screamed shipboard romance and loose woman. But suddenly the idea of walking away after a week with flesh-and-bone memories seemed in-finitely better then walking away with a hollow fantasy.

She dragged her eyes away, drawn back to his face,

his mouth. The air crackled with awareness, attraction imploding into need.

She licked her lips again. Her head was talking so much she couldn't remember what had been said out loud. 'Did you say something?'

'I said, do you want to invite me in?'

Then she said, 'Lord, yes.' His eyes flared. 'But I don't think so.'

He blinked. Not surprised but definitely disappointed. 'Very sensible.'

She smiled but she could feel the vulnerability in it. The fine line between changing her mind or being safe. If he'd pushed it would have been easier to say no but he was ever the gentleman. 'Goodnight, Nick.'

A final glint of mischief. 'It could be.'

They stared at each other and Tara wondered what was stopping her from just reaching out and touching his hand. That was all it would take. One movement on her part. She was a grown woman. A widow, not some teenage girl who needed the illusion of love to bestow her gift.

Maybe this was the way to healing. To finding her path back to the woman she'd been before the Sudan, maybe before she'd tried so hard to be everything Vander had thought she was. Before she'd failed.

Nick didn't have expectations of perfection. He couldn't have because she'd arrived here a wreck and he'd still befriended her.

Maybe if she kissed him again, just once more, properly, she'd know what she really wanted to do.

CHAPTER NINE

N$_{ICK}$ had accepted the no. Expected it. That wasn't to say he didn't carry condoms in his wallet.

So when he saw Tara's pupils dilate he was willing to adapt. Even so, when she leant towards him one more time, he hadn't intended the kiss to get quite so carried away. But he'd wanted this with a depth of need he hadn't anticipated.

The devil whispered.

They both wanted this. Both grown adults.

Suddenly they were plastered together and before he knew it they were through her door and across the room and up against a wall in her cabin, lost to the rest of the world.

One hand captured her head and he couldn't get enough of her delectable mouth, while the fingers of his other slipped inside her robe and captured the silken, peaked glory of Tara in his palm.

Her indrawn shudder softened his mouth and he raised his face and breathed in her hair before his lips skidded down the side of her cheek, skin so soft, so vulnerable, like the petals of a blushing rose, until he found her mouth again.

'I could kiss you for ever.'

'Nick.' A whisper back against his lips.

'Hmm?' He opened his eyes and eased away so that she wasn't jammed against the wall. Ran his hands down her back in apology. Gazed down at the open robe and the perfection that was Tara and lost the plot again. Leaned in.

'Nick.' Another whisper.

He shook himself. 'Sorry. Yes?'

She was smiling. And what a smile, but the vulnerability had grown. He felt his insides melt and rush of emotion he didn't recognise.

'I'm not very good at this. Never have been.'

Nick shook his head. She was incredible. He pulled her even closer and hugged her. 'It takes two to tango. And you are perfect.'

'Not what my husband said.'

He held her soft bony bits against him. 'Then he was a fool...' and a creep, Nick thought but didn't say it '...who didn't know how lucky he was.'

But he saw her fear of letting him down, saw the undermining of her self-belief, her lack of faith in her natural instincts, and for the first time he decided cholera wasn't all bad if it had carried off Tara's husband.

'So why did you marry him?' Stupid time to ask this but suddenly he had to know. Not something he'd ever cared about with other women in his arms. Especially a semi-naked one.

'He was a friend of my parents. From their church. And I'd just been let down by a man I thought I'd loved. Who turned out to be married.' She shrugged. 'I thought at least I'd get no lies from Vander.' She sighed. 'Could have done with a few less home truths.'

'Hey.' Nick tilted her chin. 'Maybe he did lie. About the part of you that scared him.'

He kissed her and when she responded, when she'd relaxed again from the tension he'd created by asking, he slid one finger under her chin until she looked at him again.

'Crazy woman. Can't you see the seductress inside you? She's one hot lady. The one who captured my attention from the first moment I saw you.'

She looked away. Shook her head. 'I was a wreck.'

'Not to me.' He kissed her and when she opened her eyes again he stared straight into them. 'You are the most beautiful and sexy woman I have ever seen.'

She lowered her eyes. Unconvinced. 'Can we go to bed?'

Yes, please. And he would prove it to her. He bent, slid his hands behind her shoulders and knees and lifted her until she was safe in his arms. Squeezed her to him and the robe fell open further. Gentle hills and valleys stretched out before him, silver pale in the dim light, and the darker toffee from her exposure to the sun like a chocolate frame around the white centre of her sweetness. The pink in her cheeks deepened at the way he cherished her with his eyes and he had to kiss her again before he moved. 'Quite happy to stay here and just look—but your wish is my command.'

He carried her gently to the bed, settled her like the feather she was onto the white bedspread, and gazed down at her unwrapped like a morsel at Christmas. 'You are an incredibly beautiful woman.'

When he said it again, for the first time she almost believed him. Her mother had always said she was plain. Vander had once said she was pretty but she didn't want to think about him now. The way Nick was looking at her at this moment was a gift greater than she'd expected and she pulled him down towards her and kissed him. She could take this moment and cherish it. The last two years had taught her a lot and life could disappear at a whim. No way was she going to regret time she shared with Nick.

Nick was in no hurry. 'I'd like to savour this time with you.' He trailed his finger down her cheek, leaned in and kissed her gently but thoroughly, and like magic she relaxed bonelessly back onto the bed under him and he followed her. Forgot what he was going to do as he was lost in Tara, couldn't stop these long, slow, drugging kisses that he'd never really included in his repertoire until today. Kisses that came from a well of need he hadn't known he had. A need that was matched by Tara's because when he went to move she pulled him back and they both drifted away again.

He murmured against her lips, 'You are the most glorious kisser.'

Tara opened her eyes. Her brain screamed, *Not true,*

but the sexy curve of his mouth said she had to believe him. She felt the tears scratch, but not form, as a piece of her heart broke off that this gorgeous man thought she was a good kisser.

She of the B minus in the bedroom.

And she had to believe him because he was looking at her as if she was the eighth wonder of the world. Nobody had ever looked at her like that before.

So she pulled him back and opened her soul for some more of the same and slowly his hands began to worship her. And he encouraged her gently to do the same to him.

When he moaned, she stopped until he encouraged her on and slowly she began to smile. Began to seek those movements that tortured him, nibbled at the edges of knowledge that was growing, nibbled at the edges of Nick with a curve of her lips that made Nick smile back, and they murmured on through the night. Learning, teasing, sometimes devouring, and occasionally dozing.

Much later Tara rested back in Nick's arms and traced the taut curve of biceps. 'Oh, my. So that's what they mean by sexy and satisfied.'

Nick smiled and squeezed her shoulders. He felt ten feet tall and he never wanted to let her go. So why did it feel like his heart was going to break?

Because he didn't do this stuff. The lying back and loving. It was supposed to be all light and fluffy and giggly…and then he was gone.

He leaned across and kissed her forehead. She'd be gone in a week. And he'd be gone in the other direction.

This was dangerous territory and he'd survived this long because he knew the rules. Get out. Now.

But he had to kiss her one more time, which led to more, and afterwards he just closed his eyes for a moment. Soon he'd get up and go.

An hour before dawn he left. 'You are amazing.' He shifted his arm out from under her and tried not to see the way her face stilled when she realised he was going. The ridiculous thing was he didn't want to go. Ached to lie the whole full night just listening to her breathe, or moan, but if he didn't get out now something bad was going to happen. He just knew it.

Nick left and Tara lay in her tumbled bedclothes and sighed at the ceiling with a soft incredulous smile on her face. Her arms crept around her tender breasts and she just had to hug herself. Her body still glowed in a languidly sated way. There was so much to learn and Nick cared enough to show her a world she had never known existed.

She shied away from the reminder that this world had six nights to go and even with the way she'd opened to Nick last night she knew there was a closed-off centre he'd never reach. But she felt way more alive than yesterday. 'Oh, my.'

Nick didn't go to bed. He walked the pre-dawn decks like an automaton, head up, peripherally avoiding obstacles and late-night revellers, but only seeing Tara as he'd left her. It had just been sex. But she'd gazed up at

him like he was some kind of god, when in fact he was
the other bloke. The one with the horns.

The gift she'd given him was priceless. Her faith in
him, her belief that he could be trusted with teaching
her about her own innate sensuality, allowing him to
see into her damaged core of self-belief when it hurt
her to show anyone.

The responsibility for that sat like the weight of the
whole ship was on his shoulders. What if he let her
down? Which he would when he left.

She'd better not fall for him because he felt guilty
enough. He was no hero and she deserved one. A genuine one.

If Tara wanted fun and fluff, that's what he was offering. Just sex.

As a middle child and the only boy in the family, he'd
always tried to be the opposite of his serious sisters.

He'd had to cut himself off from all the girly stuff
like crying and analysing emotions to protect his mas-
culinity and the belief that he was solely responsible
for his own happiness. With his mother's betrayal exposed, he couldn't be the rock, 'cos even though he
loved women he didn't trust love. He'd lost that trust on
the same day. He didn't want to get too close or be depended on by any woman. Because he knew he couldn't
depend on them and they couldn't depend on him.

Except maybe for Kiki. His youngest sis. The one
he was replacing now. She'd been all for taking the fun
side of life and he'd encouraged her. She had no issues

that he was the playboy and entertainer of the family. That was his job.

Had he been stuck in a groove? Did he really want more? No! And if it was changing then he'd put a stop to it right now.

They were docked at Piraeus, for Athens, when Tara turned up at the hospital at ten the next morning. Nick was showing a worried young mum and her baby into his room. Good.

That gave her a minute to let her blushes die down before she had to face him because, to her surprise, after he'd left she'd actually slept the sleep of the very wicked!

She didn't know about dreamlessly because when she'd woken up she'd had a grin plastered on her face like the Joker out of *Batman*. She suspected the dreams had been almost as amazing as the real thing.

Tara followed him into the examination room when he smiled and inclined his head and there was just a flash of naughtiness that made her compress her lips and look at the floor.

When she looked up at the patient she noticed the child's eyes had that exhausted, rolling back look that sick infants had. Her gaze sharpened. Last night receded even further as she studied the infant.

Nick's voice rumbled quietly as she visually assessed the patient. 'I'm Dr Fender, Nick, and this is Dr McWilliams, my colleague. She's very experienced with children.'

Tara smiled. 'Hello.'

The mum gave a perfunctory smile and then looked worriedly down at her baby. 'Joey's eight months old. He's got a cough and he's crying a lot.'

Nick leaned forward and gave Joey the end of his tie to hold. Tara loved the way he did that while he used his stethoscope to listen to Joey's chest. Then he ran his fingers gently over Joe's skull and even though Tara knew he was checking Joey's fontanelle wasn't sunken, the sight made her stomach warm. He was so gentle and caring that even a baby recognised he was safe with him. Even *she* felt safe with him.

When he'd finished Nick prised Joey's fingers free and stepped back to reach for the thermometer, which he slid under Joey's arm. Joey wriggled and whimpered and Nick gave him back the end of his tie. 'I can hear some rattles in Joey's chest.' The thermometer beeped and Nick pulled it out. He looked at the mum. 'Thirty-nine degrees Celsius. Or a hundred and two point two in Fahrenheit. So he has a temperature. When did you first think he was unwell?'

Aimee's concern deepened. 'Last night. He wasn't feeding as long as he usually does and he felt hot.'

Joey started to cough and Nick and Tara looked at each other with mutual concern. Joey's lips were tinged blue and Tara crossed the room and came back with the little pulse oximeter, which she clipped onto Joey's wrist, and a mask connected to oxygen, which she held off using until they had a reading in room air.

Nick put his hand gently onto Joey's to keep his hand

still, and finally they could read the result. Joey's oxygen saturation was down at ninety per cent instead of around a hundred.

Tara waved the mask. 'He needs a little bit more oxygen than he can get out of the air, so do you mind if we pop a little mask on him?'

Aimee nodded tearfully as Tara slipped the oxygen onto Joey's face. It was a measure of how unwell he was that the little boy didn't fight her.

Aimee wrapped her arms around her own chest. 'I should have brought him earlier.'

'Children go down quickly. You did the right thing.' Tara had wanted to say that but Nick beat her to it and she loved him for it.

Vander would never have said it, even though Aimee was here and had done the right thing.

Nick went on. 'Joey's picked up a chest infection, and I'm afraid he needs to be admitted to the hospital.'

Aimee looked at Tara. 'Can't you keep him here?'

Tara shook her head. 'I'm sorry. No. We could if we had to, if we were out at sea. But, like Nick said, children go down very quickly and we're in a major port. It's safer for Joey to be under the care of a paediatrician in Athens in a proper hospital. He needs intravenous antibiotics, nebulisers to help break up the gunk in his chest and follow-up X-rays.'

Aimee chewed her lip. 'But I can't speak Italian.'

Tara nodded sympathetically. 'That's going to be hard.' She'd found it difficult enough the other day even though the senior staff she'd dealt with had all been able to speak English. 'But your specialist will probably speak much better English than your Italian.'

Nick glanced at his watch. 'Tara's come to take over from me here. You'll need an escort anyway and I've got time to take you. I speak fluent Italian. We'll get an ambulance because Joey needs oxygen.' He squeezed Aimee's arm. 'How about that?'

He met Tara's eyes over the top of Aimee's head and she nodded. He wondered if he would normally have got involved like this. Pre-Tara. He could feel the changes, the idea of taking his care a little further with his patients. Like she did. Nick closed off that train of thought.

He went on, 'I'll get you settled before I leave you. Find an interpreter you're comfortable with.'

They were lucky Nick was here, Tara thought, and she couldn't help being proud of the care he was giving. He was a great guy.

It seemed Aimee thought so too. 'Would you? Thank you.'

Tara listened with half an ear as she settled Joey into a cot and checked his oxygen was attached properly. She wrote down the readings of both oxygen and oximeter and took Joey's pulse.

Nick touched her shoulder and she looked up. 'I'll start the arrangements and see what antibiotic the hospital wants us to start him on. We can give his first dose before he goes.'

Nick realised he was finding it hard to work with Tara. Harder than before. Not to the detriment of his work but to reassure himself that she was still there.

Still felt the same. Wasn't regretting last night. Stuff he didn't need on his mind.

She was looking at him like he was a hero again. 'I'll put a cannula in, then,' she said, 'so we can give the antibiotics IV?'

She'd be better at it than him. So whose fault was that? He handed children onto a paediatrician, whereas Tara had had no choice but to gain the skills.

'Thanks. That would be great. I'll send Gina in to help while I phone around.'

Nick and Aimee left with Joey in the ambulance an hour later. Gina tidied up and restocked while Tara finished off the computer notes before she emailed them, together with all the observation and medication charts they'd used, on to the hospital.

The clinic was finished and Tara locked up as she left. She had two hours until she was needed back at work and the idea of a lunchtime nap in her cabin was more attractive than food. Funny how a night making love made you tired.

CHAPTER TEN

TARA fell asleep with a smile on her face as soon as her head touched the pillow and woke an hour and a half later with the afternoon sun streaming in the window. She stretched, ached a little in odd places and her mouth curved, but she felt fantastic.

The phone rang and she picked it up still half-asleep.

'Have you had lunch?'

'Hello, Nick.' I was just thinking about you. Tara smiled into the phone. 'No. But probably won't have time. I have to be at work in twenty minutes.'

'I'm on my way.' The phone went dead.

She looked at the silent receiver, shrugged and put it down. Then she assimilated his statement and bounced off the bed and into her bathroom, where she cleaned her teeth and brushed her hair just in time.

The doorbell buzzed.

Her stomach rumbled and when she opened the door Nick was holding a covered plate on a tray.

'You're trying to fatten me up.'

Nick winked. 'Lucky you.'

Tara took the tray and went back to put it on her

table, and Nick followed. 'Chicken salad rolled in a wrap. I saw you have one the other day.'

'Quick and easy to eat and just what I fancied.' She glanced at him. 'When did you see me eat?'

'The day before Amalfi. I watched you come in but you didn't see me.'

'And you didn't say hello.'

'I was scoping you out.'

Tara chewed the bite she'd taken thoughtfully. 'Why are you always feeding me?' He didn't answer.

'Don't get me wrong. It's nice.' She pointed to the tiny dish of hulled strawberries that had appeared every day, fresh on her table, since the first day he'd sent them.

Nick looked away. 'You like strawberries. They're good for you.'

She frowned. 'Yes, but *why* are you feeding me?'

She realised he was actually feeling uncomfortable. The moment stretched and Tara wished she hadn't asked.

Nick's problem was that he didn't know why. It just made him feel good. But that was a dumb thing to say. And he couldn't say it was because she was too skinny when, in fact, to him she was perfect.

A new fetish? He'd never wanted to feed a woman before. Though he could remember when Kiki had been sick as a child he'd ride to the shops on his pushbike and bring her home sweets.

The devil helped him out. 'Maybe I like to watch your mouth and it gives me an excuse.'

He watched her blush and lick her lips nervously,

and he realised it was true. He really liked watching her mouth. 'But you have to get to work and this conversation could lead to you being late.' He stood up. 'And I know how you hate to be late.'

Tara fought down the heat in her cheeks and concentrated on normal things. Served her right for asking such a stupid question. She realised he had changed out of his whites and was back in the black trousers of the hospitality staff. 'So you're going back to being a bar manager now.'

'Just this afternoon. Though if you get snowed under the captain will probably let me come back for an hour or two. I'll still do the early shift tomorrow, you do the mid-morning and Will should come back in the afternoon.'

So she wouldn't get to see him at work any more today. Funny how after two days she was used to working with him. Would miss his smile. 'So when will we catch up?' Even to her own ears she sounded needy and she wished the words back in her mouth.

They'd both said they were there for the fun and not the future. Nick had also said, 'Never say never,' but that was a just a line from a smooth guy and they both knew that.

Thankfully his response let her know he was still fine with a bit of clinging. 'We could share dinner. I could watch your mouth again.'

He made her smile so easily. It was going to be hell when this cruise ended. 'Same time. Same place?'

'Sounds good.' He turned back at the door and

stepped up to her. Dropped a kiss on her lips that had
her eyes shut one second into it.

When he lifted his head they were both a little
spaced. 'Mmm. Like to do more than look sometimes.'

Then he was gone and Tara was late.

Dinner was a blur because the whole time Tara was
waiting for the time they could finish and go. She had
no idea what she ate. And judging by the darkness of
Nick's eyes, his mind wasn't on nutrition either.

He held her hand all the way back to her cabin and
she didn't remember much of that trip either. She fum-
bled the swipe of her card in the door, tried again without success, and Nick took it from her and did the deed
himself. Then he stepped back to allow her to enter and
followed so close behind she could feel the heat from
his body.

She stopped suddenly so that he bumped into her
and she was grinning when she turned. 'Excuse me?'

'Certainly.' Then not much more was said as their
clothes seemed to peel away along with the conversation and Nick lifted her so that her legs were wrapped
around him and she was hard up against solid muscle.

Looking down was amazing. His face so chiselled
and alive, clearly wanting her, his body sculpted and
powerful, holding her as if she weighed little more than
a feather, her skin plastered to his as he backed up towards the wall.

His thigh nudged against hers. 'Have you any problems with this wall tonight, my love?'

My love? She wished but she wasn't going there. She grabbed hold of the cold that seeped in with her own acknowledgement of illusion and forced it away. Tonight she was his love. That's all she wanted. She dug her fingers into the rippled muscles of his shoulders and bent down to gently bite his neck. 'I love this wall tonight.'

He growled softly in his throat and she felt the beast within herself respond and not much more was thought, all was sensation, and want, and need, and Nick. And the wall.

Afterwards, as they lay entwined back on her bed where Nick had carried her, chest heaving, silly grins on their faces, Nick stroked a line between her breasts. 'Kissing's not all you're amazing at.'

'I've had a good teacher.' She stroked his chest in turn. 'And you are amazing. Wanna play again?'

He shifted his arm. 'I've got the late shift.' The second lie he'd told her. But inside he was still shaking.

This had been too much. Too amazing. Transcending 'just sex' and lust and all the other names for the things people did when they were searching for this moment he'd shared with Tara.

The moment he hadn't been searching for.

When the earth had spun off its axis like it wasn't supposed to.

'I have to go.'

She frowned. 'You didn't say that earlier. At dinner?'

He didn't meet her eyes. 'I had other things on my mind.' He kissed her and rolled off the bed. Glanced back over his shoulder at her. 'I was watching your mouth.'

To his relief she closed her eyes and giggled. Though that hurt even more. He turned his back and picked up his shirt from the floor. Scooped up the rest of his clothes and disappeared into her bathroom.

Stared at himself in the mirror when the door was shut and hated the man looking back at him with a passion born of fear. He was falling in love with her and he didn't want to.

Another amazing night's sleep and Tara bounced out of bed in the morning, scooped up her yoghurt from the mess, and ate it as she walked towards the hospital.

When she arrived, Nick was showing out Gwen and Tommy, and Tara waved at them. Gwen looked happy, which was nice for a change, and Tara vaguely wondered what the problem had been this time.

'Satisfied customer,' Tara murmured as she followed Nick into the consulting room. She wasn't sure if she was talking about the patient's mother or herself. That made her ears heat.

This man could charm the birds off the trees, let alone cheer up a harassed mother on a ship. And now she came to think about it, she'd seen Gwen yesterday and the day before that as well.

Gwen did seem a tad over-protective. The boy had his arm in sling and the woman smiled at Nick as she left, like he'd made her day.

She looked again. 'What's with Gwen? And Tommy? Boy, is she having a holiday with problems.'

'Sorry?' When he turned back to Tara Nick wasn't smiling, although she thought his eyes did soften when he looked at her. Maybe his gaze did drift over her face as if he needed to see something good.

And he thought that was her? Was she becoming needy?

She resisted the urge to lean up and kiss him.

Nick had gone back to frowning. 'What do you mean?'

Thank goodness she hadn't moved on the kiss impulse. 'Um. Gwen. With Tommy. She's been in most days, I think?' Because now she could see he was on a totally different planet from her at this moment.

She tried not to be disappointed. 'I think Tommy and cruising don't mix.'

Nick clicked on the computer and scrolled back through the doctor's notes. 'Every day, in fact.'

He was looking past her. She thought he'd forgotten she was there until he began to speak in a cold, distant voice she'd never heard him use before. 'A long time ago, when I first started private practice, I met a woman who scared the hell out of me. Gwen reminds me of her.'

'What do you mean?'

'That woman was the wife of a friend. And I tried not to see what was happening. But I became more suspicious every time she came with her little girl. A beautiful little girl I let down.'

Tara didn't like the sound of that. So much so she

wished he'd stop, but perversely she needed to hear it as much as he needed to tell the story.

'In the end she nearly killed that little girl and I almost let it happen. I went off and did a stint on a cruise ship while she continued to make that child suffer. You can't always believe what you want to, Tara.'

He looked at Tara and frowned. 'I may have a nasty, suspicious mind but I'd like to rule out something more serious before that mother does any more damage.'

Tara blinked. She turned back to look at the empty waiting room. The woman had gone. 'You think she's making the child's illness up?'

He tapped the computer screen and the list of visits. 'Have a look at how many times she's come to the clinic. We've had one presentation every day since we sailed. All different reasons. All gaining her lots of sympathy for having a sick child.'

He ran his hand through his hair. 'Today was a red rash on the arm that had suddenly appeared.' He chewed his lip. 'She's given me a list of allergies a mile long, some different from what she's given Wilhelm.'

'So?' Tara couldn't see where this was going. 'She's over-protective?'

He sighed and ran his hand through his hair before he went on.

'She seemed pretty excited about how painful it looked and that set my alarm bells off. I remember that and I'll never forget it.' He glanced at Tara. 'This may seem incredibly far-fetched, but have you ever heard of Munchausen syndrome?'

Tara's brain clicked back into medical mode—away from memories of last night. 'Like a hospital addiction syndrome? They make up illnesses to gain attention? Even have surgery for fictitious illnesses?'

Tara had trouble imagining that in the context of her last two years and survival being paramount to her patients instead of gaining attention.

He nodded. 'And then there's Munchausens by proxy, which is even worse.'

Tara took a step back in shock. 'You mean she could be harming her child to gain attention.' She shook her head vehemently. 'Surely not. I've never seen a case.'

Tara could feel Nick's agitation and she tried to remember what Wilhelm had said after the mother had left the day before.

'I have. Not pretty.' Nick was still in the past. 'That mother's child nearly died before the state removed her. I came back. Saw the damage. Diagnosed my patient with psychosis and she's still in an institution. Her husband, my friend, almost killed himself with remorse. And I had suspicions before I went away. I was one of many who ignored the signals. Because I was having such a good time playing locum, I almost didn't come back and make the diagnosis.'

He rolled his shoulders as if the weight of those memories sat heavily on him, and in a moment of clarity she saw that frivolous Nick had his own nightmares, like she did.

In his normal voice Nick said, 'I just wonder if our

Gwen has rubbed something irritating onto Tommy's skin to make it red.'

Tara winced and her stomach tightened with distress. She visualised the pale child who'd just left. 'That's ghastly. Tommy's only just turned three.' She shook her head. They had horrors out here in the real world too.

'Surely not.' She worried her lip with her teeth. What if it was true? 'What were you thinking? What can you do?' What could they do?

Nick lifted his head and there was no lightness in his sea-blue eyes. Today they were cold, reflecting the steel in his voice, and she felt the chill go right through her. She hoped he never looked at her like that.

'We can try and catch her out.' She could see him clenching and unclenching his fingers and she wanted to soothe him from whatever guilt was eating him up.

'Okay.' She touched his hand and his fingers stilled as he looked at her. 'How, Nick?'

He shifted his hand out from under hers and jammed it through his hair. 'I've asked her to bring him back in half an hour to see if the cream works. I've given her lots of sympathy so she should be feeling good and maybe craving a little more attention.' There was a thread of self-disgust in his voice she didn't think he deserved.

'You didn't know.' He wasn't listening.

'Then if I knocked on her door in fifteen minutes? See if I can catch her in the act of trying to make the rash look worse before she comes down here?'

This was no light and airy cocktail waiter. This was

a man willing to stick his neck out for a child who might be at risk. Tara tried to visualise the scene. 'Can you do that?'

Action Nick was a whole different person and she was having trouble merging the two Nicks. She didn't know if she'd be so decisive about a suspicion but then she doubted she would have even suspected a mother of such a thing. She was more used to mums worrying about finding enough food for their children than manufacturing illnesses.

Nick glanced at his watch. 'I could get a cabin steward to knock on the door with towels or something. He'd unlock the door and I'd follow him in before she can hide her intention, if she has any. If I caught her doing anything I'll just say I was worried and we want to keep her son under observation in the hospital because it might be contagious.'

It was a daring plan. But perhaps the situation called for it. 'What if she's in the shower or half-dressed?' There'd be hell to pay then. She tried to imagine the scene.

'Just before her appointment would be her most likely time for trying to exacerbate Tommy's rash.'

Tara shuddered. 'Do you want me to come?'

'Would you?' He thought about it. 'Maybe that could be better. If we don't catch her out this time, I don't want her to know we suspect her. You could say I asked you to look in because the clinic got busy suddenly. To save her waiting. Would you be comfortable doing that?'

'I guess.' Tara thought of the little boy who could be

at such cruel risk. 'No. Not guess.' She lifted her chin. 'Of course I can. And it looks better if a woman forces her way into her cabin rather than a man.'

Nick rested his hand on her shoulder. 'Thanks, Tara. I know you must be thinking this is pretty much out of left field but I let that other child down and I'm not letting this one suffer if it's happening.'

'I understand.' She did. Feeling like you'd let someone down was the worst feeling in the world. She looked at him. 'I would never have suspected this, you know, Nick. I would have let Tommy down too. And Wilhelm saw her yesterday.'

'It's a picture once seen never forgotten, I assure you,' Nick said grimly, and glanced at his watch.

Ten minutes later Tara knocked on the door of Gwen's cabin and the steward inserted the key in the lock. Tara drew a deep breath and pushed open the door.

Tommy was whimpering as his mother held his arm. Tara glanced and blinked at the label of the spray can that sat on the bench and bile rose in her throat.

She forced a smile and glanced away from the bench. How not to strangle the woman? 'Hi, Gwen. Remember me? Dr Fender sent me.' She made strong eye contact and Gwen stared back. 'Dr Fender is tied up with another patient but he asked me to drop in rather urgently.'

She strode forward and gently took the little boy's arm, which glowed angrily. 'He's had another thought about Tommy's reaction and it does seem red and worse. I think Tommy should come with me in case he's heading for an anaphylactic reaction. It could jeopardise his airway, you know.'

Tommy's mother bustled forward from where she'd fallen back at Tara's assertive stance.

'No. I'll bring him.'

Tara grimaced—as close as she could get to a smile—at Gwen. 'Perhaps you could find his pyjamas and medications and I'll meet you down at the hospital. I'm quite concerned, and I'm sure you are too.' The mother gaped as Tara picked up Tommy.

'But...'

Tara didn't wait to hear. She cradled the boy in her arms and carried him from the cabin. The steward followed her before she shooed him ahead urgently to hold the lift for them.

Nick was waiting and Tara rushed straight for the tap at the side of the room with Tommy in her arms. The little boy sniffed forlornly as she ran the cold water over his arm. 'Oven cleaner.'

Nick turned away and bunched his fist and then slowly straightened out his fingers until they were rigid with control. Not again. His stillness showed his feelings better than if he'd hit the wall, and he glanced at Tara to see if she'd noticed.

He couldn't help the past but he was damned if he'd ever see anything happen like that again. He reached into the fridge and removed the white creamy burn salve that would soothe almost instantly.

Tara watched him gently comfort the little boy and Tara's heart squeezed when she realised the child expected it to hurt. 'Where does this sort of illness come from? I can't believe someone would do this to their baby.'

'Historically? It's a mental illness.' Nick's voice was low and gentle so as not to alarm Tommy. 'Psychotic behaviour. Maybe it happened to them as a kid. Or maybe they had no attention as a kid and it's turned into an irrational need. At this minute I don't care. All I know at the moment she will be diabolical with her lies and knowledge of conditions that backs up her imagined scenarios. When they do it to themselves it's bad—but to a baby like Tommy…' He shook his head.

'She'll be here in a minute.'

They both glanced at the door. 'We have to keep Tommy here tonight. The ship docks tomorrow in Mykonos and we'll have him transferred to the hospital. I'll ring them tonight and set it up.'

When Tommy's mother walked in her eyes were intense and fixed on Tommy with concern. Tara couldn't equate the woman she'd seen doing damage to her child to this caring mother. And just as hard to believe was Nick.

He spoke gently. Calmly, as if to Tommy. 'Sit down, Gwen. We need to talk about Tommy's rash.'

'What's wrong with him?' Gwen rushed over and cuddled the little boy who, to Tara's horror, snuggled up to his mother. 'Will he be all right? He's my whole life.'

'I believe you.' With those words Gwen seemed to settle and Tara tried not to let her mouth gape. How could he say he believed her? Tara wanted to strangle her and discreetly she drew a deeper breath than normal to calm her own agitation.

Not discreet enough for Nick apparently. 'Do you think you could get Gwen a glass of water, Tara? Please. And send Gina in if you would.'

Tara nodded with relief while he glanced at the mum. 'I can see you're very anxious and we can't have you getting sick. Tommy needs you.'

It seemed this was the sort of appreciation Gwen needed because she relaxed into the chair Nick guided her to. 'Thank you, Doctor. You're very kind.'

'The thing is, Gwen,' Tara could hear him as she left the room, 'we'd like Tommy to stay with us tonight. Keep an eye on him, and I know that will be hard on you.'

The door shut behind her and their voices became a distant rumble.

'You okay?'

Gina, the nurse second in charge after Marie, was tidying the waiting room. The clinic was over and wouldn't open again for another two hours. They still had one child in the sick bay who was being nursed one on one by the other clinic nurse.

'We have another stay-over tonight.'

'The little boy with the rash?'

'Long story. Nick can tell you later.' She crossed to the water cooler and poured a paper cup full of water. 'Can you take this in for the boy's mother, please, Gina? Nick asked me to send you in. I'm going to look up something on the computer.'

'Sure. No worries.' Gina took the cup, crossed to the consulting room, knocked and went in. Tara stared as the door shut and shook her head. Tommy's mother was a darned good liar. In fact, Nick was a darned good liar too.

She tried not to dwell on the second thought as she sat down at the computer but maybe she needed to remember his skills at fabrication when she looked at him next. Or maybe she should try not to look at him.

A bit like he hadn't looked at her that morning. And she had a horrible feeling it wasn't just Gwen.

But that was pretty hard considering what they'd shared last night. She only had to go within three feet of him and the hairs on her arms started waving hello to him.

She heard the key turn in the door Gina had locked at the end of clinic and Wilhelm poked his head in.

Tara gave a forlorn smile. 'Hello, there, chief. Are you supposed to be out of bed?'

He shrugged and smiled back. 'I'm the doctor. I said I could.' He narrowed his eyes. 'You okay?'

Tara nodded but couldn't dredge up any other facial expression. 'Better than you, Mr Pale and Interesting.'

Wilhelm came in with purpose. 'I feel pale. But remarkably okay, actually. Must have been a twelve-hour bug. I just ate a horse and feel much better.'

'Poor horse.' Tara said it with a straight face and he frowned, worried. 'You're not a vegetarian, are you?'

Nick would have got it. Mentally she shrugged and couldn't help the thought about the last two years' staple diet of vegetable soup. 'Only when I have to. Loving the red meat here.'

It was Wilhelm's turn to study her. 'Suits you. More colour in the cheeks and not so bony.'

'Already.' Maybe her boobs would come back. Unwillingly she smiled. 'Better slow down, then.'

Wilhelm looked worried again that he'd offended her, and Tara held back a sigh. 'Nick's in there with a mum and her son. He's keeping the boy overnight.'

'Nick?'

'He replaced you for the last twenty-four hours.'

Wilhelm grinned. 'Nick's a champion. He's used to stepping in.'

She wasn't real sure if she needed to hear more glowing testimonials about Nick, not while she was wondering about how good an actor he was, but that didn't stop the curious part of her. 'So you two know each other well?'

'Last ten years. Catch up every couple of months at least. Depending where he's working and where I am.'

'So he's versatile?'

Wilhelm looked away and grinned. 'Oh, yeah.'

Enough. She didn't want to know. 'If you're determined to stay on I might take a walk, get some air.' She pointed to the computer screen. Her voice lowered. 'Better warn you this is what Nick thinks is the problem…' she inclined her head towards the shut door '…in there.'

Wilhelm peered over her shoulder at the screen and she heard his indrawn breath as he scanned the page on a parent causing illness in a child to gain attention. 'Unpleasant. And Nick's sure?'

Tara sighed. The whole episode had upset her. 'I think she sprayed oven cleaner on her son. Makes me feel a bit sick, actually. I'll come back for afternoon clinic. That okay?'

'Sure. And thanks for holding the fort, Tara. Bit of a stressful introduction for you these last few days and you're due some extra time off. Not a lot of people who would have coped as well.'

Nick would have. Apparently. 'Thanks, Wilhelm.' She stood up and he slid into her seat to finish reading the medical article. 'Catch you later.'

Wilhelm looked up briefly. 'Sure. Don't rush. I can always page you.'

CHAPTER ELEVEN

TARA drifted around the ship, trying to come to grips with Gwen's illness. With the idea that if Nick hadn't cottoned on, Tommy would still be suffering.

The hardest thing to come to grips with was the fact that he'd hugged his mother despite everything she'd done to him, and poor little Tommy was going to suffer when his mother was taken away.

Still, maybe one day Gwen could be well, medicated, psychoanalysed until she could be a safe mother again. Who knew what was in her own past? But at this moment Tara had trouble caring. The picture of Tommy squirming in the cabin haunted her. She couldn't help wondering what had happened to the child Nick felt he'd let down.

Tara did the whole walking track around the outside deck thing while most of the passengers were having their morning tea then climbed the stairs to her favourite place.

The bow of the ship, where most of the outdoor activities were grouped, always seemed semi-deserted. It was a good place to think, despite the mini-golf, half-tennis court, basketball rings. She walked past the two empty green tables and of course thought of Nick and his offer to beat her at table tennis and wished she'd embraced the simple things before it had all got complicated with these new feelings she was having for Nick.

Served her right for sleeping with him. Not that they'd done a lot of sleeping.

At least that morning since she'd been at work she hadn't thought much of last night, thanks to Gwen, and suddenly her problems weren't as huge any more.

She glanced into the window of the children's play centre and saw the laughing faces as the teacher read a picture book. Poor little Tommy should be in there, not in a sick bay for protection from his own mother.

She wondered how Nick and Wilhelm were doing with Gwen and decided she didn't want to think about it.

She went down to the crew's dining hall and Miko was there with the first mate. He gestured her over.

'Come, Tara. Grace our table.'

Classic diversion. Why couldn't she have found Miko attractive? He was much less complicated than Nick. 'Hi, guys. What's happening?'

After an early lunch Tara returned to the clinic but her mind was on Nick when she unlocked the door and the sight that greeted her took a moment to sink in.

At first thought Tara assumed Gina must have fainted but when Tara fell to her knees beside her and rolled her over she saw the blood from the blow that must have knocked her out. Gina lay stretched out on the floor and as Tara's hand reached to staunch the blood she heard Wilhelm's raised voice.

'Take him, he's in the obs ward. Just get out of here so I can see to my nurse.' That was followed by an 'oomph' of pain and a crash, and Tara winced because the sickening thud boded ill for the recipient.

She needed help. Fast. She needed Nick. She scrambled for her phone and texted, 'Security, clinic,' and sent it before whoever was here could realise she'd sounded the alarm. She tucked the phone away quickly and glanced frantically around for somewhere to hide because footsteps were coming and there was no time to get out.

Too late. A wild-eyed Gwen burst from Wilhelm's office into the waiting area, wielding a metal stand used to hang intravenous fluids. She saw Tara, stopped and frowned as if confused, but it didn't last long enough as the element of surprise wore off.

Tara shifted backwards as Gwen launched herself at her just as Nick burst through the door and dived in to tackle Gwen to the floor.

In seconds Nick had Gwen pinned face down and, disarmed, and shortly after that four burly security guards arrived, followed closely by the officer of the watch.

The next few minutes were a blur as Gwen was heavily sedated, and Tara could feel her fingers trembling as she tried to staunch the bleeding on Gina's head.

After one fierce embrace to assure himself she was unharmed, and a quick glance over Gina, Nick hurried through to Wilhelm.

An hour later Tara and Nick stood side by side as they watched through the window into Gwen's locked room. Deeply asleep, she'd been placed on monitoring while one of the security guards sat in the room with her. In repose her face seemed calm but Tara didn't think she'd ever forget the maniacal eyes of her attacker.

'You okay?' Nick was hovering.

Tara could tell he was upset she'd been in danger and she didn't know what to do with the feeling that she actually liked it that he cared enough to be upset. But he looked more than upset. He looked distraught.

She tried to reassure him. 'I'm okay. Thanks to you.' He really had dived right in. Anything else and she would have been flat on her back with a steel pole between the eyes. 'I couldn't believe how fast and powerful she was.'

Nick shook his head. Paced. 'No. I should have seen she was dangerously unstable. I thought we'd found a solution that would carry us through safely until we docked. I made an almost lethal mistake. Again!'

Tara put out her hand to catch his arm but he paced right past. 'You didn't make it on your own. Wilhelm agreed with you.'

'Wilhelm and Gina paid for it.' He jerked his hands through his hair and this time she reached out and touched his shoulder. His muscles were like steel bands, tension oozed out of him, and she slid her hand down and squeezed his upper arm until he looked at her.

'Looks like a fair amount of self-flagellation is going on here. Stop it. I'd say you've blamed yourself enough.'

Her hand dropped as she looked him up and down. 'You'd probably have preferred to be where Wilhelm is now, nursing a sore head. Wouldn't you?'

'Too right.' He paced away from her again and then back, and she couldn't help the tiny whisper in her head that said she was sorry, but glad that it wasn't Nick on neurological observations in Room Two.

'Men!' She shook her head. 'I'm upset about Gina but relieved I'm not sporting a black eye or worse.'

'So am I.' He actually shuddered. 'Poor Gina.'

'Looks like we're back on duty together.' And here was a danger of a different sort. Not that she really minded as long as she kept reminding herself this was only short term.

Since that morning she couldn't deny that her body went into receptor mode every time she went near him. Now they'd be seconded in here together, again, with so many patients to stay and supervise, and she didn't know how that was going to go, not being able to touch him.

Today had left her feeling especially vulnerable. And not a little shaky. The idea of being cradled in Nick's arms, to find a haven of peace in a crazy world, and mutual comfort from a rather horrific day that had gone from one ghastly moment to the next, meant if he knocked on her door tonight she'd probably haul him in by the collar. And the idea was growing more attractive by the minute.

She wasn't quite sure if she was going to be able to hide that from him or whether she'd bother trying.

Nick was a mess.

The picture of Gwen almost smashing Tara with that pole played over and over in his head. He wanted to pull Tara into his arms and run away with her. Bare his teeth and keep her safe from crazy people. Protect her with his life. There was that life thing again.

Well, he couldn't. That wasn't who he was. So he shuddered all the way down to his toes at the thought of her being unsafe. And that was madness of a different sort.

He couldn't remember ever being so scared, well, yes, he could, but he'd been just out of med school then.

His mother. Dying in the hospital after the accident and all his brand-new skills hadn't been able to save her.

Then later, going through his parents' things, finding out his beautiful mother had had a secret. Written in her own handwriting, in his father's wallet, so he couldn't explain it away. That both their parents had lived a lie.

Of course he hadn't told the girls. Though he often wondered if Kiki knew somehow. God, he'd been wild, and bitter, and lost. And unable to tell anyone. He'd lost more than his parents that day.

Today had at least pointed out, with ironic fingers, how he was setting himself up to create the same mis-

takes his parents had made. The figment of an imagi-
nary utopia. With Tara.

No way. How had he forgotten the basic rules? Don't
get involved. Don't get attached. Good-time guy.

He had to get out of here before he cracked. 'Why
don't you let me know if you get snowed under with
work?'

He saw the confusion on her face and hardened his
heart. It was for her good too. 'I'll do the call for night
shift tonight.' He backed away towards the door. 'Keep
Security here. I'll send another man down just in case.
Page me if you need me. I need to check my other job.'

Nick barely saw the carpet on the stairs as he jogged
up towards anywhere away from Tara.

Level after level. Upwards. Five floors, six, seven,
eight, his breath starting to come a little more unevenly.
Nine, ten, eleven, starting to pant now and he slowed to
a walk. The plastered barman smile on his face was a
caricature that would fool no one so he took himself to
the stern and leant against the rail and breathed deeply.

He stared out over the green waves and felt the sick-
ness of impending loss that he'd promised himself he'd
never feel again.

He was in a dilemma. Last night with Tara had been
incredible. She'd amazed him, reached him in ways nobody had ever reach him, had made him question his
goals and expectations and want to be the man for her.
But he didn't have the faith. Not in himself, not in life,
not in relationships.

It wasn't fair to keep coming back for more, to be

there when she turned around, to pretend he was laying foundations when he was really hoarding memories to carry away for when he was gone.

He knew it but couldn't stop himself.

He hadn't meant to go back to her cabin last night. Get in deeper. Fall more in love with the moments shared with her. But the clock was ticking until the cruise ended. Then Tara would be gone. He would be gone. They were both going to be miserable and it was all his fault.

What was going on here and how had he let himself get this entangled by a pair of long legs and a woman with an acquired phobia about death and disaster?

Then his initial agenda filtered in through his cold funk and he began to breathe again. He was just trying to help her. He could even feel his face relax with the thought. Okay. That wasn't so bad. He wasn't trying to fulfil her life, or his, he'd been trying to help. But now he needed to get out otherwise he'd be the one who needed help.

He just needed to ease away. Create distance again. Maybe a little diversion could put last night back into perspective.

Now he was kidding himself again. Last night with Tara had had the power to redefine his life if he let it, and that was what had rocked his mind this morning as he'd paced the deck. That and what he'd been going to say to her when she came down to work.

In the end Gwen had put paid to any discussions he might have had with her, and the reality of her being almost critically assaulted had destroyed his concept that it would be easy to walk away.

He didn't know what to do.

Back in the hospital, Tara listened to Nick's footsteps jog away. Nick had left? With a blankness in his eyes that said he wasn't coming back unless the walls fell in.

Tara frowned at the empty doorway and suddenly she felt alone, despite the half-dozen patients, the security guards and the need to start the quagmire of paperwork this incident had caused.

It was all very well for her to consider keeping her distance and then the rules had changed. It wasn't nice when Nick did it.

She wondered what this hollow pain in her chest was. Like someone had just scooped out her belly and let the wind in to whistle around.

Her hand crept to cover the cavity in her abdomen and she realised that Nick had the power to hurt her. Hurt her a lot. Perhaps more than her worst nightmare.

What had happened to that theory of spending time with Nick as a fast track to healing? Was this because of last night and the night before or in spite of it? But when it all came down to blame, she'd allowed it.

Tara winced and concentrated on the computer. Fool. That had been close. Imagine if she'd spent the next few days in his bed. She'd have been head over heels in love with him before they got to Venice. Well, she'd better snap out of it. No wonder he'd walked away.

Must have seen the threatening love light in her eyes.

And discovered she didn't have much to offer. Just a hollow, damaged shell that had promised all she'd wanted was the quick fix of Nick holding her. Anyone with half a brain would be able to tell an empty shell wouldn't be enough for any man, let alone a man like Nick.

She sat at the desk and began to type up the incident. Concentrate. Document. Work.

Work had helped last time, until the cure had been worse than the disease. But she was supposed to be wiser now. Her mind went back to Gwen and the moment Nick had reassured the woman. The moment Tara had realised he could lie if he needed to.

She stopped and stared at the wall. But.

A part of her was whimpering, What if Nick had lied again? Like just now, when he'd made it obvious he just wanted to get away from her. It didn't make a lot of sense when she thought about it.

Because earlier, when he'd saved her, the expression on his face, the fierce hug he'd given her when he'd seen she was okay, that had said he cared. Really cared. What if he was just as scared as she was of being hurt?

Imagine.

Then the world intruded on her thoughts. Vaguely she realised the ship was rolling a little, like it had the first two nights she'd been on board. Not much, but enough to roll the pen off the desk and ensure she did a round to secure any loose objects.

Wilhelm was awake, and cross with himself for being caught unawares, and Gina asked for a cup of tea. No time to stew over her doomed relationship with Nick.

Then Miko arrived with an injury to his arm. 'You coming out tonight, sweet Tara? To dance?' Mico's chocolate eyes crinkled with mischief. Tara decided that cruise personnel certainly knew how to flirt.

'Not tonight, Miko.'

'Ah, but Mykonos is the party capital and we dock at midnight. The dancing is good. Very romantic.'

Tara laughed. 'You know I can't dance with you, Miko. You tread on my feet.'

'One mistake.' He threw up his hands. 'I could learn to dance with a dominant woman. The idea grows more enticing.'

Tara laughed. 'Yeah, right. But I'll be tucked up in my little bunk at midnight, after the last couple of crazy days.' She had a quick flashback to what she'd been doing last night and hurriedly picked up his chart and studied it. 'The only reason I'll be up is if there's a medical emergency.'

'Ah. So you are on call, then.'

Even though Nick had said he would do it she would be available, so she smiled and agreed as she taped the end of the bandage to Miko's damaged arm. 'We're down on numbers at the moment.'

'It is a shame you cannot come. The discotheques are very popular here and most of the crew will disembark and return around five in the morning.' His eyes appreciated her. 'It is not as if you need beauty sleep for you are already beautiful.'

Yeah, right. 'Maybe you shouldn't be going. You should rest that arm. It may not be broken but I'm pretty sure you've damaged ligaments. What on earth possessed you to try and catch an urn that size?'

He shrugged philosophically. 'It is the centrepiece for my restaurant. I did not want it to break.'

'Next time let it go.'

When the night nurse came on to relieve her she knew she had to find out where she stood with Nick.

She just hoped he wasn't asleep so when she was standing in the corridor, waiting for him to answer his doorbell, she doubted her logic. This was dumb with a capital *D*.

But just as she turned she heard the door open and he was standing there, a towel slung around his hips, his hair tousled.

She thought at first it was okay but then his face changed and he didn't look pleased to see her. 'Déjà vu. Is this my turn for you to check on me?' he said.

No invitation, then. 'I wanted to know if you were okay.' The echo from yesterday was there and they both heard it. That was good, wasn't it?

Nick didn't say anything and she couldn't read his expression. Tara couldn't stand it any more. 'Can I come in?'

There was still no indication what he was thinking and she wished she could see just a glimpse of the Nick she'd met those first few days.

He shrugged and she winced. Even if he was pretending, it still hurt. 'Are you sure that's what you want?'

Tara felt a shaft of pain slice right through her followed immediately by a wave of heat in her face. He was knocking her back.

She spun on her heel and walked away and she could feel Nick's eyes on her. A rebuttal just like Vander had given her many times, and never had she felt so mortified. Because Nick had made her believe.

A few seconds later she heard the cabin door shut.

Tara walked the length of the ship to the bow and felt the spray slap her in the face. Like reality. She'd been incredibly stupid. And blind. And she couldn't believe how gullible. But he'd never promised fidelity. Had said he flitted from month to month, changing girlfriends like socks. Well, he was sick of this pair obviously.

The bizarre part of it all was that if she could take back what had happened on the last two nights she doubted she would. How could she when Nick had made her feel like a real woman for the first time in her life? Maybe she just needed to leave some money at his door and then she could carry that into the future.

The guy obviously had a gift but she just wasn't cut out to be fast and loose—like him.

She guessed she'd known there were men like that in the world, she just hadn't actually met them. It was pretty hard to take.

She walked slowly back to her cabin where the memories were no easier to deal with but she assured herself the experience wouldn't kill her. Just toughen her up. Maybe that needed to happen.

Nick sighed and watched her hurry away. He shut the door and tried not to think about the distress on Tara's face.

Wilhelm's words floated back at him. 'I'd hate to see her hurt.' Well, he'd done that.

But since last night he'd been able to think of little else except how he was going to stay away from her.

CHAPTER TWELVE

SPLIT, Croatia, and a beautiful blue-sky day. Tara decided to get off and get away from the damn ship. Create some distance between Nick and herself, if only for the day.

Wilhelm was again back on duty, looking a little the worse for wear, but just as determined for Tara to get away for the day.

A sedated Gwen had been picked up by an escort nurse and the coastguard for transfer back to Rome, and Tommy had been rescued by his aunt on Mykonos for temporary care.

Tara had been reluctant to hand him over without being sure his aunt was normal, but a bevy of giggling children in the car had helped, as did the children's services aide, who assured her she would be checking on his wellbeing.

Nick she didn't see, which was a good thing because, thinking about the next time he approached her, she wasn't sure how she'd handle that. Maybe sightseeing would help the emptiness she'd felt inside since she'd discovered the truth about Nick. After today there was only Venice and she'd seen little of the cities they'd visited.

She was still nervous about getting back on board if something went wrong, but the fact that if she climbed any structure above sea level she'd be able to see the ship helped.

She hailed a taxi.

Nick followed Tara off the ship and watched her stride along the long dockside car park to the taxi rank.

Nick's night had been plagued by regrets. How badly he'd handled it. How much the hurt on Tara's face had replayed in his head. He'd been a fool and a coward not to tell her the truth.

He must have been insane to use Tara's visit as a golden opportunity to get out from a situation that freaked him.

Stupid, thoughtless oaf that he was, she'd never talk to him again and he couldn't blame her. But he needed to apologise and at least assure her she'd done nothing wrong. God, he'd crushed her just like her husband had done.

When he saw her climb into the taxi he picked up the pace and with two desperate strides opened the opposite rear door before they could drive off.

Tara considered opening her own door and climbing out again but the vehicle pulled away from the kerb.

'Please leave me alone, Nick.' She saw the taxi driver glance in the mirror and raise his eyebrows, and she wondered if he was offering to throw the extra passenger out. She doubted Nick would go peaceably but the gallantry made her feel a whole lot better and she declined the unspoken offer with a shake of her head.

Nick was oblivious to Tara's new protector. 'I will. Just as soon as I've apologised.'

She angled her shoulder towards him and gazed pointedly out the opposite window. 'For what? Being yourself?'

'You don't know me.'

She looked at him. 'Biblically?' She raised her own brows and he had the grace to glance away before he sighed and leaned her way.

'Look, Tara.' He lowered his voice. 'I'm sorry.'

She breathed in slowly and let it out. Felt a little of the tension she'd carried since yesterday ease away because breathing always helped.

But that didn't mean she was diving back in for a Nick-fest. 'Great. Can you get out now? Or should I feel less brushed off as an annoying groupie of yours? Funny how I didn't like the feeling.'

She thought about it some more. 'So why was it easy for you to let me think what we shared was nothing?' That had stung and she glared at him. He was a low-life. 'Are we not even friends?'

Nick glanced up at the avidly curious taxi driver. 'Can we get out and talk about this?'

Should she? Tara checked with the taxi driver, who shrugged.

'Maybe?'

The man driving screwed up his face in the mirror.

Not decisive enough for him. 'Okay.' Tara gave in. Mostly because it had hurt so much when she'd thought Nick had been unmoved by something she'd almost call life-changing. 'We can walk into the city and then I'm going to have the rest of the day to myself. Here, thanks,' she said to the driver.

'Fine.' He owed her that. He glanced at the alfresco restaurant on the edge of the park. 'It's our last stop before Venice, give me a chance, let me buy one drink as an apology, while I explain.'

She closed her eyes. It still hurt. Maybe she needed to hear. 'One drink. I don't want to force myself on you again.'

'You didn't force yourself on me, Tara.' That would be my undoing, Nick thought, and tried a smile. He could do light-hearted and platonic. He owed her that. 'Let's just enjoy the day. Like friends. The cruise will be over soon. Should we climb the bell tower?' And he would pay the price of another collection of memories to hold onto when she'd gone.

Tara loved bell towers. Was looking forward to the hundreds in Venice. There was even a voice inside her head that whispered she might even find the truth about Nick and herself up there.

Irrational, ridiculous, but so compelling it pushed her up the sharp steps, through the tiny tunnel built for smaller people hundreds of years ago and around and around through thick stone walls, feet gingerly climbing worn stone steps and sections of steep iron ladders that echoed and swayed, always enticing her up to the view she knew would be spectacular.

'Whoa. That was pretty hairy, coming up.' Nick was grinning, his hair blown across his forehead in an unruly heap, so handsome and devilish and so like her pirate that she ached just looking at him.

'So where do we go from here, Nick?'

'Back down again.' He didn't meet her eyes.

'Don't get me wrong. We both wanted a commitment-free two weeks of fun.' She waited until he looked at her. 'So in two days we go our separate ways.'

'I hope we'll be in touch.'

She couldn't believe how much those words hurt. 'But without touching?' Why was she so surprised at being sad?

Tara looked woozily down from the church tower at the sprawling ancient city of Split below her, could feel Nick at her shoulder, and like the vertigo that had grown unexpectedly the higher she'd climbed the fear that what was between them was as flimsy as the guard rail that seemed so incapable of stopping her fall down the stairwell.

It had always been just a holiday affair. But what was really making her sad was how she was starting to believe that Nick would never find true happiness. And she wanted that for him, even if it wasn't with her.

'So can you tell me what happened? What made you like this?'

'Like what?' Stone walled Nick. Just like the tower.

'Come on, Nick. I know what happened to me.

Indifferent parents. Difficult-to-please husband. Burnout at work. What spoiled you for happy-ever-after, Nick?'

She saw his shock. His assimilation of things she'd barely mentioned before but she hadn't said them to sidetrack him. Didn't want him sidetracked.

'There's something inside you that allows you to reach a certain point and then the safety catch kicks in.' She tilted her head and ignored the vertigo. 'What is that?'

She thought for a moment he was going to brush her off. They were alone, but she could hear the clatter of more people coming up the stairs. A very brief window of privacy. She almost didn't expect it when it came.

'A letter.' He shifted until he was beside her. His shoulder next to hers as he put his hands down to lean on the parapet. They looked into the city from above and it was like a thousand dolls' houses gazed on by giants. He didn't look at her.

'There was an accident. We were going through my parents' things after they died and I found a letter. From my mother to her lover. In my father's wallet so he knew. She'd been cheating for years, and I couldn't tell my sisters. They'd been heartbroken enough, so I burnt it.'

His voice was so quiet, unhurried, as if talking about someone else's tragic revelation.

'I burnt the proof that my parents' lives were a farce. That their marriage was a charade. I guess I lost my ideal of marriage that day, as well as my parents. I never told anyone. Then there was my friend's wife. Living a lie while she tortured her child. Two bizarre illusions of happy marriages I couldn't talk about.

'I just let it sit there and fester all these years. Became the good-time guy you see before you.' He tapped his chest. 'Definitely no plan for permanency.'

It wasn't what she'd expected but it made a lot of sense.

But it underlined the real reason they would never make it together. Trust. He didn't have any.

She looked away from his profile across the roof-tops. An empty square with a gaping wound, the dome of ruined church vestry without a roof. Just grey walls going down into the dark hole with the hint of internal archways.

That's how her heart felt. Exposed and open, although the sun had turned to rain and now she knew what the future would be like without the comfort of a soul mate.

She sighed. 'My husband never trusted me. He'd had a failed marriage before me and I guess it came from there. I was young, idealistic and thought I could change him. He died before I saw any change but I think if he'd lived to be a hundred he'd never have changed. Never trusted me enough to open up and show me the real man.'

She sighed and looked away. 'Looking back I don't even think he trusted my medicine in those few months we had. I guess that was why I stayed. To prove to myself I really could help. Did have skills to offer.'

She could never again live with a man who didn't have faith in her. This would never work with Nick. Ever.

The vertigo increased exponentially. She could feel the ground rush up at her, along with the roaring in her ears. She swayed.

'Tara? You okay?' Saw Nick's concern tighten on his face.

'No. I don't think so.' The devastation was physical and manifested like a beast on top of the tower. Vertigo rose in her throat like hot bile. 'I don't think I can get down.'

Nick's concern was almost palpable but it didn't help. 'I'll guide you.'

If she didn't feel so sick she would have laughed. Nick couldn't guide himself. 'You can't help me, Nick.' Now she knew. All because of the letter found by a fresh young doctor.

She honestly hoped he'd heal one day.

Maybe talking about it today would help—down the track—too far away for her, though. 'At some stage you'll have to let go, Nick. Because that's what you do.' And she was talking about two journeys here. One down the tower and one into life.

She would be okay. She was strong. She might spin a bit but she knew her strength now. 'I'm better on my own.'

'That's not true. And has nothing to do with now anyway. Come on, I'll help you down.'

She shook her head but that wasn't good. Everything

rotated so she stopped moving it. Or she'd throw up. 'No. I think I'll have to do it myself.'

Nick looked around for help, found none, saw the options and knew he'd have to do it her way. 'Then I'll follow you.'

'No. Go in front. At least I'll be able to see you.' Watch you walk away from me, she thought.

So he led, slowly, and she watched his dark hair float below her then pop back from around the curved walls to make sure she was still coming, and then he would go away below her on the steep steps.

She kept her hand on her flimsy rail and her eyes on Nick's hair. Once she slipped on the worn stone edge of an ancient step, and once she skidded down two instead of one, each time her heart in her mouth, but always her eyes returned to Nick's hair.

Funny. She could almost feel it under her fingers.

Then right at the bottom the section that was so narrow and steep she couldn't see him was upon her and his voice floated back. 'You okay, Tara?'

She couldn't answer, leant against the wall and breathed deeply for a few seconds. This was the last bit before it was over. She tried to move her feet forward.

'Come on.' His voice was beside her now as he gently took her arm. 'Nearly there.'

But once they got to the bottom she was going to say goodbye. They both should. Because the way she was feeling about Nick the unobtainable wasn't funny.

When they got to the bottom Tara reached out,

squeezed his hand, said, 'Thank you, Nick, but I want to go back to the ship alone.' Then walked away.

When he tried to follow she held up her hand to stop him and such was the resolution on her face he didn't follow.

Nick stood at the bottom of the cathedral steps and watched her go. What had just happened up there?

Nick started to walk back towards the dock where the tenders ferried people back to the ship.

Well, for a start he'd just told the first person ever about his mother's infidelity—something he'd never thought he'd blurt out up a bell tower—and admitted to Tara, and himself, that he wasn't looking to find the happily-ever-after he didn't believe in.

It sounded pretty stupid when you said it out loud. But there was no guarantee of lifelong fidelity. He'd seen plenty of examples on the ships where he'd worked, and the hospitals he'd locumed at that hadn't made him change his mind.

Relationships did fall apart. People were unfaithful. Lies were told. Wasn't it better to know up front not to expect too much? Then you wouldn't be faced with the dilemma of creating a web of lies that destroyed people.

'But this was Tara?' He said the words out loud and he kept walking but he wasn't seeing the narrow stone archways and alleys of Split, he was seeing his parents before he'd known, and for the first time in a long time he just let the memories come without judging. There were some pretty good memories. Some great times they'd had as a family.

But all the time the lies must have been there.

CHAPTER THIRTEEN

NICK woke the next morning and stared at the ceiling. He wanted Tara. He ached for the gnawing emptiness of his arms. For the feel of her hair against his chest. To be able to run his fingers down over the contours of her head and across her silken cheek.

Something he'd chosen never to feel again. He wanted to hear her stride across the room with that determined walk of hers, a rhythm of footsteps he would never lose the memory of. The subtle scent of violets, his new favourite flower, a token he would never pass without seeing and feeling Tara's presence.

He was in love. Irrevocably. And he'd blown it.

With his new insight he just hoped that in the past no women had ever felt like this about him while he'd been oblivious.

He wondered if his parents had felt like this when they'd first met. They must have because he had four sisters and a bag full of memories in their big old house that made him smile if he let them. About time he did.

Instead of the usual anger against his parents he only

felt sadness. Poor them. To have lost this feeling would be the most tragic loss in the world.

He loved Tara and to hell with it. He'd rather have felt this and lost it than never felt it at all.

He looked out his porthole and saw they were coming into the waterways of Venice.

That first island greeted him. He always loved this moment and usually he was on deck for it.

A spot of land on the ocean, green and lush but not joined to the world of men.

He was sick of being an island. Admittedly a party island but at the end of the day there was just him and his illusion of fulfilment and friends.

Maybe his parents had messed up, maybe they had broken each other's hearts, but at least they'd tried. He was the coward. He wanted to be so much more. For Tara.

The dawn touched her cheek on the pillow with greypink fingers of light, drawing her up to look out the porthole. Venice was coming.

Tara wanted Nick. Wanted to see the mischief in his face when he teased her, the solemnity in his eyes when he loved her. To feel the tenderness in his hands, those elegant, masculine hands that could be so powerful in protecting her yet so gentle with reverence when he touched her skin. She loved him. She knew that now.

Tara pulled herself up reluctantly in the bed, still in denial that today was the last day. A breakwall made of rock—like a long bony finger—pointed towards the shimmer of the city in the distance.

The waves slapped against the side of the hull as they cut through the pastel water towards their destination and the ship ignored the tearing pain in her heart that wanted to plead with the captain to turn back out to sea.

How could she have fallen so deeply in love with a man who couldn't love? What if she'd been able to let go of the memories that had kept her from being the woman Nick needed? Would that have changed the outcome? Would he have met her halfway? She'd never know.

Tara dressed silently, her face tight with distress, yet as always the tears stuck stubbornly in her throat in a big dry ball.

She walked the full length of the ship through the empty corridors. The passengers would be packing last-minute hand luggage, all the cases had lined the corridors the night before and were stowed below decks, ready for rapid removal and claim.

Passenger doors began to open. People moved towards the rails as the islands began to appear. Finally she reached the café at the bow.

She felt the rock in her chest grow heavier until it lay like a huge lead fist crushing her heart.

'Coffee, Dr Tara?'

Miko had a cup and saucer in his hand, his Slavic accent quietly kind with sympathy, and they shared a bitter-sweet smile.

She looked down at her cup. Her last cradle of fine

ship's crockery, her last freshly brewed Colombian from a friend, a gesture of respect—and farewell.

'Thank you.' Her throat hurt from those unshed tears and the burning-hot coffee helped disguise that pain as it went down.

She put the cup down and climbed to the highest point on the deck, gazed out, and the breath stilled in her throat. The ship sailed blithely onward towards Venice.

Another island. Another. Ancient buildings, church spires, the increase of boat traffic. Vaporettos, water taxis, car-carrying ferries and tiny blue transport vessels.

More buildings as the sun rose and the ship drew nearer to the port. She stood there alone, no one beside her to share the moment, and she wondered if the rest of her life would be filled with moments with no one beside her.

Nick came upon her silently, stood for a moment oblivious to the landscape of Venice he normally adored, and absorbed the distress and loneliness he'd caused in Tara. He felt the sting of remorse and regret and sighed at his own stupidity.

How could she forgive him? He wasn't sure he could forgive himself. He absorbed her profile, saw how despite the pain she held her head high, shoulders straight as if she knew she would survive. This woman who had known such turmoil and heartbreak yet was still so strong.

His mind flashed back to the roadside scene when

she'd first shown him her core of steel, and he loved her even more.

He prayed she could see he'd changed. That she'd encouraged that change by believing in him. Encouraging him to let the past go and stride into the future—hopefully with her.

But he'd understand if she said no. And he would be strong too, and try not to look back with regret but forward to new goals he'd avoided for too long. Thanks to a woman he'd once loved.

Suddenly the vista became overwhelmingly beautiful, spires and domes and long rows of arched buildings, snatches of greenery, and always the wash of the waves on the stone steps of an island as their ship glided past. This was the way to see Venice for the first time.

Sixteen stories above, gliding along the water, the whole orchestra that was Venice was laid out before her in the pastels and golden rays of sunrise.

Tara leaned back and closed her eyes. She wished Nick was there.

'I'm sorry, Tara.'

The breath jammed in her throat and she tried to swallow. 'Nick?'

'I'm so sorry I didn't tell you I loved you.'

She chewed hard down on her lip. She couldn't take his lies right now. 'What do you know about love?'

'Good question.' His voice came from behind her until he leaned down and kissed her. For a moment she weakened and shut her eyes and pretended.

He went on. 'I love you. It scares the living daylights out of me but when I wake up in the morning it's your face I want to see beside me. Every day.'

She turned and his smile and the light in his eyes blinded her more than the sun that lifted above the water, and suddenly she was unsure if this was a delusion.

'I dreamt of you big with my child.' A soft, sexy smile. 'Actually, there was more than one child.' Was this Nick saying these things?

Her heart seemed to be beating too loudly in her chest. Her face felt hot and then cold and she stared up into his face. The face she loved so much and had given up on seeing again. She saw the certainty there. But she couldn't believe him. 'When did you decide you love me? What happened to "long term isn't viable"?'

There was sympathy in his face. For the pain he'd caused her. And regret. And a promise to make it up to her. Shining out at her like the new dawn she'd just witnessed. 'I've let it go. Because I've loved you every minute since I saw you. I was just too frightened to admit it. And long-term viable isn't a quarter as scary as short term and gone.'

She looked around. The city was closer. Time was running out. 'Why now?'

He pulled her into his chest. 'Because I can't lose you. Can't have you disappear into Venice without me.' His voice dropped and his mouth came closer. He whispered, 'I know I'll want to feed you strawberries. And watch your mouth.'

She wanted to cry. For the tragedy of it all. But she couldn't. She wasn't worthy of him. Couldn't give him what he needed. A whole woman. Not a frozen hull of a woman.

I'll always love you, she thought, but she didn't say it. She watched the city grow through stinging eyes as it rose before her.

She hadn't expected Venice to be this achingly beautiful. Heart-wrenching, devastating, with Nick holding her right at this moment. His arms were around her and nobody else's would ever feel the same.

'It's okay to cry,' he whispered in her ear with her backed into his chest, hard against his hips, and her body recognised all of him.

When an unexpected sob tore from her throat she shuddered, frightened by the power of it, and he held her tightly, safely, and that was when the tears began to fall.

Suddenly she was drowning in a flood of silent, choking tears cascading down her cheeks as the glacier that had been frozen for the last two years began to crack and splinter and melt into flooding trickles of pain that dripped into the canals of Venice.

She wiped them away but more just soaked her fingers and ran off her chin. Of course she hadn't brought a tissue.

'Here.' The handkerchief was pushed into her hand and she hid her face in the white cotton of his handkerchief as the floodgates opened even more.

As if Venice had released the gate to the torture she'd stored in her heart but, in fact, it had been Nick.

The faces of the people she'd lost, her husband who'd died an unhappy man, the babies who had never breathed, the men who had walked away broken because she'd failed their wives.

And the loss of Nick. But this man had not walked away, even though she'd failed him.

She cried for herself, and for Nick, and for the world she couldn't change, and Nick held her safe, gave her strength, warmed the last ice from her heart, and finally the weight eased from her shoulders. When she looked up from the safety of Nick's arms Venice was before her.

Wise and wizened, smiling with benevolence in all her aged splendour and determination to stay afloat. Like Tara and Nick would together.

They glided past the Doge's Palace silvery in the morning light, the huge tower of St Mark's Church soaring above the cobbles as the bells pealed a welcome, and she could see right into the almost empty square as they glided past the covered gondolas waiting for their morning passengers.

And then the sun blinded her as it rose above the horizon and she turned her head to rest her cheek against his chest.

Nick's finger came under chin and he turned her all the way and then lifted her chin. Her beautiful body was wedged against him and her scent wrapped him in a mist of lust and insanity. He breathed her in.

'I though you weren't doing this?'

He opened his eyes and studied the face he loved

as she looked up at him. 'Well, that's the thing. I can't resist you.'

She smiled. Slowly and sweetly as she sighed into him. 'Damn,' she said as she kissed him.

'Welcome to Venice, my love. This is where we start our new life together.'

CHAPTER FOURTEEN

MR AND MRS Nick and Tara Fender stayed in Venice for six months and when they left they left in style. The honeymoon suite on the rear of the Sea Goddess. A huge suite filled with flowers and baby clothes from the baby shower Kiki had hosted for them that afternoon with all their old friends on board.

Tara was gazing with delight around the huge cabin. 'Next year, when we've had our babies, and they're big enough, can we come back and cruise again?'

Nick couldn't think of anything he would enjoy more. 'I could work and you could play.'

'And Kiki might even have decided to leave the bar and head down to the hospital to join you.'

'I think she's nearly ready. But let's talk about us.' He lifted her fingers and kissed her wrist. 'I need to tell you something.'

The steward had just delivered their daily chocolate-dipped strawberries for the VIP couple and Nick leaned over the back of Tara's deckchair and held the strawberry above her mouth.

She giggled, and he swore he would never tire of that

sound as he brushed the glistening fruit against her lips and then couldn't resist a taste. 'Yum. Strawberries, and not surprisingly chocolate ones, and best of all you.'

When they parted she held up her hands. 'No more. I swear you want me as fat as a pig.'

'Sweet wife, you eat two a day and only if I encourage you. It's not the chocolate that's putting on your inches.' He stroked a gentle finger down the mound of her stomach. 'It's our twins.'

Tara's hand floated down to rest on his and their hands entwined as they both looked into the future that was as golden as the afternoon sun as they sailed out of Venice.

* * * * *

A sneaky peek at next month...

Medical Romance™

CAPTIVATING MEDICAL DRAMA—WITH HEART

My wish list for next month's titles...

In stores from 7th December 2012:

☐ From Christmas to Eternity – Caroline Anderson

& Her Little Spanish Secret – Laura Iding

☐ Christmas with Dr Delicious – Sue MacKay

& One Night That Changed Everything – Tina Beckett

☐ Christmas Where She Belongs – Meredith Webber

& His Bride in Paradise – Joanna Neil

Available at WHSmith, Tesco, Asda, Eason, Amazon and Apple

Just can't wait?

Special Offers

Every month we put together collections and longer reads written by your favourite authors.

Here are some of next month's highlights— and don't miss our fabulous discount online!

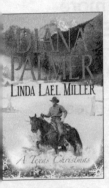

On sale 16th November

On sale 16th November

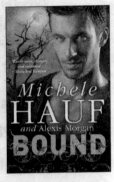

On sale 7th December

Save 20% on all Special Releases

Find out more at
www.millsandboon.co.uk/specialreleases

Visit us Online

1212/ST/MB392

MILLS & BOON® Book Club

2 Free Books!

Get your free books now at
www.millsandboon.co.uk/freebookoffer

Or fill in the form below and post it back to us

THE MILLS & BOON® BOOK CLUB™—HERE'S HOW IT WORKS: Accepting your free books places you under no obligation to buy anything. You may keep the books and return the despatch note marked 'Cancel'. If we do not hear from you, about a month later we'll send you 5 brand-new stories from the Medical™ series, including two 2-in-1 books priced at £5.49 each and a single book priced at £3.49*. There is no extra charge for post and packaging. You may cancel at any time, otherwise we will send you 5 stories a month which you may purchase or return to us—the choice is yours. *Terms and prices subject to change without notice. Offer valid in UK only. Applicants must be 18 or over. Offer expires 31st January 2013. **For full terms and conditions, please go to www.millsandboon.co.uk/freebookoffer**

Mrs/Miss/Ms/Mr (please circle) _____

First Name _____

Surname _____

Address _____

_____

Postcode _____

E-mail _____

Send this completed page to: Mills & Boon Book Club, Free Book Offer, FREEPOST NAT 10298, Richmond, Surrey, TW9 1BR

Find out more at
www.millsandboon.co.uk/freebookoffer

Visit us Online

0712/M2YEA